TERI POLEN

THE COLONY SERIES : BOOK ONE
SUBJECT A36

Black Rose Writing | Texas

The author grants the final approval for this literary material.

First printing

ISBN: 978-1-68433-415-5
PUBLISHED BY BLACK ROSE WRITING
www.blackrosewriting.com

Printed in the United States of America
Suggested Retail Price (SRP) $17.95

Subject A36 is printed in Calluna

*As a planet-friendly publisher, Black Rose Writing does its best to eliminate
unnecessary waste to reduce paper usage and energy costs, while never compromising
the reading experience. As a result, the final word count vs. page count may not meet
common expectations.

For Michael

Also by Teri Polen:

Sarah

The Gemini Connection

SUBJECT A36

ASHER

Elsa's small feet stumbled across the gnarled tree root, and I grabbed her elbow to steady her. You'd think she'd be more sure-footed after playing around the knotted, decades-old apple tree nearly every day, but her skinned knees and elbows told a different story. Every day it was a hazard for her to navigate without incident. To us, it wasn't just a tree. Some days it was the wall of an enemy castle we stormed. Other days, it was a majestic ship, its sails billowing in the wind as it carried us to distant lands.

This morning, the tree was something to occupy our time while we waited for Mom outside. With the closest town nearly a hundred miles away, market day was a monthly event for us. Lists were made, then double and triple checked, because if something was forgotten, we'd have to do without it until the next month. Multiple strategic routes in and out of town were planned to avoid any soldiers in the area.

"Elsa, remember to grab a hat before we leave." Cami, my other sister, had already clambered up the tree and waited patiently a few branches above us.

The roots of Elsa's natural ash blonde hair formed a pale strip down the part at the center of her head. Mom touched them up monthly with a mousy brown color, but Elsa's hair had grown faster than the weeds in our ample vegetable garden this month. Due to rumors of heavy numbers of Colony soldiers in the area, our monthly market trip had been delayed a week. Elsa's hair color and wavy texture had been in high demand by wealthy Colony residents since before she was born four years ago, and Mom had kept it closely-cropped and dyed since Elsa was a baby. If you didn't live behind the walls of The Colony, you were an Outlier, and caution was our first priority.

"Pull me up, Asher." Elsa's tiny hands reached for me. I'd already swung myself up to the lowest branch.

Cami rolled her eyes—her ocean-blue irises camouflaged by muddy, brown-tinted contacts. Colony citizens would pay well for the color beneath them. "Quit being a baby, Elsa. Just sling a leg over and pull yourself up."

Elsa stuck out her bottom lip and stomped her foot. "I'm not a baby! I can't help it that my legs are smaller, and I can't run and climb as fast as you and Asher."

I jumped down beside her then wrapped my hands around her waist. "Here, I'll lift you up." With me pushing her and Cami pulling, Elsa was soon several feet above the ground.

"Hold on this time and watch where you're stepping," I cautioned.

"Let's go higher and get some apples," Cami said. Breakfast was less than an hour ago, but there was something irresistible about pulling the fragrant fruit directly from the tree, then biting into it. Mom warned us constantly that we'd get sick if it wasn't washed first, but we were still alive.

"I'll get the apples," I said. "You stay here with Elsa." Cami glared at me, but we both knew I could climb faster and reach the taller branches easier. I'd experienced my fair share of tumbles and injuries, but they'd healed almost overnight. Mom said I was as surefooted and graceful as a cat, but that hadn't stopped her from holding her breath every time she saw me scaling the trees. Not that I could ever show off those talents anywhere in public. Like Elsa and Cami, I had to keep my desirable traits concealed.

Never draw attention to yourself. Our parents reminded us of this almost every day. Not that we'd ever forget it. I could never be the fastest. Cami could never be the smartest. Wanting us to have as normal a childhood as possible, our parents sent us to public school for a couple of years, but after too many comments about my athletic ability and Cami's intelligence, they concluded homeschooling was the only option. Allowing us to continue our education in public school was a risk they weren't willing to take.

I'd understood the danger but was still disappointed and missed interacting with other kids my age.

When I was much younger, I'd been really sick and basically quarantined. Dad was the local physician in our small community and treated me himself. Our closest neighbors, the Wallaces, had two children—

Noah, my best friend, and his sister, Brynn. The two of them and Cami had been my only playmates whenever I was strong enough to go outside. I remembered days of lying in bed, with barely enough energy to sit upright.

Hide and Seek was their favorite game to play. I'd watch from the window, so I could still feel like I was a part of the game. Brynn was always the best seeker. I didn't know if she sniffed Noah and Cami out or possessed super hearing, but she never searched for long. She'd always find Noah first, like she wanted to prove how easy it was. He accused her of cheating, but I knew she didn't. I watched her. They scuffled in the dirt over it, but when the dust cleared, Brynn sat astride Noah's chest, his arms pinned overhead, and demanded an apology. When Cami accused Noah of cheating after the next round, Brynn tackled her, defending his honor.

Whatever treatment Dad gave me had worked. I was healthy now, and had spent many days playing games and sprinting through the woods with the three of them. Dad swore all my running and climbing was an effort to make up for lost time.

After ensuring Cami and Elsa were secure, I climbed higher to reach the biggest apples, their deep red skin peeking through the leaves. As the oldest at eight-years-old, I felt my sisters' safety was partly my responsibility. Maybe I was a little overprotective sometimes, but if I allowed them to follow me this high, we'd all be grounded—literally—for at least a week.

I stretched out the bottom of my shirt to form a makeshift basket for the apples, then descended the tree one-handed. I tossed the biggest fruits to Cami and Elsa, then bit into my own. With hands and mouths sticky from apple juice, we sat on a low, thick branch and listened intently while Cami outlined a treasure hunt for later this afternoon when we returned.

When the back screen door slammed, my head spun in that direction. We'd been scolded several times over slamming doors, and with the three of us outside, I wondered who the guilty party was.

It was Mom.

"Asher!" She gripped the porch railing and called for me. Her voice cracked and was laced with tears. Dad vaulted over the porch railing, landed solidly on the grass, and frantically scanned our expansive yard.

My stomach clenched. Something was very wrong. "Over here!"

Dad's gaze locked on mine. "Code Exodus! Now, Asher. Run!"

Was this another drill? We'd practiced twice a week, the times always unexpected, without fail for as long as I could remember. Drills were a regular part of our life, like eating, sleeping, and homework. Protocol was pounded into our brains. There could be no hesitation.

But this felt different. Dad's expression was tight and urgent. Tears streamed down Mom's face, and I knew. This was no drill. It was real this time. We'd been found. Code Tribe—we leave together. Code Exodus—we leave without our parents.

Code Exodus rules.
Find Cami and Elsa.
Grab the backpack.
Leave immediately.
Don't stop for anything or anyone.
Run to the Wallaces.
When my sisters could no longer keep up, hide them and keep running.

I remembered the day Dad had first gone over this plan with me. "Cami and Elsa aren't as fast as you and won't be able to keep up. Get them as far away as possible, then hide them. Protect them as long as you can. But you have to keep going, Asher. It's crucial that *you* not be found. Do you understand me?"

My heart surged into my throat. Surely I'd misunderstood about going without him and Mom, and then abandoning Cami and Elsa. I shook my head in confusion. "Dad, n-n-no. We can all leave and stay together, we can..."

"No." He cut me off. His voice was firm, his eyes glistening. "With Code Exodus, that's not a possibility. I know this is difficult for you, Asher, and sending the three of you away without us is the hardest thing I'll ever do— if it comes to that. But it's imperative you not be found. Patrick and Anna Wallace will know what to do if this code is ever called." He pulled me into a hug and whispered in my ear. "Whatever happens, know I never regretted what I did. Not for a second. Your mother and I will come for all of you when it's safe. I promise."

A low rumbling vibrated in my chest, snapping me out of the memory. Choppers. We had to move. Birds skittered and took flight from branches above us, startling Elsa, and she grabbed onto my arm and hid her face against my shoulder. Our apples fell to the ground, all but forgotten in the chaos. I pushed off the branch and jumped down, then crouched low so Cami could help Elsa onto my back.

Leaves blew wildly overhead from the helicopter rotors, and whirlwinds of dust flitted around us. While Cami grabbed the backpack from its hiding place under a nearby rock, I stole a last glance back at our parents. Dad stood tall with his arms around Mom, her head buried against his chest, hair blowing in every direction as the choppers grew closer. Our parents didn't look in our direction, not wanting to alert the soldiers to our location.

With Cami at my side and Elsa on my back, her small hands clasped around my neck, we took off through the forest to the Wallaces' house. They were the closest thing we had to extended family, and Dad and Mom trusted them implicitly.

Somehow, I'd get all three of us to their house safely. No matter what I'd told Dad, leaving my sisters wasn't an option.

My speed was one of the reasons I'd been noticed at school. When we raced, I'd always beaten other kids by yards. Now, even with Elsa's weight on my back, I had to stop several times and wait for Cami to catch up. And we were still over a couple miles from the Wallaces' house.

"Cami, hurry, we have to move faster." We dodged dead tree limbs and craggy rocks on the uneven forest floor as best we could. Elsa clung tightly to me, crying softly.

Questions darted through my head. I'd always known people were looking for us. But why? When I'd questioned Dad, all he'd said was it involved his past, and he'd explain when I was old enough to understand. Why couldn't he and Mom run away with us? We were a family, and families were supposed to stay together.

"Ow! Ash, wait!" I stopped abruptly, and turned to see Cami collapsed on the ground, wincing as she clutched her ankle. "I twisted it."

I jogged back, then knelt beside her. Elsa slid gently to the ground. "Can you walk?" Maybe I imagined it, but the skin around her ankle already seemed puffy. "Here. Put your arm over my shoulder." I slid one arm around her waist, grasped her hand draped over my shoulder, then pulled her up.

Cami shrieked in pain the second she put weight on her foot, and I lowered her back to the ground. "I can't. It hurts too much."

I sighed, wondering how I'd manage this. "You'll have to lean on me. We'll be slow, but we have to keep moving."

Her eyes shimmered, and she leaned in closer and spoke softly so Elsa couldn't hear. "You can't carry both of us. And you know the protocol. You have to keep going."

My eyes widened. I'd thought those instructions were only between Dad and me.

"Dad knew you wouldn't want to leave us, and I have to make sure you do."

I shook my head. My hands clenched into fists. "I'm not leaving you. Without Mom and Dad here, it's my job to take care of you."

"If we all get caught, none of us is safe. Hide us, like Dad said. He and Mom will come for us, and then we'll meet you at Noah's."

Everything about this felt so wrong. I couldn't abandon my sisters. Protecting Cami and Elsa was my responsibility now, and leaving them to fend for themselves wasn't part of my plan. "Hurry, Ash. Dad said you have to run. Elsa and I can find a place to hide. He wouldn't have told you to go on without us if it wasn't important." Cami put her arm around Elsa and pulled her closer. Her eyes pleaded for me to go, but I also saw a hint of fear.

I huffed out a breath. Dad must have had his reasons. And he'd come for all of us. He'd promised. "Elsa is too small to help you walk. At least I can find a place for you." I hurriedly scanned our surroundings. I could put both of them in a tree, but there was no way Cami could climb. A low outcropping of rocks caught my eye. Shrubs, young trees, and vines concealed most of it, which meant my sisters would be hidden from sight. But it didn't make me feel any better about leaving them behind.

I carried Cami behind the shrubs, then gently lowered her to the ground. Elsa trailed behind me carrying the backpack.

"Elsa, I need you to stay and take care of me while Ash goes for help. Can you do that?" Cami's voice wavered, but I knew she was trying to stay calm for Elsa's sake.

Elsa's teary eyes looked at me. Her lip quivered.

"You can do this," I said gently. "Just stay here and be quiet. No peeking to see if anyone's coming, you understand?" My own voice was shaky. I had to have faith in Dad, and trust he knew what was best for us.

My trembling hands unzipped the backpack and shoved the gun and extra ammunition aside. I took out a couple bottles of water and some protein bars and set them on the ground within Cami's reach.

"We'll all be together again soon. I promise." I slung the backpack over my shoulder, then pulled both of them into a tight hug and kissed their foreheads. After one last look at Cami and Elsa, I made sure they were completely camouflaged then sprinted through the forest, dodging trees and jumping over moss-covered logs. The wind dried my tear-stained cheeks.

That morning was the last time I ever saw my parents or my sisters.

ASHER

I jolted upright, wide awake and disoriented in the room lit only by a small lamp in the corner. My heart hammered in my chest, convinced I was still running. After nearly a month without the dream, I'd believed its grip had loosened, finally allowing me a peaceful night's sleep.

I was wrong.

Releasing a long breath, I lowered my head back to the pillow and reached beside me for Brynn. I hoped I hadn't woken her. Her side of the bed was empty, and the cool blankets told me she'd been gone for a while.

I huffed in annoyance. Once again, she'd ignored my request to wake me when she got up. Yes, I'd gotten in late from the supply run last night, but this morning was the strategy meeting for tonight's raid. And she knew I operated just as well on four hours of sleep as eight. Besides, I was Alpha team leader and needed to be there.

I shoved the covers off, the damp coolness of the room a shock to my skin after the warmth of the blankets. The clothes I wore last night lay in a crumpled heap on the floor and were my fastest option, so I slipped on the wrinkled black jeans and hoodie then shoved my feet into boots. When I opened the heavy metal door, it screeched in protest. We'd been in this long-abandoned factory for a few years now, but the smell of oxidizing iron and stagnant water from a leaking roof never lessened. Dank smells were a small price to pay for safety.

The corridor outside was empty, and my footsteps echoed off the walls as I strode toward the common area, wondering if the strategy meeting had already begun.

"Asher!"

I halted then turned toward the voice. Elijah jogged to catch up and stumbled over an uneven spot on the cracked concrete floor. If he was here, I hadn't missed anything. Without Elijah and his wicked tech skills, we'd be going blind into our missions. He was our eyes when we couldn't see. Not only did he supply the three-dimensional images of our targets during strategy and briefing sessions, he'd developed a radar shield soon after we'd moved into this compound. It was because of him The Colony hadn't found us yet.

He stopped beside me and looked up, grinning sheepishly. "Mind if I walk with you?"

I shrugged and resumed my brisk pace.

Elijah had to jog again to keep up.

"Late night supply run. Brynn didn't wake me this morning."

Elijah continued talking—about what, I really couldn't say, since I tuned him out. He was a genius with the tech stuff, but his endless chatter was like an annoying mosquito that buzzed around your face. My mind was focused on the rescue scheduled for tonight.

"Well? Can you, Ash?"

"Sorry, what?"

"Help me with extra target practice? Please?"

From the residence halls, we emerged on to the catwalk overlooking the common area below then took the stairs down to the main floor. After turning left, raised voices from the conference room drifted around the corner.

"Can we talk about this later? Sounds like I've got something to take care of."

Having spent the better part of the last ten years living with them, I knew those voices well. Noah, my best friend, and Brynn, his sister and my... what? Girlfriend didn't really cover it. Soulmate sounded too cheesy. Reason for existence? Purpose in life? Nothing seemed to fit. She filled all the empty spaces inside me. How do you label that?

Brynn would snort with laughter if she heard me say those words. I knew she loved me, but flowery declarations weren't really her thing, and she accused me of being a romantic at heart. Secretly, I think she enjoyed hearing those cheesy declarations from me.

Noah and Brynn butting heads over procedures or strategy was a regular occurrence. Or butting heads over anything, really. I guessed it was a sibling thing. Their backlog of arguments ranged from differing opinions on complicated tactical maneuvers to the five best foods to douse with ketchup. Over the years, I'd learned to lay low and stay out of their disagreements as much as possible.

When I rounded the corner, brother and sister stood on opposite sides of a long table, facing off. Brynn leaned over, arms braced on the hard surface possibly—probably—to prevent her from leaping over the table and tackling her brother. "That's not the most optimal place for transport, and you know it. It should be obvious there's not enough cover."

Noah stood with his arms folded over his chest. The small, gold hoop earring that had belonged to his mother glinted in the sunlight streaming through the window behind him, and his right index finger sported his father's ring. He wore them to remember his parents, just like the pendant necklace my dad gave me hung around my neck. With the perpetual dampness of the factory, Noah had taken to wearing a dark tan leather coat that fell to mid-calf. The color nearly matched his eyes and was only a few shades lighter than his skin. Brynn teased him about wanting to catch the attention of the new raven-haired guy who worked in the supply section, but I knew Noah was too professional to have a relationship with someone from his own sector. Besides him being Noah's subordinate, it would make things all kinds of awkward if they split up, and Noah avoided drama as much as possible.

Unless it was the drama he and Brynn created when they disagreed.

Noah's expression remained detached as he explained his reasoning. His ability to shelve his emotions was in direct contrast to Brynn's inability to restrain hers. "According to intel, there are more children in this group, and we need transport closer. With our limited timeframe, getting hostages to a more sheltered area would take too long. The transport van can wait further back until they're alerted." He might have looked calm on the outside, but I knew all too well the crease between his brows and his clenched jaw were signs of barely restrained anger. Which made me think this 'discussion' had been going on for quite a while and Brynn had pushed him to his limit today.

Paige turned when I walked in, caught my eye, and threw up her hands in exasperation. Her inky black hair fanned out behind her as she strode away toward a more neutral zone. When diplomacy was handed out, she'd received a triple dose, and it was her natural inclination to act as mediator. Today, it appeared her efforts were in vain.

Brynn wore her usual attire—utility pants, boots, and a snug black t-shirt, its sleeves stretched over toned arms. A leather tie gathered umber-colored, long braids that cascaded down her back. Her slightly crooked nose was the result of an altercation with a Colony soldier's fist meeting her face during a mission a couple years ago. Seconds later, she'd shattered his knee cap with the heel of her boot then rescued the child the soldier was loading into a van. She hated the way it looked, but I loved tracing my finger down its length. It was a reminder we both fought for those who couldn't help themselves. To us, that was more important than our physical attributes—unlike residents of The Colony.

I placed my hand gently at the small of her back, and her body relaxed a bit as it recognized my touch. Which was a relief. I'd seen her incapacitate team members in seconds who hadn't been quite as cautious when approaching her.

"Elijah's here now, so why don't we look at the layout of the harvest center and surrounding area, then come up with a plan that makes everyone happy?"

Noah's mouth twitched slightly at my undisguised attempt to bring peace to the negotiations.

Brynn slid her gaze sideways in my direction then turned to face me. Her lips grazed mine briefly, then she lowered her voice. "How are you awake and alert? It's only been four hours since you got in, and you were on patrol duty the two nights before."

I shrugged. "You know me. A few hours of sleep, and I'm good to go. I feel fine."

She brought her hand to my face. On the outside, Brynn was an obstinate, fierce operative who had no patience for anyone who wasted her time. Underneath that was a woman who cared deeply for those closest to her. Anyone she allowed in her circle discovered a loyal friend and protector who would defend her loved ones to the death. She was someone you wanted on your side.

Her mahogany-colored eyes were filled with concern. "You need to rest."

I brought her hand to my lips and kissed the tips of her fingers. "I'll nap later. If I have time."

"I'll make sure of it."

Noah cleared his throat. "If you could keep your hands off my sister, Ash, maybe we could get started."

A glance around the table revealed eight sets of eyes staring at us. The rest of my team—Paige and Oz—along with Beta team, their expressions a mix of amusement, annoyance, and envy. I'd been so focused on Brynn, I hadn't noticed them waiting.

Brynn smirked in Noah's direction, and I shrugged in apology as we took our seats. A 3-D hologram of the harvest site rose from the middle of the table, courtesy of Elijah.

Noah said, "According to our intel, soldiers raided the northern sector of Lancaster last night, and this harvest lab received a delivery of one hundred people. At least half of them children. As you've probably already guessed, most of these children are now orphans."

Words of outrage and sympathy were uttered, Paige's louder than anyone's. When Colony soldiers came for their children, Outlier parents usually put up a fight—as any loving parent would. Unfortunately, it was an action that sealed their fate. The Colony took what they wanted.

"Word has come down from Central that our window of opportunity for rescuing these people has narrowed considerably. Instead of the usual three-day processing period before harvesting, that timeframe has been shortened to one day."

Surprised gasps and curses flowed around the table, until Noah raised his hand for quiet. "The reason for change is due to a malfunction with the freezers when the nitrogen became too warm. An enormous number of products were lost, and Colony residents are making their displeasure known. To make up for the loss, scouting and harvesting have tripled."

Products. The word repulsed me and was something I'd never gotten used to in all the years we'd been fighting The Colony. As Insurgents, we used the word in an attempt to distance ourselves from its true definition. The real word invoked a flood of emotions that snowballed into outrage over something we had little to no control over. It was best to focus that energy where it would be better utilized helping those victims we could reach.

Twenty years ago, a few years before my birth, scientists developed and perfected the process of gene editing in embryos, which changed the futures of the unborn population. Genomes that carried both life-threatening and non-life-threatening diseases could be altered before a fetus was born. Changing the DNA of an embryo, or germline engineering, meant genes for that disease would never be passed down to any subsequent offspring. Inherited disorders were essentially eradicated. Not only would these babies grow up disease-free, so would their descendants. In the future, people would no longer suffer from conditions such as cancer, heart disease, HIV, diabetes, and so many others. The population would be healthy. Natural causes, fatal accidents, or murder would be the primary causes of death. This unparalleled, miraculous discovery would eliminate pain and suffering for untold millions of people in the future.

But what about the people who suffered from those diseases now? What about their quality of life?

It turned out gene editing in children and adults was trickier. Monumental mistakes by scientists resulted in numerous deaths of those who'd volunteered for the experiments. After such disastrous results, funding was withdrawn, and the program shut down.

But some of the bigger egos couldn't accept all those failures, and with donations from an undisclosed organization, a group of scientists continued their experiments. Eventually, they discovered a solution.

Gene stripping.

This technique required healthy genomes to be stripped from one person then implanted in another, replacing the affected genes for the inherited disease. Once the method was perfected, it was just a matter of time before those with the means to afford it clamored for traits and characteristics.

Say an Outlier, those who weren't high enough in society to reside behind the gates of The Colony, possessed an enviable characteristic or quality—an attractive eye color, curly or straight hair, or heightened intelligence. If it was marketable or desirable, the Outlier was captured, taken to a harvest site, then stripped of their genes. Screaming, helpless children ripped from their parents. Moms and dads dragged away from their children. Families split up. Age wasn't a deterrent. If an Outlier had a covetous trait, they were taken. All because Colony residents desired a different hair color, wanted to be better at math, or decided they shouldn't have to live with diabetes.

Once the genes were stripped, there was only one outcome.

Death.

So, in reality, 'product' was a moniker for genes stripped from Outliers, sold, then implanted into wealthy Colony residents.

That's why the Insurgents had fought against them since the inception of harvesting. It's the reason we lived in this abandoned, rusted out factory. Why all of the Insurgent sectors were located in secluded areas. If we were found and captured, thousands—tens of thousands—of lives would be lost because we wouldn't be there to save them.

Noah directed a laser pointer on the holo of the harvest site to indicate our positions. "Our inside contact will shut off the power at exactly midnight. The tech van will be a half mile away. Elijah, you'll have thirty seconds before backup power kicks in to hack into their system and deactivate the security alarm."

Oz glanced at Elijah, his left eyebrow raised in skepticism. "You got this, E?"

"Through sheer talent." He ducked his head and glanced up sideways at Oz. "I may also have been given backdoor information to their system by the inside contact."

For Elijah, I doubted the backdoor was even necessary. Probably best not to take chances, though. Especially with all the children in this intake group.

Noah continued. "We know they'll have four guards patrolling the perimeter behind the fence. Alpha team will handle them then make their way inside from the delivery ramp out back. At that time of night, there should be minimal employees, if any, in that area of the building. Beta team will hold until further instructed."

As Noah continued, my mind drifted. I'd helped him outline the plan yesterday and already knew it inside and out. My purpose for being here was to make sure the other operatives understood the importance of this mission. Not that they didn't take their jobs seriously and use the utmost caution when raiding harvest sites—it was the number of children involved this time. So many things could go wrong, and from previous raids, I'd seen first-hand their scared and confused faces. The ray of hope in their eyes when they understood we were there to help, not hurt them.

I'd also witnessed utter resignation. Blank expressions and dull eyes accompanied by the knowledge that no one was coming for them. Death was a certainty. They'd never see their families again. Their lives were forfeited because people considered them less than human, expendable—nothing more than a walking display of merchandise for purchase.

The dream that woke me this morning seeped back into my mind, the last day I'd spent playing with my sisters. The last time I'd ever seen my parents. My last day as a child, really. We'd never found a trace of Elsa or Cami after I'd left them hidden in the forest, but I'd always been pretty certain of their fate. Elsa's untamed, wheat-colored hair and Cami's sapphire blue eyes had always been in high demand.

"Questions?" Noah's voice snapped me back to the briefing. His gaze landed briefly on each of us gathered at the table, but no one replied. "All right, then. We leave in twelve hours." He strode from the room in the direction of his office.

Directly across from me, Jonah turned to Mason. "Noah's being a real hardass today, did you notice? Do you really think all our bases are covered on this mission?"

Jonah was a fairly new arrival to our compound, having joined us about six months ago. After we'd lost four operatives over the course of two weeks, sector twelve supplied us with some of their new recruits.

Brynn tensed beside me, then shoved her seat back and planted her hands on the table. "Hey, newbie. You've got what, around twenty missions under your belt? The first three you froze in the field and required remedial training. Two weeks ago, the transport van had to be hosed down because you hurled your dinner after seeing a couple of dead bodies. Do you really think you're qualified to question the judgement of your Controller? Someone with almost five years' experience in the field and who grew up in this environment? Keep your mouth shut and listen to operatives who know what they're doing. Maybe you'll learn something. Quit giving the maintenance guys extra work. They shouldn't have to deal with your messes. And if I hear you talking about my brother like that again, I'll see you in the sparring ring."

Jonah gulped, his face tinged crimson from his collar to the tips of his ears. I'd seen him in the sparring ring, and with one armed pinned behind her back, Brynn would put him down in a couple of minutes. It would only take that long because she'd enjoy teasing him first.

Luciana, Beta's team leader, met my gaze, and she looked angry enough to take Jonah into the sparring ring herself. She nodded, indicating she'd handle him, then Beta team followed her out of the room.

"Remind me to never get on your bad side, Brynn. I value certain parts of my anatomy too much to part with them." Oz slung an arm over Paige's shoulders. She immediately stiffened and angled away from him, pulling her jacket from the back of her chair. Oz tried to hide it, but I saw the flash of disappointment in his eyes as he pulled strands of his dark blond hair forward to cover the burns on the left side of his face and neck. I'd noticed this habitual response when he felt insecure or embarrassed. I suspected it was why he wore his hair longer and only tied it back for missions.

Brynn's eyes narrowed. "Just keep doing your job, Oz, and you and I will be fine." She and Paige wandered away, chatting to each other. About what, I couldn't tell you. Paige was an exceptional operative, but even after living in close quarters for the past couple years, she remained all business. Always polite, but she maintained a boundary around herself no one had successfully penetrated.

And Oz had tried. If I had gold stars to give out for effort, he'd shine brightly from head to toe. For months, he'd used every angle he could think of to learn about her interests outside of missions. We all had other hobbies or activities that distracted us from the stress of what we did. We were encouraged to take breaks and allow our minds and bodies to recharge. For Brynn, it was something physical. Rock climbing was her drug of choice, or really any activity that got her heart pumping. If it involved a sliver of danger, all the better. She'd fixed up an old dirt bike last year and rode the local trails.

Noah could be found reading anything he could get his hands on. Some of the collaborators made an effort to send him new books along with our monthly supplies. I suspected his deepest desire was to form a book club, but considering our way of life, I doubted he'd be able to maintain it. Especially if members kept getting killed off during missions.

For me, it was games of strategy. Chess, checkers, cards—calculating moves, planning ahead, forming backup plans—my mind loved the challenge. Noah had loaned me some books on war strategies, and I'd gotten through a couple of them, but it really wasn't my thing. I preferred hands-on learning.

Oz possessed a strong sense of curiosity and a need to learn how things worked, whether it was machinery, technical equipment, or organizations. He'd hung out in every area of the compound, questioning people about their jobs and absorbing their information.

To my knowledge, Paige remained the only puzzle he couldn't crack. He tracked her as she left the room with Brynn, his eyes full of hope and longing. Oz was persistent, but after this many months, I was almost certain he was fighting a losing battle.

"Got any advice for me, Ash?"

"Wish I could help, but I've got nothing."

Oz dropped his gaze and scuffed the toe of his shoe on the floor. "It's the scars. Paige is beautiful. Those jade green eyes... she's truly stunning. Why would she want to be seen with a guy like me?"

"Paige is a lot of things, but shallow isn't a word I'd ever use to describe her." I clasped his shoulder and squeezed it reassuringly. "Maybe just relax for a while and see where it goes."

He fell back into a chair and scrubbed his face. "Brynn scares the crap out of me most of the time, but you guys are really lucky to have each other, you know? Everything we go through, the uncertainty we face—it sure would be nice to have a partner to share things with. Especially someone who understands what we do. The two of you make it look so easy."

I snorted. "Easy? You have no idea." I dropped onto the seat next to him. "I almost ruined everything between us before you got here, and she called me on it. Told me to walk."

"No way. You guys broke up?"

Regret swept over me when I remembered how I'd nearly let my own stupidity and insecurities ruin our relationship.

3

ASHER

Growing up, Brynn had always been Noah's annoying younger sister, butting in when we were playing, following us around, and generally being a nuisance. I'd teased her as much as—or even more than—Noah because she was essentially my sister, too.

Until one day, she wasn't.

I'd been hiking in the woods behind the compound. Sometimes I needed time alone to remember my family and relive memories. It scared me to think those memories could disappear as easily as my family had, and they were all I had left. When I'd talked to Anna, Brynn and Noah's mom, about it, she'd encouraged me to write them down, then even if I forgot things over time, I'd always remember our home filled with love.

Emerging from a group of trees, I'd come upon Brynn stretched out along a fallen log, eyes closed, her hands resting on her stomach. It was fall, and only a few stubborn leaves remained on the trees. Late afternoon sun illuminated her body, and her skin glowed a dark bronze. Ebony braids trailed toward the ground. Even then, she'd preferred her hair long.

I halted abruptly. Stood still, silent. My mouth felt dry, and my heart galloped as though I'd run for miles instead of ambling. This wasn't Brynn, my annoying kind-of-sister who hid in trees and around corners, jumped out hoping to scare me, and stole my chocolate chip cookies when I wasn't looking. I wasn't sure where she'd gone, but some kind of alluring creature had taken her place. When did this happen and where had I been during the transformation?

As if she sensed my presence, she opened her eyes and rolled her head in my direction, a slow smile spreading across her face. "Are you going to keep gawking, or do you want to sit down?"

I blinked slowly, then moved in her direction, half stumbling while I wiped my suddenly sweaty palms on my pants. She eased herself to a sitting position and straddled the log, while I swung my leg over and mirrored her.

"Thinking about your family again?"

"Yeah." My voice was unusually rough. "It's been worse lately. Next week makes another year they've been gone. I was remembering how Elsa loved it when I attended her tea parties."

Brynn giggled. "I remember that shirt of your mom's Elsa made you wear one time. Floral prints did wonders for your coloring."

I laughed with her, but then the pain overwhelmed me, and I choked back a sob. "I failed them. If I'd stayed with my sisters..."

She reached over and gripped my knee. "No, Ash. Don't ever think that. You were a good big brother to her and Cami and only following your father's directions. He had his reasons."

"That's what I keep telling myself. But what possible reason could there be for me to leave my sisters behind? I didn't want to, but Cami's instructions were to make sure I followed through."

Brynn shrugged. "You may never know what happened. But you have to quit blaming yourself. Maybe your parents and sisters are still out there somewhere."

"Yeah, right." I broke off a piece of dead wood from the log and threw it toward a hole in a tree across the clearing. It sailed through the middle of the opening. "If they were still out there, why haven't they come back for me? I'm exactly where my dad told me to go."

"Ash Solomon, you look at me." Brynn's tone left no room for argument. She'd inherited it from Anna, and I'd heard it plenty of times over the years when Noah and I hadn't picked up our room or we'd tracked mud in the house.

My gaze raised to hers, and I peered out through dark blond strands of hair falling over my forehead.

"Quit feeling sorry for yourself. Your parents loved you, which is why you're here, safe with us. Nothing could have stopped them from getting to you if they were able.

"I know it hurts every day they're gone. But you have us, you know. We're your family, too. When you're old enough, maybe you can go look for them." A dazzling smile slid across her face. "Maybe I'd even help you."

And that was the day Brynn first flashed the smile reserved just for me. The day I quit looking at her as my sister and felt the stirrings of something more between us.

Since then, we'd only been apart for one week. It was devastating, soul-crushing, enlightening, and my own stupid fault.

It was before Patrick and Anna died. We hadn't been working as operatives for very long and had just received the location on a harvest center. Everyone was gathered around the table, and Patrick had just finished outlining the rescue strategy. Nothing out of the ordinary, but problems were anticipated with this one. Intel told us The Colony were providing extra soldiers, as this intake group contained 'specimens' in high demand. Extra vigilance was required. Another Insurgent team had attempted a rescue at this facility a couple months ago and had suffered several lost operatives during the mission.

I'd pulled Brynn into an empty seating area for privacy. "I think you should stay here, sit this one out."

"Stop, Asher. Just stop right there." She held up her hand in front of me in a halting motion. "You have no right to tell me what to do."

I rubbed my hands over my face in irritation and leaned against the wall. "It's a dangerous mission, Brynn. I don't want you to get hurt."

She tilted her head to the side, narrowed her eyes, and looked at me questioningly. "Really. Haven't we both taken the same self-defense classes and spent an equal amount of time sparring and in the field?"

"We have. But so many people were hurt or killed just last month. I don't want to see anything happen to you." We'd been going at this for a while, and frustration had taken a deep hold. On both of us.

She crossed to the opposite side of the room muttering to herself, then turned to face me. "I'm a good operative, Ash. Next to you, I'm probably the best in the field, and you know it."

"Damn it, Brynn, I know you're a good operative."

"Then what is it? We both know I'm not the delicate type or an indoor girl, and I'm not going to stay in the compound and work behind a desk. That's not me." Her voice had an edge to it. A tone I'd never heard before. And it scared me.

I strode over and took both of her hands in mine. "I don't know what I'd do if something happened to you, okay? There's no way I could handle it. My instinct is to protect you." I pressed my lips to her knuckles.

She jerked her hands from mine. "I know how you feel about me, but your insecurities about my safety aren't going to put limits on me. I won't change who I am for you, and you're out of line for asking me to. I'm capable of taking care of myself, and if you can't get that in your head, then maybe we shouldn't be together."

A chasm opened beneath me, swallowing me whole. I couldn't lose her. What happened? How did we get here? Everything I said came out all wrong. "Maybe you should take some time to think about things."

"No!" I reached for her with trembling hands. "Please. I'm sorry, okay?" My voice shook.

Brynn's eyes softened, and she placed a hand on my cheek. "I'm not ending things between us, Ash. You're as essential to me as breathing. But maybe some time apart isn't such a bad thing for us while you come to terms with this." She tiptoed up and kissed my lips softly. "I'll be here waiting when you're ready."

Brynn spent a week away from me. In close quarters like this, that wasn't an easy feat, but she requested Patrick put us on separate missions. Passing her in the halls was torture. The questioning glances and whispers from others made me want to punch a hole in the wall.

I asked Noah for advice, but he refused to get in the middle of it. Said we needed to figure things out for ourselves, but wondered what, in all the years I'd known Brynn, made me think I could change her?

I wasn't a therapist, but the root of my fear for Brynn's safety was obvious, and it was carrying over into our relationship. Logically, I knew I couldn't keep her locked up in the compound. But remaining here instead of taking missions in the field increased her odds of survival or avoiding serious injury. Brynn was deeply committed to fighting The Colony, and she'd never been the type to sit on the sidelines and watch. I'd known this about her even when we were children.

Loving her meant loving every proud, stubborn, and challenging part of her. I needed to have faith in Brynn's ability to know what was best for her and be responsible for her own safety. It didn't mean I wouldn't worry, but that was just a part of loving someone so completely.

4

ASHER

Under cover of night, Alpha and Beta teams sprinted through the trees flanking the north side of the harvest facility. Besides our dark clothing that blended into the shadows, clouds shielded the nearly full moon and provided extra cover for us. It was a perfect night for a raid. The transport vans waited for our all-clear signal half a mile away and were equipped to handle over a hundred people.

Noah and Elijah were on the other end of our comm devices in the tech van. Noah was running the operation, and Elijah would soon infiltrate the facility's security system then stand ready to alert us of any obstacles.

Alpha and Beta teams took cover behind the trees while Oz and 1 surveyed the fenced area with night scopes. Most of the harvest facility was built back into the hill behind it, and the part that jutted out was a pale gray, two-story, windowless building with a single door at the front entrance. To the right of the building was a parking lot and not much else, but on the opposite side was the delivery area. Captured Outliers were unloaded, brought into the harvest center against their will, assessed for their characteristics and qualities, and then put to death.

Anger ripped through my veins at the thought of any hostages being roughly shoved inside, especially the children who were terrified beyond reason.

"Sitrep on the perimeter, Oz." Noah's voice was calm and controlled.

"Intel was correct. Four armed guards, evenly spaced." At some facilities, we'd seen guards on the night shift who took it as an opportunity to slack off. Staffing was at a minimum, and deliveries of Outliers usually arrived during the day, so their nights were often slow.

Which made it the perfect time for Insurgents to strike.

In contrast, these guards scanned the trees and stopped at regular intervals to assess their surroundings.

In the back corner of the delivery area was a collection of several barrel drums. I pointed it out to the teams. "When the power goes down, that's our point of entry. We'll have sixty seconds to cut through the fence and get ourselves inside. The barrels are our cover."

I shoved the night scope into my bag then motioned for both teams to head toward the entry point. Luciana's Beta team trailed behind us. Using the tree line as camouflage, eight of us moved swiftly through the forest. What little noise we made was covered by the usual nighttime chatter of birds and insects. In minutes, we reached the fence, then we crouched behind the barrels.

"Luci, keep your eye on the perimeter. Standby for backup."

"Got it, Ash."

I dragged my gaze over Oz, Paige, and Brynn, and they all nodded their readiness. We'd worked together as a team for months, and I trusted each of them with my life. I knew without a doubt we'd all look out for each other.

"In position," I said to Elijah.

"On my mark, you have sixty seconds."

Spotlights around the perimeter went dark when the power was cut by the inside contact. Perimeter guards called out to each other in confusion, unsure if it was merely a power outage or something more. Over the comm unit in my ear came the sound of Elijah's fingers flying across the keyboard as he deactivated the security system, then he said, "Go."

I nodded to Brynn, who already had wire cutters out of her bag and at the ready. With no electricity or alarm on the fence, she safely snapped through the first several links, but the last two presented a problem. No matter how she angled the bolt cutter, it wasn't working.

"Brynn?" I asked.

She ignored me and continued maneuvering the cutter.

"Losing your touch?" Oz teased.

Paige shot a warning glance at him.

Brynn increased her efforts.

"Twenty seconds," I said.

Oz moved to grab the cutters from her, but Brynn shoved him off and growled, "I've got this."

With only seconds to go, the links finally gave way.

Oz sprang forward, rolled the fence back, then held it open while we dove through, loose dirt forming a cloud around us. He then followed behind. We'd made it with only seconds to spare. Oz's remark had angered Brynn, and even though she'd probably wanted to throttle him, she'd stayed on task. I'd lay money on a confrontation later.

Oz and Paige headed toward the guards closest to the front entrance, while Brynn and I targeted the other two by the loading dock.

Clouds shifted, and a shaft of moonlight fell across Brynn's face. Her mahogany eyes sparkled with excitement. When Brynn, Noah, and I had been old enough to choose our areas of training, Noah tried to steer Brynn in the direction of tech support rather than field operative. Even though he was less than a year older, his big brother instincts were strong, and he'd wanted to protect her. It was the same stupid mistake I'd make later on. But Brynn let him know in no uncertain terms what he could do with that suggestion. After only a few months of training, her accuracy rate on the shooting range and speed on the obstacle course made it clear she was a natural. Scaling a wall came as easily to her as brushing her teeth. But where she really excelled was in hand-to-hand combat. Brynn had bested everyone in our training class, Noah included. To his credit, he'd taken it like a champ.

Correction. Brynn had beaten everyone except me. Though not from lack of trying. Besides our routine workouts with the other operatives, the two of us regularly sparred with each other a couple times a week to stay sharp. Brynn was always a challenge, but to let her win would be an insult. She'd see right through it and expected nothing less than my best effort.

That's what I always gave her. And why I knew she could handle herself in the field.

Guns drawn and movements cloaked by the shadows, Brynn and I sprinted toward the guards. When power was restored, the element of surprise would no longer be on our side, so we had to be fast.

Our targets were in conversation with each other, still trying to figure out what went wrong with the lights. We stopped behind stairs leading to the loading dock.

"You take the one on the right," I whispered.

"Gladly." Her eyes gleamed in anticipation.

We holstered our guns then charged our marks, accelerating out of the shadows from behind them. I hooked one arm around the guard's throat and put my other hand behind his neck in a choke hold. Seconds later, I lowered him to the ground before he knew what happened.

Although I'd reached my guard only seconds before Brynn, it was enough time for her target to be alerted.

The guard spun around to face her, as his hand reached for the gun holstered at his side. But before he could draw the weapon, she took a running leap and used his thigh as a springboard to propel herself up. She hooked her right leg around his neck then used her momentum to take them both to the ground. With his air supply cut off, he was unconscious in seconds.

She was so graceful—it was like watching a deadly ballet.

"Very nice."

"He went down quicker than you."

Brynn had practiced the move on me over the past few weeks, wrapping her legs around my neck dozens, possibly hundreds of times.

I grinned. "Maybe I enjoyed it more."

She smirked in reply.

Brynn ripped the radio from the belt of her guard then smashed it with her boot. I kept the other guard's radio, turning down the volume before clipping it to my belt. Didn't need any static announcing our presence. Brynn tossed me zip ties she'd removed from her bag, and we secured their wrists and ankles. Then we gagged them, just in case they woke a little early. The perimeter lights sputtered back on as we dragged the guards into the shadows.

Oz and Paige jogged around the corner and joined us. "Problems?" I asked.

Oz smiled. "Nothing we couldn't handle."

I nodded and gave Elijah our status. "We're moving."

Guns drawn, the four of us slipped back into the shadows then sprinted toward our entry point at the loading dock.

Every individual sector of Insurgents spread across our country was headed by a Controller—in our case, Noah—who reported to Central. Central was like a brain regulating the body. They kept tabs on Colony soldiers and harvest centers, handed down missions, and oversaw the running of safe houses for Insurgents and rescued hostages. When Noah assigned those missions, he devised a plan to infiltrate the facility and get the team and hostages back to the compound, but how we handled obstacles and life-threatening situations was left to the team leaders. And the approaches tended to vary.

Rule one on my team—we don't kill needlessly. Other team leaders didn't share my views, but that wasn't something I could control. Life was precious, and most of these people were only doing their jobs, trying to survive in a world controlled by The Colony. The soldiers had families to provide for, and I had to believe the majority of them loathed what they did but had no other choice. They'd taken my parents and sisters, but thanks to The Colony, there was an excessive number of orphans in the world, and I wouldn't be responsible for increasing their numbers if I could help it.

When two new operatives to my team killed two soldiers on their first mission, I'd learned the circumstances weren't life threatening. Those lives could have been spared. Back at the compound, I'd raged at them while they cowered in a corner, their heads hung low. After I'd booted them from my team, Patrick had reassigned them.

Their lives hadn't been threatened in that particular situation. But if any of the captives or our team were endangered, Insurgents were trained to kill without hesitation. And we had.

When we reached the loading dock, Brynn and Paige covered my back while I tried one of the double metal doors leading into the facility. Despite its heaviness, it opened easily, but a rusty creak echoed against the high walls. If anyone waited for us inside, it would definitely draw their attention in our direction.

While I held the door open, Brynn and Paige entered and scanned the large room, guns raised. Then Paige said, "Clear."

Oz and I followed behind them. The east wing housed the captives, and three hallways and a guard station stood between us. At this time of night, most hostages should be sleeping and staff was at a minimum. But that didn't mean we wouldn't encounter any resistance.

We weaved through rows of supplies stacked on towering shelves. "Look at all of this food," Oz whispered, gaping longingly at the cans and boxes of nonperishable items. "Peanut butter! It's been so long since I've tasted it. Don't we have time to stuff a few jars into my bag?"

Brynn grabbed the back of his collar and pushed him forward. "Keep moving."

I regretted having no way to transport everything to our compound. The food could feed us for months, and the medical supplies taking up the rest of the shelf space were always useful. We received adequate food deliveries from a network of collaborators, but when we returned with rescued hostages after a mission, they sometimes couldn't be transported to safe areas for a couple days. That was a lot of mouths to feed and injuries to treat, and these supplies would allow us a nice cushion—rations wouldn't have to be quite as severe. Maybe we could return and clean out their shelves at a later time, but after a breach, it was likely security would be heightened and patrols doubled.

We continued through the rows until we reached the wide, double doors leading out of the supply room and into the hallway.

"Elijah, are we clear?" My voice was barely above a whisper, but I knew he heard me.

"Two guards headed your way. Security cameras are looped and will show nothing but empty hallways. No motion sensors."

I cursed under my breath. They must have heard the door when we entered. Oz and I immediately flanked the doors on either side, while Paige and Brynn took cover behind a pallet of boxes. My muscles tensed in anticipation of an attack.

The doors swung outward into the hallway, and the one closest to Oz began to creep open. Through the narrow crack, the nose of a rifle appeared. Before its owner could enter behind it, Oz pushed the barrel toward the ceiling, jerked the rifle out of the guard's hands, and shoved him to the ground. His partner rushed in behind him, but didn't get far after I thrust the heel of my boot into the side of her knee. She yelped and grimaced in pain, then toppled to the ground and dropped her weapon. I kicked it out of reach and motioned for Brynn and Paige to come forward.

Four zip ties and a couple gags later, we were ready to proceed.

"Elijah?" I asked.

"You're clear until the second hallway. Three unarmed people are headed in your direction."

We slipped through the doors then jogged down the darkened corridor. Although the overhead fluorescents weren't on, dimmer lights gave off an eerie orangish glow. Where the hall took a right turn, we waited behind the corner for the three unarmed people. They could possibly be support staff or off duty guards, but they might be the scientists who stripped the genes from the hostages. Just the thought of that made we want to override my rule, but at this point, we had no confirmation of their occupation.

Their voices echoed through the hallway just before they rounded the corner. Brynn, Paige, and Oz scuffled briefly with them but covered their mouths before they could call out. After lowering them to the floor and securing them in the same manner as the guards, we continued.

"You're clear to the entrance of the hostage wing," Elijah said.

Had my sisters wound up in a place like this? Maybe even this very facility? I shuddered thinking what their fates might have been. What their last moments were like. I'd promised to come back for them. Were they alone after they'd been taken? Or did they at least have each other? Had they blamed me for leaving them?

I shook my head to clear it. Now wasn't the time to think about them. I needed to focus on the mission and save the people I still could.

The corridor dead-ended, and the only option was a left turn. We came to a halt at the corner, backs to the wall. Arms bent with my gun pointed at the ceiling, I sneaked a look around the corner, then pulled back. Nodding at Brynn, she spun out into the hallway, gun at the ready on the off chance we were met with opposition. Elijah said we were clear, but extra precautions had saved us more than once. The four of us moved quickly down the last corridor that ended in front of a door with a keypad to its right. Behind this lay the guard desk outside the entrance to the east wing where the innocents were being held. I trusted Elijah to assist with the code.

"Update?" I asked him.

"Two guards inside. The key code is 85432."

I craned my neck up toward the security camera directly overhead that would show an empty hallway on the guards' monitor. When the door slid open unexpectedly, their moment or two of surprise and hesitation would be an advantage for us.

I closed my eyes and forced down all the doubt and visions of ways this could go sideways. We were well-trained. Considering what we were about to do and the risks involved, my pulse should have been galloping. From what Brynn told me, that was a typical reaction. But my rate had always been normal—even slower than normal—on missions. I told myself it was because I was in excellent physical shape, I'd calculated the risks and outcomes, and our briefings left us well-prepared. Deep down, though, I knew nothing was guaranteed. Anything could go wrong. And it had on previous missions.

Yet still my pulse didn't spike.

Oz and Paige flanked one side of the door, and Brynn stood behind me on the other. My team crouched in readiness. I punched in the security code, the light on the pad switched from red to green, then the door whooshed open.

"Go!" I yelled. Paige and I spun in from opposite sides, guns pointed at the surprised guards to cover them.

One of them leaped to his feet behind a desk. "What the..." The other fumbled with something at his side. Probably his gun. Before he could draw, Brynn and Oz rushed past us.

Oz jumped to the top of the desk. Towering over the seated guard—who gaped up at him with a shocked expression—he raised the butt of his gun then thrust it down. It impacted his opponent's forehead with a dull thud, then the guard slumped from his seat, unconscious. As Oz secured him, he said, "Well, he was kind of useless."

Brynn's guard put up more of a struggle. While she matched him blow for blow, I saw the realization come over his face that he'd severely underestimated her.

Elijah's voice crackled in my ear. "Ash, six armed guards incoming."

Now it was getting interesting. "Luci, launch Beta team."

"On the way," she replied.

Brynn landed a brutal punch to her opponent's jaw, his head snapped sideways, then he dropped hard to the floor.

"Brynn, you and Oz take cover behind the desk. Paige and I have the door. Be ready." I took my place opposite Paige at the only entrance to the room.

Guards streamed through, guns at the ready. In this situation, my life preservation rule would have to be suspended. Our lives were in imminent danger, and I wasn't losing anyone tonight.

Paige and I quickly put down the first two guards when they entered, but that alerted our presence to the other four. Brynn slid out from the left side of the guard desk in a low crouch and shot a guard in the chest. He got off a few rounds before he fell, but they went high.

Oz popped up and clipped the fourth one in the shoulder, but he took a bullet to his left upper arm, spun, hit the wall, then went down. He was exposed, and an easy target.

"Oz is hit," Brynn yelled. She lunged forward, grabbed Oz's uninjured arm, then pulled him back to safety behind the desk.

Two guards whipped around toward me and Paige. Before her guard had turned completely, she raced toward him, leap-frogged across a table, then thrust her legs out in front of her. She was like a human missile when her feet connected with his face. After he hit the ground, a swift kick to the head put his lights out.

Compared to the girls, Oz and I were totally outclassed when it came to style.

I ran at my guard, dropped to the floor, then slid into her legs. As she toppled over me, I wrenched away her gun. After tossing it to Paige, I straddled her chest. One hard punch to her jaw and she was out of the game.

Brynn had a cut over her left eye, but had taken care of the guard who'd wounded Oz. His arm was bleeding, but it was only a superficial wound, and he'd be fine after medical patched him up. The whole altercation had taken only minutes and was over by the time Beta team swarmed through the door.

"Nice," said Luciana as she surveyed the damage. "Guess you didn't need us after all."

I shrugged. Extra help was something I'd never turn down. "Stand guard with your team while we bring out the hostages."

"Affirmative."

"Elijah?"

"Clear for now."

Alpha team entered the holding room containing the 'donors' as The Colony referred to them. As if it had been their choice to generously donate their genes. Hostage was the correct term.

I was surprised there was no code on this door. It would have added an extra layer of security. Did they really think Insurgents would never make it this far into their facility? Even more evidence of their overconfidence and arrogance. They assumed no one was a threat to their way of life, thought they were entitled to take what they wanted without regard to anyone else simply because of their station in life.

We entered a dim room. The stench of mildew, sweat, and waste was overpowering, and I nearly gagged. Two rows of beds lined either side of the room. Privacy was nonexistent. Not even curtains to separate the occupants. Men, women, and children were all housed together. Although it was the middle of the night, several of them were still awake, undoubtedly disturbed by our scuffle outside their door. Paige's head whipped in the direction of the muffled sounds of children whimpering.

I'd never understand how someone could knowingly take the life of a child. I hoped karma ensured those who were responsible for the loss of their innocent lives would suffer the same pain for eternity. Since inherited diseases, cancer, and other illnesses had been all but eradicated, people were living longer and population numbers had increased. With their warped reasoning, The Colony justified their actions by claiming harvesting helped control the growth rate, which was a benefit for all.

All of *them*. I didn't see any Colony citizens volunteering to be 'donors'.

The clang of metal on metal echoed through the lofty room. Brynn's narrowed gaze snapped to mine in question. I caught movement out of the corner of my eye and pivoted to the first bed on my left. A young boy, no older than eight-years-old, crawled slowly toward me on his mattress. His movements were awkward, and he dragged one leg behind him. That's when I saw it.

Everyone here, children included, was restrained by metal ankle cuffs chained to their beds. I gaped in horror at the young boy, his ankle raw and bleeding from the attached hardware, as he looked up at me with pleading eyes. "Can you help us? Please?"

Hatred for the people who'd done this bloomed hot in my gut. We'd infiltrated numerous harvest facilities and rescued thousands of people, but the conditions had never been this horrendous. My gaze darted over pots holding the occupants' waste, to the surrounding beds where thin blankets covered the stained, lumpy mattresses. The Colony treated their animals better than this. With the lack of mobility, adults were restricted from moving to the beds of children, unable to provide the little ones even the smallest bit of comfort before they were forcibly dragged to their deaths.

"Oh, no." Paige's eyes rimmed with tears. Oz muttered curses under his breath.

"Yes. We're getting all of you out of here." I caught a glimmer of hope in the boy's shimmering eyes, and the corner of his mouth twitched upward in a half smile. "Oz, you and Brynn search the guards for master keys. This was unexpected, and we need to move fast. Noah, we've got a delay. The hostages are chained to their beds. All need to be released before we can get them to transport."

"We're not leaving without them," he replied. "Luci, move your team into the hallways leading to the egress point. We may have more company."

"On it," she said.

Paige sat beside the boy and tucked him under her arm, pushing his hair away from his face. He collapsed against her, eyes closed. Few people ever saw this side of her. She might have been a closed book with adults, but she opened her heart to children.

Brynn and Oz returned with two handheld tubular devices that emitted a red pinpoint of light. When pointed at the sensor on the ankle restraint, it snapped open. Brynn and I quickly moved down each row, releasing hostages, while Paige directed them toward the lobby where Oz stood guard.

When the last person was freed, I alerted Elijah. "Send the transports."

"Affirmative."

We escorted the hostages down the long corridors, making our way back to the loading dock. Beta team fell in behind us and covered our backs. Two large transport vans waited. The four of us stood watch while Mason and Luciana assisted the rescued into the vehicles.

Several of the adults held small children, and my heart jolted when I saw a young girl, her long, blond curls bouncing as a woman carried her. Elsa's hair had been the same color, her curls just as untamed. When the child turned her head toward me, I anticipated Elsa's iridescent blue eyes, but was greeted with dark brown instead.

What was wrong with me? If Elsa had lived, she'd be fourteen-years-old now, not four. Maybe it was my dream from the night before that brought thoughts of her so close and caused me to keep seeing her here tonight.

"It's not her, Ash." My head snapped in Brynn's direction. Of course she'd noticed my lapse in attention. Sometimes I swore she could read my mind and knew me almost better than I knew myself. Many nights I woke Brynn as I cried out in my sleep, reliving the nightmare of leaving Elsa and Cami behind and saving myself. She'd always been there to wrap her arms around me and offer reassurances that it hadn't been my fault.

I bolted straight up in bed covered in sweat, my heart racing.

Brynn gently cupped my cheek and wiped away tears I hadn't known were there. "Shhh, Ash. It was just a dream."

Her soothing voice reached my ears, but I was still in the forest. Dark trees formed a canopy overhead, mossy ground made a carpet beneath me. I stared at the boulder I'd hidden my sisters behind. My gaze darted around the shrubbery in search of them. I pushed Brynn away, shaking my head. "No, no. I'm not leaving them again. Never again."

"You're here with me, Ash. What you're seeing happened a long time ago. Come back." Brynn spoke quietly, while gently guiding me back to a prone position. She pulled my head to her chest and ran her fingers through my hair to calm me.

The familiar vibrations of her voice were like a rope spanning the years between the past and present, and I clung to it desperately to find my way back to her. I breathed deeply, and my pounding heart slowed to a normal rate. But the dampness on my cheeks remained, and I blinked away unshed tears.

"It wasn't your fault."

Our voices were near whispers in the stillness of the night, the only other sound the faint dripping of water hitting concrete. "I should have known better. If I'd stayed with them or brought them with me to your house, maybe my sisters would still be here."

"You can't know your presence would have made a difference. Cami was hurt, and there's no way she could have kept up. You couldn't have carried both of them, and all of you would have been in danger."

We'd had that conversation more times than I could count, but Brynn always talked me through it. Impatience never seeped into her voice. No matter what she said, guilt was a part of my life, just like eating, breathing, and sleeping. I'd never be free of it.

There were two constants in my life—living with the uncertainty of what my family's fate had been, and knowing that whatever happened, Brynn and Noah loved me unconditionally.

"Ash," she hissed, catching my attention. "Don't lose focus. We're not clear yet."

Damn. That could have been dangerous letting my mind wander like that. Anything could have happened. The first van had already departed, and the second was at near capacity.

I scanned the loading dock and the perimeter. Still all clear, but our luck wouldn't hold out forever. The last of the hostages entered the van. I'd just taken off my gloves when a small red ball bounced through the door, stopping when it knocked against my shins.

A young boy being carried by a woman cried out at its loss. He couldn't have been more than six-years-old.

I bent down and picked it up.

"Is this yours?"

His tear-rimmed emerald green eyes stared back at me. Those irises were probably what had landed him at this harvest center. He smiled weakly when I held it out to him.

"Here you go. Make sure to hang on to it."

Mason climbed into the van, slid the door shut behind him, then gave me a thumbs up.

I pounded the passenger side door a couple of times to let the driver know we were clear, then the van sped away. One hundred more people saved from a certain death after being harvested.

It was a good day.

5

OZ

When we arrived back at the compound, medical was a hive of activity. Most of the hostages required treatment for minor injuries caused by the ankle restraints, a few had sprained limbs, and a handful required stitches. My arm throbbed, but it was a minor injury. I'd taken worse hits, and this one wouldn't keep me out of the field. A couple days of rest, then I'd be ready for action.

This had been a difficult mission. Not completing it—the horrific conditions we'd found those children in would haunt my dreams tonight. But for now, maybe I could put some smiles on their faces. Several of them were gathered in a circle near me playing with some of the toys we kept around for situations like these. A few of them scrutinized me warily and kept their distance. I was used to it. The burn scars tended to frighten them, but I had ways of overcoming their hesitancy. The easiest was to pull my hair forward to cover the burns on my neck, which I did. The others were more subtle.

A little girl who looked to be around four-years-old held a teddy bear close against her chest, her tiny hands white from clutching it so tightly. "What's your name?" I asked.

She ducked her head shyly, and strands of auburn hair fell over her face. She whispered, "Addy."

"It's nice to meet you, Addy, but I was talking to your bear."

Her head snapped up, and she giggled in response.

"Did he tell you his name?" I asked.

She inched a little closer. "No."

"Then maybe you could give him a name. What do you think?"

She tilted her head to the side, considering her stuffed friend. "Brownie?"

I laughed. "That's a perfect name. Brownie the bear."

Some of the other kids had listened in on our conversation, apparently decided I wasn't a threat, and moved closer.

"My dog's name is Bo," said a boy on the other side of Addy. He clutched a stuffed Dalmatian wearing a red collar and smiled brightly.

My heart slammed against my ribs. He had a strong resemblance to my younger twin brothers, Riley and Logan. The similarity was uncanny. It had been years since I'd seen them—I assumed they were dead—but I'd never forget those smiles.

I was originally from a small town hundreds of miles away where I lived with my parents and brothers. It was nestled in a valley far from The Colony's normal harvesting area, and our citizens considered themselves safe. We led relatively normal lives.

Until one sunny spring morning, when our illusions of safety were shattered. The Colony had widened their hunting territory and ventured further south.

I was ten-years-old, and my twin brothers and I, along with thirty other children, were aboard a school bus. My best friend, Matt, sat beside me while I repaired his handheld gaming device. Riley and Logan, two years younger than me, sat in front of us arguing over some video game they'd played the night before. It was a normal day like any other, with kids complaining about homework and teachers and making plans for later that day when they were released from the confines of school prison.

The bus came to an abrupt stop. My head slammed against my brothers' seat in front of me, and several kids were thrown to the floor. Some of the younger ones cried out in confusion and pain.

"Ow! What's going on?" I asked, rubbing my forehead and peering out the window. We'd come to a stop in front of a housing development, still about a mile away from school. A trickle of blood ran down Matt's nose to his upper lip. I leaned over the seat in front of me to check on my brothers. "Are you guys all right?"

Riley's eyes were rimmed with tears, and a bluish spot on Logan's cheek looked like an early sign of a bruise.

The front bus door opened. The driver stood, hands raised. Two Colony soldiers boarded the bus, pointing rifles at all of us.

"No one move," said the male soldier. "You'll be happy to hear there's no school for you today. Instead, you're going on a field trip. We've got a special van parked just across the street. Everyone stay calm and exit the bus to the front. If any of you feel like being a hero, I promise things won't end well for you."

Fear skittered down my spine. Everyone knew about The Colony and the horrible things they did, but we were hundreds of miles away from their territory. They might as well have been in another world. Harvesting happened to other unfortunate people. It wasn't something anyone in our neck of the woods worried about.

We should have.

"Oz, what's happening?" Riley's voice quivered. Logan's lip trembled as he looked to me for reassurance.

"We're getting out of here, that's what's happening." I couldn't let them take us. I knew what waited at the end of the "field trip."

My gaze darted to the emergency exit at the back of the bus only a couple of rows behind me. I'd never opened it before, but assumed it wasn't difficult. Their intended purpose was to help students get to safety, not to have them stop and read complicated directions first. Riley and Logan could crawl under the seat to my row, and Matt and I could get them off the bus. Then we'd run.

My plans were crushed when I spied soldiers waiting outside the exit door. They surrounded the whole vehicle. Maybe we could break away from the line before being loaded on the Colony bus. "When we get outside, stay close to Matt and me, okay? Do exactly as I say." They nodded and grasped each other's hands.

Kids were crying—some quietly, others openly sobbing. "Quiet!" the guard yelled, which only caused them to cry louder. It was Riley's and Logan's turn to fall into line, and they both looked back at me for reassurance. I wished I could give it to them, but all I could do was nod.

"Are you with me?" I whispered to Matt.

"Nobody's stripping anything from my body." His voice quavered, but his eyes were full of determination.

The row beside us should have gone next, but I jumped up first and pulled Matt behind me, wanting to keep my brothers close. We shuffled single file to the front of the bus. The guard who'd spoken earlier sneered down at me, and I held his gaze, summoning all of the hatred within me and pushing it toward him. I hoped he felt it and somehow it would penetrate his body and twist his vital organs. He turned to the other soldier beside him and chuckled. "Looks like we've got some rejects on our hands."

When we stepped off the bus, I took Riley's hand and Matt grabbed Logan's. I expected us to be split up at any moment, so we'd have to move fast. To our right was the entry to the housing development. One of my other friends lived there, so I knew it covered a vast area and held a couple hundred houses. Houses with yards where we could hide.

Catching Matt's attention, I gestured toward the development and he nodded. Sweat trickled down my back, and my heart pounded in my ears. I tightened my grip on Riley's hand.

A shot rang out ahead of us. Heath Miller, a grade ahead of me, lay fifteen feet away from the line face down on the street, a pool of blood seeping out around him. We'd shared the same idea about escaping into the sea of houses, but he'd been killed during his attempt. A few seconds later, and it could have been one of my brothers. Or all four of us.

The world tilted, and my body shook all over. Matt turned toward me, his eyes wide with fear. We had two choices—try to escape and die here on the street, or board the van and die at a harvest center. I had to stay alive as long as possible for my brothers. Maybe we'd have another opportunity.

We didn't. Soldiers escorted us on and off the transport vans, and if we'd tried anything, we'd have met the same fate as Heath. Logan and Riley clung to me. The tears had stopped, but their expressions were blank, as if they were resigned to what would happen.

After we reached the intake center, we were led into a sorting room. I knew we'd be separated. My brothers' genes had been edited before they were born. With no inherited diseases and the coveted physical attributes they'd received from our mother, the two of them would be sent for harvest. My genes were unedited, and I resembled our father—who wasn't the most attractive guy in the world but was the best dad there was.

When we reached the front of the line, I hugged my brothers tightly before soldiers pried them away from me. I watched, numb inside, as both of them kicked and punched the soldiers and screamed my name while they were carried to another room.

Matt and I were deemed 'average' and loaded onto another transport van along with ten other children. You might think we'd been lucky to escape certain death. That when we were released, it would be back into the custody of our parents or guardians.

We weren't.

Instead, we were shoved off the van in the middle of nowhere, left to fend for ourselves. Like we were animals released into the wild.

Animals know how to survive.

Children don't.

Two kids, a brother and sister, wandered off on their own. The remaining ten of us stayed together, and after two weeks of scrounging for food in the forest and sleeping outside in sometimes below freezing temperatures, we'd come across an abandoned cabin in the woods. Dry matches and a fireplace inside meant safety and a warm place to sleep. We were hungry and exhausted, but ecstatic at our turn of fortune.

Popping embers started the blaze that took the lives of six of us sleeping around the fireplace that night. I managed to escape with three others, but suffered burns on the left side of my jaw down to my neck trying to save Matt. I'd failed. Uneven patches and craters of pink and brown skin were a permanent reminder of how I'd lost another person I'd cared about.

A ranger at a station only half a mile away saw the blaze, and help arrived, but it was too late for most of us. If only we'd hiked a little further, we would have been found. Of the twelve of us abandoned, ten made it to the cabin but only four survived. The other two siblings were unaccounted for.

My parents never came for me. Word was sent to them, but no one ever showed up. Maybe they'd been killed by soldiers or taken in themselves. Whatever the case, I had no home to return to and no other relatives. After living in various shelters over the next couple of years, I came of age then joined the Insurgents.

In my quest to avenge my family, I'd been a gun happy new operative when I was assigned to Ash's team. And boy, did he let me have it after that first mission. It was my own fault. Before being accepted to his team, he'd gone over his defined boundaries and the reasoning behind them. I'd nodded in agreement at everything he'd said. Sure, I wanted to rescue hostages, but my other goal was to take out as many soldiers as I could. Preferably the ones who'd taken us off that school bus or carried my brothers away if they ever crossed my path.

Look up the definition for short-sighted and you'd find my picture. Ash had immediately kicked me off his team, and Patrick was reluctant to assign me to any other team leaders right away. He told me I'd have to get my head straight before being allowed in the field again. I couldn't help anyone else until I helped myself.

And Patrick had been right. I was full of anger and hatred for The Colony, a beast that was bigger than all of us put together. Ash helped me see that killing soldiers wouldn't destroy the beast, but I could still make a difference. Rescuing hostages ripped away from their families, like my brothers, soothed my soul and helped put me back together one piece at a time. After living with them for the past few years, the other Insurgents had become my family. It wasn't quite the same as with my parents and brothers, but considering what our world had become, it wasn't a bad alternative.

I still longed for more.

Paige came around the corner with the young boy who'd begged for our help during the rescue. I'd overheard someone say his name was Miguel. Thinking about the conditions the hostages had been forced to endure, I cringed again. She squatted down in front of him and said something I couldn't hear, wiped his tears with her shirt sleeve, and then drew him into a hug. When she pulled away from him, Miguel offered her a half smile, and then Paige led him by the hand from the direction of registration.

I wanted more.

6

ASHER

After debriefing with Noah, I went to check on Oz. His wound hadn't looked serious, but I still wanted confirmation. I found him sitting on the floor surrounded by several children, their eyes wide as they listened in rapt attention to whatever wild tale he'd created this time. His upper left arm was bandaged, but the way he waved it around, it couldn't be that serious.

I chuckled to myself. Once again, he'd won over and distracted a group of traumatized children with his animated personality and entertaining stories that made them forget, even for a little while, everything they'd been through. Kids connected easily with him because he was essentially a large kid himself. They laughed hysterically over something he said, and I shook my head, amazed at their resiliency. Many of the rescued adults stared into space in a state of shock, while others sat silently, tears streaming down their faces.

Paige passed by with the desperate young boy who'd been chained to the bed. Oz tracked her until she was out of sight. He looked as wistful and lost as I had during the time Brynn and I were apart. Brynn was more observant than I was when it came to people, and until she'd pointed it out, I'd been oblivious to the way Oz felt about Paige. Watching him now, I don't know how I'd missed it. Sadly, I was afraid he was in for a world of hurt because Paige didn't appear to feel the same way.

Paige led the boy away from registration. After hostages arrived at our compound, they were registered and usually stayed a couple days before being transported to another Insurgent facility that worked to locate their families—if they had any left. In their endeavors to enhance their already extravagant lifestyles and in their misguided attempts to achieve perfection, The Colony destroyed families, leaving broken parents who'd lost their children and orphans who had nowhere to go if they were rescued. Their only hope was to be taken in by a loving family or form new families together.

Noah and I had been friends for as long as I could remember, and I'd spent so much time with the Wallaces, they were like family. But after my parents disappeared, I was sure they hadn't counted on raising another kid. I'd gone to Patrick and Anna and told them I'd leave or they could take me to an orphanage.

"Ash, what makes you think we'd want to do something like that?" Anna had asked. She truly looked puzzled, as if my offer was the most nonsensical thing she'd ever heard.

I shifted nervously from one foot to the other and couldn't look them in the eyes. "You already have Noah and Brynn, and I don't want to be a bother to you. You shouldn't have to take responsibility for me, too. I'll be fine at a shelter."

Anna knelt down and gently lifted my chin to meet her gaze. "Now you listen to me. In the early stages of Garrett's evacuation code, the plan was to put you and your sisters in the custody of other Insurgents who would get you to a safe house. Patrick and I told him in no uncertain terms that his plan didn't suit us at all. You, Cami, and Elsa were like our own children, and no matter what happened, we wanted the three of you with us."

Patrick squatted down beside Anna. "You're our child, Ash, the same as Noah and Brynn. This is your home now, and you're stuck with us, whether you like it or not."

I could barely see their faces through the tears in my eyes, but I'll never forget the tight hug the three of us shared. They raised me, provided a stable home, and couldn't have loved me more if I'd been their biological child. I could only hope other children in the same situation found similar good fortune.

I walked over toward Oz and the crowd of tiny groupies circled around him. Storytime was over, but the children lingered, and he listened as they talked to him and each other.

"You're all right?" I asked. "Looks like the wound wasn't serious."

"You know me," Oz smirked. "Takes more than one bullet to put me out of the game. It went straight through. Only took a couple stitches." He reached for a handful of hair and pulled it around his neck.

"Good to hear. We've got another mission coming up in two days."

He saluted. "I'll be ready."

As I was leaving, the delighted squeal of a child made me glance back over my shoulder. Oz was on all fours playing pony, with two little girls sitting astride his back. I grinned. He was definitely a large child.

Paige sat on a cot reading to the young boy she'd led back from registration. He was lying with his head in her lap, eyes droopy. Sleep wasn't far away. Taking care of the children wasn't technically part of an operative's job description, but everyone in the Insurgent compound worked towards the same goal, and the lines of responsibility often blurred. We all cared about the hostages and their well-being.

Paige had been here a couple years now. She was an intelligent, skilled, and trustworthy operative, and I was fortunate to have her on my team. But she was intensely private, and I didn't know anything more about her now than I did when she first crossed our threshold. Well, I'd learned one thing— the girl was a workaholic. When she wasn't on a mission, she volunteered constantly to fill in for others if needed and regularly served on beta teams. She seemed to need as little sleep as I did. Don't get me wrong, Paige was cordial and would go out of her way to help those she worked with, but when it came to *really* knowing her, I don't think any of us did. Only children seemed to draw any emotion from her. She blossomed in their presence and spent as much time with them as she could after rescues. It might have been the only time she smiled.

After ruffling the young boy's hair and lowering his head gently back to the pillow, she tucked the blanket around him and approached me.

"Problems, Ash?"

"No. Just happy to see that little guy warm in a bed without any restraints." She glanced back at him, and the corner of her mouth nearly tugged into a smile. "You're good with the kids, you know. Both you and Oz. Even though we have them for a short amount of time, you make them feel safe. And that's a rare thing in the world we live in."

"Thank you. Everything we go through on missions, getting shot at, injured... they're what makes it worthwhile. Kids still believe there's good in the world. For me, they're the only good thing I've found." Her voice fell away, and her eyes softened as she stared at the sleeping boy. When she turned her attention back to me, the shutters closed, and her face took on its usual amicable but detached expression.

I cleared my throat. "Brynn's off for the night, and I'm headed back to our room. Want to walk with me?"

She nodded and fell in step beside me. We walked in companionable silence through the common area filled with mismatched worn and patched couches and chairs, then we climbed the stairs. The dimly lit hallway leading to the sleeping quarters was empty at this late hour. Although we tried to walk softly, our footsteps echoed off the rusted steel walls.

"We may be looking for a new team member soon. I was talking to Noah, and Oz may split time with the tech department. Seems like he's got a knack for it."

Paige's jaw tensed. "I wouldn't mind less time with Oz."

I quirked an eyebrow. "What? Is someone finally immune to his charms?" From the first day he arrived, Oz seemed to blend in seamlessly with our compound. Other than Paige, only Brynn kept him at arm's distance. She trusted him to watch her back and everyone else's on our team while in the field, but she still hadn't welcomed him into her private circle. I told her she was jealous people liked Oz better, which resulted in her putting me in a headlock until I nearly passed out.

Paige shrugged. "Don't get me wrong, he's a great guy and an asset to the team, but it seems like every time I turn around, he's there. It's kind of creepy."

"So you *have* noticed his interest. I think you're the biggest enigma he's come across."

"He's not very subtle."

"And you're not interested?"

Paige cast a sideways glance at me.

My question was too intrusive. I touched her upper arm, and she stopped and turned to face me. "Sorry, Paige. It's none of my business. I didn't notice his interest until Brynn pointed it out, but it seems like the guy's really fallen for you."

She stared up at me with narrowed eyes and cocked her head slightly to the right like she was evaluating me. "No need to apologize. Let's just say I'd be more likely to date Brynn than Oz."

I furrowed my brow. But Paige knew Brynn and I were together, so why... oh. Ohhh.

Brynn always said unless a mission was involved I was slow when it came to connecting the dots with people. That was a huge reveal for Paige. She'd never shared anything this personal.

"Got it."

"Relationships aren't something I'm interested in. It works for you and Brynn, but personal attachments are a distraction for me. My focus is on the missions."

My eyes widened. "Of course, and you're an exceptional opera—"

"I know. Goodnight, Ash."

"Night, Paige." I stood there a few moments longer, stunned that after all this time, Paige trusted me enough to reveal a personal detail. That plus her being a dedicated operative and loving kids meant I now knew three things about her. Make that four. I'd also noticed in the cafeteria that she never ate peaches.

Poor Oz. He was pining for someone who'd never feel the same way about him, and he was in for some serious heartache.

I continued down the hallway toward my room, anxious to slip into bed and wrap my arms around Brynn.

7

ASHER

The group of new rescues waited in line to board vehicles that would take them to a safe house where they'd be processed then hopefully reunited with their families. Or, if not, would make a family of their own with others who'd lost loved ones. Just in time, too, because we had another mission tonight. We hadn't been scheduled to go out until tomorrow, but Noah received word from a contact about a large group of children taken to a facility close to us. Normally, missions were handed down from Central, but when trusted contacts came forward with information, sectors could act independently.

Insurgents scurried about directing people toward vans, checking on the wounded once more before they were loaded, and keeping the children together. Kids bounced around in excitement of a new adventure and at the thoughts of being with their families again. Some of the adults who'd had dull, empty expressions last night now held cautious expressions of hope in their eyes.

By one of the vans, Paige knelt in front of Miguel, the young boy from last night. In one hand, he held the book she'd read to him before he fell asleep, and his free arm wrapped around her neck while she gathered him in a tight hug. After reluctantly releasing him, Miguel smiled brightly and waved back at her before bounding up the stairs of the van.

Paige discreetly wiped her eyes, then all emotion fell away from her face when Oz appeared at her side to check on her. He started to reach out his hand as if to offer comfort but pulled it back. She said something to him, then turned and headed back into the compound.

Oz watched her leave, shoulders drooped, then he dropped his head and ran a hand through his hair.

Getting overly attached to hostages could be difficult. They'd been through horrific life-threatening and life-altering experiences. Forever changed. And we were the people that saved them and offered them a second chance. Once they were transferred to the safe houses, we never knew what became of them. I liked to imagine they all found happy endings.

And I fervently wished for Miguel to find his happily ever after. In my mind, he'd grow up and create his own family in a world where he didn't have to fear for their safety every second of the day.

I'd do everything in my power to make sure that dream came true.

•　　•　　•　　•　　•

"Everything about this is wrong," Brynn said. "First, the perimeter was unprotected. Then, those guards we ran into laid down their weapons and made no effort to stop us. I'm waiting for someone to offer us hot chocolate and cookies. Maybe the hostages will have a bow wrapped around them."

Getting into this harvest center had been far less challenging than others we'd breached. Noah's intel indicated a typical Colony facility, nothing out of the ordinary. Perimeter guards, security codes, cameras—everything we typically dealt with. Logically, security should have been increased at night considering that's when our rescues took place.

"What the hell's going on, Ash?" Oz asked.

"No idea, but stay alert." Despite Elijah reassuring me we weren't showing up on the security monitors, I couldn't shake the feeling of being watched. The sooner we found the hostages and got out of here, the better.

Elijah's voice crackled in my ear. "You're clear to the hostage barracks."

"Of course we are," Oz said in a sarcastic tone, his forehead glistening with sweat.

The four of us continued silently down the corridor then around the corner leading to the area where the captives were held. Like most facilities, a keypad was installed to one side. But the door beside it was cracked open.

"I don't like this," Paige whispered. Her gaze swept the hallway behind us, then peered beyond the door.

I whole-heartedly agreed with her. "Elijah, confirm again the number of guards inside."

"I'm showing none, Ash. It's safe to proceed."

Studying the tense faces of my team, they were still vigilant, weapons raised. Simple and uncomplicated didn't mean safe. To me, it masked something else. Something that raised the hairs on the back of my neck. I just hadn't figured out what it was.

We got in position. Oz threw open the door. Paige and Brynn rushed through, guns at the ready, while Oz and I moved in behind them. The four of us scanned the room, checked behind desks and in darkened corners. As Elijah had indicated, it was empty. No guards to be seen.

A set of double doors led into the barracks. With Paige and Oz covering our backs, Brynn and I slowly pushed them open and entered the room. Dozens of children cowered in their beds and stared back at us, eyes wide with fear and suspicion. And still no guards. "Move fast," I said.

Oz stood at the door while Paige, Brynn, and I herded the children and assured them we were there to help. I was relieved they weren't cuffed to their beds, and the conditions were more sanitary than a few nights ago.

I contacted Beta team. "Luci, we're coming out, but stay alert."

"Got it, Ash. All quiet out here."

We encountered no obstacles on our exit. Still smooth sailing. With the exception of the two soldiers who'd surrendered to us when we'd entered, it was as if The Colony had abandoned this place. If that was the case, why would they have left so many of their "donors" behind?

Brynn and I stood guard while Oz and Paige assisted Beta team with loading the rescued. Her gaze met mine, and I could tell her level of suspicion was just as heightened.

"With their product supply low because of the freezer malfunction, what motive could The Colony have for letting us walk away with their hostages? This doesn't fit any pattern we've come across." Brynn wasn't a fan of anomalies, and for good reason. I still had the feeling of something sinister in the background.

"Could be they're trying to give us a false sense of confidence, hoping we'll let our guard down."

"But why would they do that? They couldn't know which facility we'd be hitting."

I shrugged. "This whole night doesn't make sense. We need to sit down with Noah and get some information from our contacts."

I closed the door of our transport behind me after Brynn and I boarded. Paige sat several rows back. She tended to keep her distance from the rest of us after missions, especially if kids were involved. We'd always respected her space. But not Oz. He dropped onto the seat in front of her, turned sideways as he released his ponytail, pulled the dark blond strands around his neck then leaned back against the window.

I sighed. Paige hadn't given him an ounce of encouragement. She'd made it blatantly obvious she wasn't interested, but I guess Oz wasn't fluent in the language. I hated to see him get hurt.

With the decline in adrenaline after the rescue, the motion of the gently swaying van rocked Brynn to sleep, and her head drifted over to my shoulder as she dozed. We grabbed rest whenever we could. Going for hours without sleep wasn't unheard of for operatives. During one very tense mission, we'd gone for over thirty hours without rest after a rescue, with soldiers on our tail. We couldn't take the chance of leading them back to our compound, so we'd had to take a different route that added hours to our travel. My team was awake and alert for anything during that trip. So, taking quick naps? Yeah, they might give you an extra boost that could save your life later. Or someone else's.

I'd just closed my eyes and started to drift, when raised voices from the back of the van jerked me awake. Since the vehicle was so small, I feigned sleep to let Oz and Paige think they had some measure of privacy. Brynn was either faking or sleeping heavily, because her head on my shoulder hadn't budged an inch.

"Come on, Paige, just give me a chance. You've worked with me for a while now, and you know I'm a good guy. Just one date."

Paige sighed heavily. "Oz, I know you're a nice guy. That's not an issue."

"Great. Then just tell me what the issue is so I can fix it."

"It's nothing you can fix."

Oz's silence gave me hope he'd drop his questioning and let his friendship with Paige be enough. I hated to see his hopes crushed, but it wasn't an easy situation for Paige, either. She didn't want to intentionally hurt Oz's feelings, but it looked like that was the only solution.

"Now I get it." Oz's voice reared up, sharp as a knife. Nothing like his usual congenial tone. "I know you're out of my league, Paige. You're gorgeous. Anyone can see that. But I didn't think looks were high on your list of priorities. Guess I overestimated you."

Paige's voice was tight, tinged with anger. "Physical beauty isn't important to me. I can't help what I look like, and believe me, it's nothing I chose." She sighed heavily. "I wish I'd had a choice. But trust me when I say it has nothing to do with you. It's me."

"Really, Paige? You're going with the "It's not you, it's me" excuse? I thought you were above that. I bet if I looked like Ash, Noah, or even Elijah, you wouldn't be sitting here tossing out pathetic excuses."

That was low and an insult to Paige. Oz had no idea it really had nothing to do with him.

She had to be fuming, but her voice was gentle. "Oz, you're so wrong..."

"Stop. We're done. I won't bother you again."

I heard shuffling and felt Oz brush against me when he walked toward the front of the van. The seat in front of us gave a high-pitched squeak when he sat down heavily. Partnering with Paige on missions would be awkward as hell now, so Brynn or I would have to do it. Or Oz would transfer off the team, and I'd have to train a new member for a full-time position instead of someone filling in part time if Oz split his time with Elijah.

With the lives we led—going from one mission to the next, knowing it was a roll of the dice every time we went out—you found a sliver of happiness wherever you could. Most of the Insurgents at our compound didn't have family, and if they did, it was a rarity to see them. Noah, Brynn, and I were some of the lucky few who were able to be with our family every day. A stab of loneliness pierced my chest when I thought about being without them—without Brynn—and an icy coldness settled in my stomach. I kissed her head still resting on my shoulder, then leaned my own against hers, reassuring myself she was still there, and thankful I wouldn't have to find out what life would be like without her. At least, not until the next mission when we rolled the dice again.

•   •   •   •   •

"Noah, I'm telling you, something doesn't feel right. Over the last five missions, we've lost two people, six of us were wounded, and both Alpha and Beta teams narrowly made it out at the Breckinridge fiasco." Like me, Noah also thought last night had gone too smoothly. Brynn's mention of the donors being wrapped up in a bow wasn't really a far-fetched comparison.

Once Brynn and I had gotten back to our room, we'd reviewed the mission backwards and forwards so many times she'd finally fallen asleep from sheer exhaustion mid discussion. And probably boredom.

Noah leaned against his desk, one ankle crossed over the other, head tilted to one side. "The intel was good."

"Was this a new source or someone we've used before?" For security purposes, only Noah knew the identities of our sources. It wasn't that he didn't trust the operatives, but on the chance any of us was taken, the less we knew about contacts, especially those on The Colony's side, the better.

"He was new, but recommended by another source I've worked with for several months. He stated security at night wasn't on par with the day shift."

I dragged my hands through my hair and slumped down further in my chair. "The guards on duty didn't even put up a fight. They practically welcomed us inside."

Noah rubbed the dark stubble along his jawline. "It's something to think about. After Breckinridge, you'd think they'd reinforce security. But Elijah also does an excellent job at disguising our presence during rescues."

I nodded. "But what could make it worth their while to lose that many donors? Even Elijah, with no field training whatsoever, might have stood a chance at bringing out those hostages by himself."

The corner of Noah's mouth ticked upward. "Did I tell you he's requesting a transfer again? He's dead set on being a field operative."

I rolled my eyes. "I thought he'd given up on that."

He shook his head. "He's been working out and training on his own, hoping it would convince me."

"No amount of training will make a difference if he doesn't possess the instincts and physical abilities. And he doesn't. I've watched him. Besides, he's brilliant at what he does and too valuable to us in his tech capacity."

"I agree." Noah chuckled. "But you have to admire his determination."

I huffed out a breath. "Look, Elijah's a good guy, but I wouldn't trust him to have my back in any of the dangerous situations we've been in. His first instinct would be to either drop and curl into a fetal position or tuck his tail and run."

"True. When it comes down to fight or flight, he's a definite flight risk, and there's no one else here who can do what he does."

"Isn't Oz working out?"

"He's nowhere near Elijah's level, but he's got potential. I have to admit, when we were critically short in tech support and I was desperate to find someone, I was skeptical when Oz volunteered to cross-train. Turns out he's a quick learner and has a knack for the tech side. He's becoming a valuable member of that team."

"Well, Elijah asked me to give him some extra training, so maybe I should. Wouldn't hurt him to know how to handle a gun. Since he's been here, Oz has cross-trained in both medical and tech. Mention a need, and he's the first to raise his hand. Maybe we should think about cross-training more people."

"It's not a bad idea."

Noah's comm unit cut in, and he removed it from his belt. "Go ahead."

"We've got a problem. The supply truck hasn't returned, and it was due back hours ago."

ASHER

I paced the broken concrete parking lot outside the back of our compound and glanced at my watch again. My jaw ached from clenching my teeth. We'd still had no communication from the supply truck. Protocol was to check in after loading, then give an ETA back to the compound. Mason and I usually did these runs at least once a week. I'd been getting in the truck to leave with him when Noah contacted me about discussing last night's mission, so Oz volunteered to go in my place. Mason never broke protocol, and we'd never been late.

That's how I knew something was wrong.

"Should we send someone out after them?" Paige asked.

I shook my head. "We'll give them another half hour." I turned to Jonah. "Try to raise them on the radio again." I peered into the darkness, searching for any sign of headlights. Nothing. We alternated supply pickups between seven different locations to avoid creating a pattern in case we were being watched. All the suppliers were reliable collaborators, and I knew none of them would have given us up. They'd been helping us for years. So, what could have happened?

"Maybe it's something as simple as the truck breaking down or a flat tire." Paige tried to be the voice of reason again, and I appreciated her efforts.

"If it was something that simple, they would have radioed us. Mason and Oz knew we'd be waiting." I looked in Jonah's direction. "Anything?" He shook his head.

I strained to listen for the low rumble of the truck over the chirping crickets and occasional hooting owl. We were down from our full roster of operatives and really couldn't afford to lose anymore. I didn't mean to sound callous—Mason and Oz were more than operatives to me, they were also friends. Living so closely in this abandoned warehouse, it was difficult not to be at least more than casual acquaintances. But the fact was, losing more operatives would put a strain on us. Earlier this week, Noah informed us the new recruits wouldn't be ready for at least another month.

It was time to take action. Just as I was ready to gather a search team, the low growl of a motor reached my ears. The glow of headlights splashed over me as a truck bounced along the dirt road leading to our compound. Relief flooded through me. Paige, Jonah, and I rushed over to meet them.

My relief melted away when I noticed the reckless manner of the driver. The truck swayed from side to side and changed speeds erratically. I grabbed Paige's arm to pull her out of its path just before it jolted to a stop.

The driver remained a mystery until the door flung open and moonlight fell upon Mason's close-cropped copper hair. He tumbled from the driver's seat, gripping the doorframe as he struggled to stay on his feet. An inky blackness dripped from his hairline and trickled down his face.

Blood.

I rushed to Mason's side, catching him just before he collapsed. I pulled his arm around my neck and wrapped mine around his waist to support him. "Mason, what happened? Were you in an accident?"

He mumbled something unintelligible in reply.

"I don't see any damage to the truck," Paige said.

Jonah came around the front of the truck from the other side, and the headlights splayed across his face. From his tense expression, I knew the news wasn't good. "Oz isn't with him."

I closed my eyes and inhaled, my nostrils flaring. There's no way Mason would have left Oz behind unless he had no other choice. This was more than a car accident. "Let's get him inside."

Paige draped Mason's other arm over her shoulder, and we half-carried him up to the loading dock, through the supply area, then into Medical, drawing several questioning looks and worried exclamations along the way.

"We need help here!" I called. Several medical personnel responded and lifted Mason onto a stretcher. As he was rolled away to an exam room, his vitals were checked and his head wound assessed. I turned to Jonah. "Contact Noah."

He nodded. "On it."

Noah joined me in minutes, and I relayed what I knew. Which wasn't very much. The doctor informed us that in addition to several scrapes and bruises, Mason had suffered a concussion but was awake and alert and demanding to speak to Noah and me.

We passed several beds separated by curtains. Since there were no missions this evening, most of the beds were empty. Those with occupants had probably sustained minor injuries from training exercises or accidents that occurred in the compound. When we'd lost people a few weeks ago, both operatives and hostages, I'd limped with a badly-sprained ankle along this same path, flanked on both sides by gurneys holding sheet-covered bodies.

I prayed Oz hadn't suffered the same fate.

Noah and I heard Mason before we saw him, and from the sound of it he wasn't a very cooperative patient.

"Don't you understand? We're wasting time. I need to see Noah! You have no idea how important this is."

Dr. Cothran's voice was calm, but firm. "Mason, you need to stay in this bed. I've already told you, he's on his way back. Now just settle down before you hurt yourself even more."

We poked our heads around the curtain to see Mason struggling to rise, and Dr. Cothran wrestling with him to make sure he didn't succeed. Mason saw us, dropped back against the pillows in relief and sighed. "Finally."

Noah nodded at the doc, and she left us alone with Mason. "Where is Oz?"

"Soldiers took him."

My eyes widened in surprise. Of all the scenarios I'd envisioned, that hadn't been one of them. Car accident, scavengers, even a scuffle with the collaborators. But not The Colony.

"Were you followed?" The calmness in Noah's voice stunned me, which was a direct contrast to how I felt. My body quivered with the need to expend physical energy. I fought the urge to arm myself, jump into a truck, and track down the soldiers who had taken Oz.

Mason shook his head. "I don't think so, but I was pretty out of it when I got back. I barely remember getting here."

Noah pulled out his comm unit. "Paige, get a team outside and make sure no one followed Mason back. Alert the perimeter to do the same." He shoved the unit back into his pocket and nodded toward Mason. "Start from the beginning."

"Everything was routine when we met with the collaborators. We were busy loading supplies when we heard screams and saw people running. I don't know how long they'd been there, but soldiers had been waiting for us. Someone had to have been hiding them. "

Noah's gaze met mine, his forehead creased with concern. This was new. Collaborators hiding soldiers? "Are you sure they weren't there to capture citizens?"

"That's what we thought at first, they were there recruiting, but they headed straight for us. Before we could get in the truck, we were surrounded by six soldiers."

I turned to Noah. "How could they know where we were?" If The Colony had somehow learned to track us, it could put an end to everything—rescues, runs for food and supplies. We'd be helpless. So would all the captives at the harvest sites. "We always vary the schedules, and it's too much of a coincidence that they'd show up while Mason and Oz were there."

"That's what I thought." Mason gripped his blanket into knots as he spoke, and I knew he understood the consequences of what this could mean for us. "But that's not the strangest part."

Noah raised an eyebrow, urging him to continue.

"The soldiers were looking for someone, but it definitely wasn't me. And I'm pretty sure it wasn't Oz, either."

Noah crossed his arms over his chest and rubbed the stubble on his chin. "What did they say?"

"They had guns on us but kept looking between Oz and me. One of them said something about it not being the ginger kid, which ruled me out. He turned to Oz and said he didn't fit the description perfectly. He was tall-ish, and kind of blond, but he didn't think their target's face was supposed to be messed up."

Noah and Mason cast questioning gazes in my direction as I ran my hands through my golden blond-streaked hair. I was a head taller than both of them. And I was also supposed to be on that supply truck. Was it a coincidence?

"While their attention was on Oz, I kicked the legs out from under the soldier beside me, then Oz and some of the collaborators jumped in. Between the five of us, we put down three of their soldiers. One of the collaborators was killed, but the other three soldiers got away with Oz on a helicopter."

I stared at Mason in stunned silence. Oz was gone. It was difficult to believe the outgoing operative who remembered every child's name who'd passed through here, who'd done nothing but help others since the day he joined us, was now a captive of The Colony. I hated to think about what he might be going through right now—interrogation definitely, torture probably—but at least he went down fighting and helped lessen the soldiers' numbers by three. We'd do whatever it took to get him back.

Mason shifted position on the bed and winced. "Have either of you ever heard the term A36?"

I furrowed my brow and shook my head. A36? Was that a code for something?

Noah's confusion mirrored my own. "In what context did they use the term?"

"I heard one of the soldiers say what sounded like "Subject A36" and "activate.""

This was becoming a bigger puzzle by the minute. It sounded like A36 was a person. But what did they mean by activate? Activate what? Equipment? An alarm?

And how were we going to get Oz back?

•　　•　　•　　•　　•

I slumped down in my usual seat on the lumpy couch in the corner of Noah's office. "This is bizarre. A36? Any idea what this means?"

After debriefing Mason, Noah and I met back here to devise a plan to locate and extract Oz. It still felt weird saying "Noah's office" because it had been Patrick's for so many years. But Noah had worked for it after the mission that tragically altered all of our lives.

Patrick and Anna, along with my parents, were co-founders of the resistance group. After my family disappeared, Patrick and Anna pushed forward with the ideas they and my parents had about developing and expanding the rebellion, and when word got out, they were flooded with volunteers who were eager to join and help in any way they could to fight against the actions of The Colony. Our numbers grew so fast, working out of the Wallace house wasn't an option, and after Anna noticed the compound on a recruiting trip, it became Central and our home. Initially, Patrick oversaw all of the sectors, but he and Anna wanted more time with their family, so he'd relocated Central from our compound and stayed on in the role of Controller.

Back then, Noah was a field operative like Brynn and me, and Anna was a doctor in medical. We'd been on a mission at one of the worst harvest sites we'd come across, and it wasn't our first rescue at this facility. The guards were abusive, and the place was filthy and probably rampant with diseases. Our assignment was to take out the guards before the captives were unloaded and moved inside the harvest center, then drive their vans back to our compound. Patrick ran the operation from the tech van about a mile away. Intel had been faulty, and eight of us were penned in behind stacks of barrel drums along the back perimeter.

"I'm out!" Oz yelled over the sounds of heavy gunfire.

I tossed him a clip. "It's my last one. Make the shots count." Outnumbered three to one, the odds weren't in our favor. It's like the soldiers had been waiting for us. I didn't see how we'd make it out of here alive, much less free the captives. The only bright spot in our dire, life-threatening situation was the knowledge Brynn was safe back at the compound, out with a sprained wrist from a mission earlier this week.

Noah crouched beside me, shooting with his usual calm precision, but sweat dotted his forehead and upper lip. He spoke into his comm unit. "Elijah, any ideas?"

Elijah was in the tech van with Patrick and Anna. Normally Anna wasn't on site for missions, but Patrick had anticipated injuries and brought her along to get a jump on tending to wounded operatives and rescued hostages.

"What about behind you through the trees?"

Noah looked behind us. "Negative. We'd be wide open for too long before reaching cover."

"Alpha and Beta teams hold where you are. We're coming for you."

"Dad, there's no way—"

"I'm your Controller. Do as I say." Patrick's voice was firm and left no room for question. "All of you, listen. Elijah, you'll drive to the facility and park as close as possible to the original egress point. Stay in the van, and under no circumstances do you leave before all eight operatives are on board. Is that clear?"

"Yes, sir," Elijah replied.

"Alpha and Beta teams, watch for Anna and me on the west side and provide as much cover as possible."

Noah's panicked expression matched my own. We were down to five shooters and nearly out of ammo. Soldiers were closing in, and I had no idea how Patrick and Anna would reach us.

Elijah must have driven at warp speed because in a matter of minutes, Patrick and Anna had moved through the trees and crept up behind the soldiers to our west, quickly reducing their number by six.

While the two of them drew fire, Oz and I slung two of our wounded over our shoulders. All of us had sustained injuries, but the rest of us were able to walk or limp and quickly escaped back to the van.

"Patrick, all eight are accounted for."

Elijah received no reply.

"Patrick, can you hear me? Anna?"

Still no response. Their comms were down or damaged. Gunfire echoed through the night.

"We're going back," Noah yelled. He, Oz, and I scrambled to gather the spare guns and ammo, then we stormed through the trees back in Patrick and Anna's direction.

They'd taken cover behind two clusters of rocks about ten yards in front of the tree line. Patrick was closest to us, and Anna about ten feet in front of him and to the right. The guards were advancing toward them. From the shelter of the trees, we cut down four of the closest ones.

"Patrick, we've got you!" I called, and signaled for him to run toward us.

He nodded, then motioned to Anna to fall back. As he turned back toward Noah, Patrick's body jerked several times, and he fell to the grass.

"No!" Noah screamed.

We'd missed the sniper on the roof.

Preserving life was important to me, and I never killed unless faced with no other choice. But that was the furthest thing from my mind. Patrick and Anna weren't just Noah's parents—they were also mine. Without hesitation and with deadly accuracy, I locked my sights on the sniper. One shot to the head was all it took. From that distance, I shouldn't have been able to see him, let alone hit my target so easily with the weapon I carried. But he was eliminated.

In the seconds it took me to take out the sniper, Anna bolted in the direction of her husband. Dark splotches blossomed on her tan-colored shirt when she was hit in the upper chest, and she fell hard on the grass close to Patrick.

"Mom!" Noah lunged in their direction, but Oz and I grabbed him from behind, knowing his fate if he was allowed to help his parents.

Our parents.

Patrick's gaze locked on mine. "Asher, go!"

We both knew there was no hope for them. I nodded and struggled to pull Noah to safety. He kicked at me and called out for Patrick and Anna. What I'd seen with a last glance over my shoulder would be with me for a lifetime. Patrick crawled toward his wife and clutched her hand seconds before a bullet left his brain matter splattered over both of them.

His last actions had saved our lives.

An interim Controller was sent to our compound, but after a couple of weeks, Noah moved into the position permanently. He was young, but since our parents were the founding members of the Insurgents, we'd both grown up in the environment. He knew the job inside and out and had spent every day since trying to live up to Patrick's legacy. Noah's biggest fear was failure. He worried he'd disappoint his parents, and they would have died in vain saving us.

If you asked me, wherever Patrick and Anna were, they couldn't have been prouder. Even though our parents were gone, their legacy lived on, and knowing they'd given birth to the Insurgents filled me with pride and made me still feel their presence in a way.

Noah leaned against his desk, arms folded over his chest. His eyes were unfocused as he stared at the wall over my head. I could practically see the wheels turning in his mind, and prior experience told me it was best not to interrupt his process.

After several moments, he spoke. "Ash, didn't you ever wonder why The Colony sent soldiers for your family?"

I shifted position and leaned forward with my elbows on my knees. "Dad never told me the whole story, but when I was old enough to understand, I thought it was pretty obvious. All of our parents were Insurgents, and I guess The Colony found out about him. They probably wanted Cami and Elsa for harvesting." Even after all these years, just saying those words was like an ice shard piercing my heart. The pain would never lessen.

"But why? Those were the early days before missions, and they'd just started meeting. Your dad had those two evacuation plans in place long before our parents formed the Insurgents. Which brings us back to why. No offense, but what made him so special?"

My hands clenched into fists, and I felt the stirrings of anger simmering just below the surface because of Noah's persistent questions. He knew how much I hated talking about that day. It already invaded my dreams several times a month. I figured my need for only a few hours of sleep per night was my subconscious way of avoiding it as much as possible. Brynn was the only person I discussed it with. "What does that have to do with anything? They found my parents, and then they killed them. End of story."

Noah sighed heavily, then moved to sit in the chair adjacent to me. "Look, I know this is painful for you, Ash, but I think there might be a connection."

I stared at him for a full, stunned beat. "A connection. Between something my father told me ten years ago and the soldiers looking for a tall, blond male. That description could fit at least ten other guys in this compound, Noah."

"Those ten other guys weren't originally scheduled to be on that supply run."

I scrunched my brows. That made exactly zero sense. Why me? We had over a hundred people in this compound alone, and that didn't include the other Insurgent sectors. Why single me out? "That still doesn't tell me why I'd be on their most wanted list."

"It's puzzling, and I admit it's a stretch to make that connection back to Garrett, but my gut tells me there's more to it. We need more information to figure it out." He was silent a moment. "Hypothetically, let's say it's you. Can you think of any way The Colony could have identified you? Something that could have linked you in their system?"

"No way, Noah. You know I'm always careful not to leave traces behind on missions. With the gloves..." I trailed off, remembering a red ball that bounced down the stairs of the transport van. Right after I'd taken off my gloves, I'd touched it. The boy could just have easily dropped it again before the doors closed.

He saw it in my face. "What?"

And I relayed my interaction with the boy.

"So stupid," I said. "A rookie mistake. How could I have been so careless?"

"Don't beat yourself up about it. I'd have done the same thing. Just maybe not removed my gloves until we were clear. We'll deal with it." Noah twisted the small hoop in his ear. "Another question we should ask ourselves is how the soldiers knew you were supposed to be on that transport."

Between this and the last hostage rescue being so easy, it was obvious. It didn't take a genius to make the connection. "This new source was planted by The Colony."

"Exactly."

9

OZ

The way my head pounded, I felt like one of those critters in the Whac-A-Mole game at the arcade Mom used to take us to when we were younger. Now I felt kind of bad for whacking them. I tried to moan, but my mouth was filled with a gag, and my cheek pressed against a cold, hard floor. Right now, I'd sell my soul for a glass of water and some pain killers.

Forcing my eyes open, I found myself lying on my side in a dimly lit room. I squinted against the pain in my head and was able to make out a small table and a couple of chairs to my right in the center of the space. An interrogation room.

I tested my limbs, but restraints held my hands behind my back and my legs at the ankles. The last thing I remembered was soldiers ambushing Mason and me on the supply run. We'd fought like hell, but I'd been whisked away on a helicopter. I hoped Mason got away and made it back to the compound to inform them what happened. The Insurgents would come for me. Since that horrible night Patrick and Anna died so tragically, Noah did everything in his power to leave no man behind. I just needed to hold on until they found me.

A high-pitched screech erupted from behind the door. The voice reached levels only dogs should have the ability to hear. "This is not Subject A36! I couldn't have made it any simpler. You had a detailed description. Even a photo. And this boy is what you brought me? The only physical traits he shares with A36 are eye color and hair color. And the hair color is stretching it. He lacks several inches in height and has facial deformities. What kind of imbeciles are you?"

Boy, did she sound like a sweetheart. I bet parts of those soldiers' anatomy were crawling up inside them right about now. These guys probably had a picture of her face on a dartboard somewhere, full of holes, no doubt. And this might be a shot in the dark, but with the mention of facial deformities, I'd bet I was the "boy" in their discussion.

"And what happened to the other three of you? Trained soldiers with years of experience taken out by two teenagers and a handful of unarmed civilians. What do you have to say about that, Colonel Ackerman? If A36 had been there, none of you would have returned alive. Clearly, I need to put someone else in charge of bringing in the subject."

A man's low baritone voice filled the air, and I swore it nearly rattled the door. "No, Dr. Everly, you don't. I take full responsibility for the loss of those men and women. They were inadequately prepared for this mission, and I underestimated the Insurgents and their accomplices. It's a mistake I won't repeat."

What was up with this A36? Screechy Everly made it sound like a person. A deadly and dangerous sort of person. And maybe I was a teenager, but I was a well-trained one and pretty proud of my performance before I was kidnapped. Don't underestimate me.

"Ackerman, you've seen the files on A36. You know what we're dealing with and how essential the subject is to the future of The Colony and our way of life. We can't afford any more mistakes. It took me years to get a positive identification on the fingerprints obtained from his house. Now he's been located. It's imperative A36 be brought in."

"Judging by their previous behavior, I believe the Insurgents will come to us instead. They'll attempt to rescue this operative. A36 will show up, and we'll be waiting for him. The boy is collateral damage. His life is only a priority until A36 arrives. After that, he's expendable."

Oookay. I didn't like the sound of that. Collateral damage. Expendable. Not my favorite way of being classified.

"I really have no other options at this point, do I?" Everly snapped. "Just make sure we don't lose the subject this time."

I swear, this Everly woman sounded like a real peach. Whoever this A36 was, no matter his skill level, I'd guard my man parts closely when coming face to face with her.

. . . . .

Days passed. Or so I guessed. They'd moved me to a cell with no windows, and food was shoved through a slot in the door. Meals were staggered and I had no way to tell how much time had passed. Since I'd been deemed "collateral damage" I was grateful they fed me at all.

But the boredom was killing me. My cell consisted of a bed with a filthy mattress, a sink, and a toilet. Nothing to read or watch, so my entertainment consisted of my own imagination. Calisthenics kept me alert and in shape. I was surprised I hadn't been questioned yet. Didn't they want to know our compound location? Or Central and the other sectors? Interrogation and torture seemed like the logical next steps.

Operatives were prepared to handle both. Patrick had trained us well, and Anna had stitched us up, cared for us, and sent us back into the field. But we hadn't been just operatives to them—they'd genuinely cared about all of us, and the night they were killed, there wasn't a dry eye among us. They'd welcomed me into the Insurgents, shown me a useful path, and helped me find a place I belonged. Given me a purpose.

When I wasn't working out, Paige occupied my thoughts. There was no denying I'd been an ass the last time we'd spoken. She deserved better. Maybe Ash was right—I should give her some space and see where things went from there.

But with the way I felt about her, it wouldn't be easy. Brynn scared the living daylights out of me sometimes, but I wanted what she and Ash had. Someone to share my life with, to care about, to tell me things would get better after yet another heartbreaking mission of rescuing frightened children captured for slaughter.

Sure, there were plenty of other women at our compound, but Paige was the only one who stirred those feelings inside me. Made my stomach quiver every time she walked into a room and my hands slick with sweat whenever I spoke to her. She was in every beat of my heart.

I heard shuffling outside my door and the metallic clang of the lock being released. The door swung open, then two burly guards entered. They nearly spanned the width of my tiny cell. "Turn and face the wall," one of them said.

"Are we going out for dinner tonight? It sure would be a treat after being stuck in here for the past few days." That comment earned me a punch to the stomach, and I fell to my knees, unable to catch my breath. Guess they didn't appreciate my humor.

"Shut up, and turn around to face the wall," he repeated.

When I struggled to get to my feet, the other guard jerked me up by my hair, then shoved me against the wall. My hands were restrained behind my back. With each guard grabbing one of my upper arms, I was dragged through the door then down a dark hallway lined with several other cells. Looked like they could house more than a couple guests at a time.

An elevator took us up a few floors, then they dragged me down another hallway and into a room with a table and two chairs. From every corner, the floor slanted inward to a drain in the center. Easier to hose down the blood that way, I guessed. It didn't take a crystal ball to know that interrogation and torture lay in my immediate future.

After tying my legs to the chair, the guards left the room. My pulse thudded in my ears. Sure, I'd been trained to handle the forthcoming abuse, but that didn't lessen the dread of the pain that accompanied it. I closed my eyes and meditated to calm my heart rate, focusing on Paige's face. Which was probably counterproductive, since thoughts of her usually sent it soaring.

"I'll be questioning the prisoner. Unless I call for you, under no circumstances are you to enter the room." Sounded like I'd finally be meeting that sweetheart, Dr. Everly, in person. Fantastic.

"Yes, ma'am."

A middle-aged woman wearing a tailored dress and white lab coat strode through the door and came to a stop on the other side of the table. Coal black hair was pulled back into such a tight, severe bun, I was afraid her eyes would bug out. No loose strands escaped. At all. It resembled a solid, black helmet.

Dr. Everly examined me thoughtfully, eyes narrowed and suspicious. I gave her what Brynn called my patented, smart ass, cocky smirk. Charm quotient engaged.

And she was very unamused. In fact, I had the distinct impression she'd like to slap said cocky smirk off my face.

She settled in the seat opposite me. "What's your name?"

"What do you want it to be?"

"I'm not here to play games. Answer my question."

"Everyone likes games. Bet you'd like them, too, if you'd give it a chance."

Yep. Definitely not amused. She plastered a fake smile on her face. "Yes, perhaps you're right. I know a game we can play." She rose, walked around to my side of the table, then glared down at me. Even sitting, I was nearly eye level with her. "What's your name?"

"I told you..."

Everly struck me across the face. My head jerked sideways, and a line of spittle flew from my mouth. She might be little, but she packed a punch. It would take a lot more than that to break me, though. Cocky smile reengaged. "Not sure I know this game."

She raised a brow. "You don't? Let me explain the rules. Every time you don't answer my question or provide a satisfactory answer, you'll be hit again. Now do you understand?" She slapped me once more to ensure I comprehended.

I spat blood on the floor. "Pardon me for saying so, but if that's the best you've got, this game could go on for a while."

"Did I forget to mention we aren't the only players?" She walked to the door and knocked once. One of the guards, the largest of the two and twice my size, entered the room. "This man will be my designated hitter. Trust me when I say he could add to the collection of scars on your face. Perhaps even deepen some of them."

My gaze darted to the soldier, then back to Everly. I lifted my chin and straightened in the chair. No way would I cooperate with her.

"Tell me about Subject A36."

And there it was again. A36. I didn't have to pretend my blank expression.

Her eyes bore into me with the intensity of a laser. "You know him as Asher Solomon."

Whaaaat? Ash? I was unable to control my stab of recognition, but quickly erased it with another blank expression. "I have no idea who that is."

She pulled a device from her pocket, pressed something on the screen, then shoved it in front of me. The video showed Ash, Brynn, Paige, and me standing in a corridor. In the dim light, Brynn and Paige's faces were shadowed, but Ash and I stood in full view. Brynn said, "Everything about this is wrong."

It was footage taken from the mission at the harvest center that had been so easy to infiltrate. They'd been watching us the whole time. The Colony must have some new technology, because no way would Elijah have missed another surveillance camera.

"You're standing beside him. Care to revise your answer?" Her eyes sparkled in anticipation.

Deny everything. And then deny some more. "That isn't me."

She nodded to the soldier. He played his part in the game well. After he was finished, she stepped around the patches of blood on the floor, and made another attempt. "If you value your life, tell me about Asher Solomon."

"I already told you, I don't know who that is." My voice wavered, and the words were slurred, but I was far from done.

The air around Everly rippled with anger. "Your false bravery isn't doing you any favors. Neither is protecting A36. It's been several days and they've made no effort to extract you. No one is coming."

Her words hit the thread of doubt that twined through my body and magnified it. Upon my capture, I was confident I'd be extracted, whether by an Insurgent team or an inside contact, but as the days passed one after another, I couldn't help but wonder if Noah and the others had forgotten about me. Maybe Mason hadn't made it back. But even if he hadn't returned, the search for us would have started at our supply run destination, and the collaborators who witnessed the attack would have been questioned.

Everly nodded to the soldier again. This time, she gave him permission to pound away, and he seemed to be enjoying himself. With his unsatisfactory work environment, he was filled with pent up frustration. Every hit jarred my bones, and I heard a crack when his fist struck my nose. Then my ribs. Pain filled my body with a white-hot intensity, and it was getting hard to remember why I couldn't answer Everly's questions. My breathing came fast and shallow.

I held onto the image of Paige in my mind. Noah. Asher. Elijah. And even Brynn. I refused to give up the people I cared about, who'd helped me find my way. Soon, the pain lessened, then drifted away completely. I felt so light—even detached—from my body, then I floated away to the sound of fists hitting wet flesh before darkness overcame me.

ASHER

It took longer than expected before our network of contacts came back with the information on where Oz was being held. Only informants who had longstanding relationships with us and had proven to be reliable over time were involved. Any sourcing of new informants had come to a halt. I tried to avoid thinking about what Oz was going through and focus on extracting him. I didn't want to leave him there a second longer than necessary, but we couldn't launch a rescue if we had no idea where to go. We'd finally received a confirmed location an hour ago.

Our meeting was interrupted by the sound of raised voices outside the door. Brynn rose to go see what the trouble was, but before she took a step, the door burst open and Mason charged in. He leaned against the door for support, chest heaving. His red face nearly matched the color of his hair.

"There's news about Oz."

Noah nodded. "We got the message, Mason. We're planning his rescue right now."

Mason shook his head. It was then I noticed his red-rimmed eyes. A pit formed in my stomach, and I was filled with dread.

"You can cancel the rescue. Oz is dead."

A blanket of silence and shock cloaked the room. Maybe if no one spoke, we could pretend Mason had never uttered those words. Act as though Oz was still alive. Like it wasn't a reality, and he was sitting in a cell or an interrogation room wearing that cocky smile and cracking stupid jokes to drive his captors insane.

And then everyone spoke at once, ten voices erupting like a volcano, spewing forth queries and accusations. Mason sagged against the doorframe, his head hung low, as if he didn't have the strength to stand, let alone answer any questions.

Noah held his hand up for silence. "Mason, what's your source for this information? How do we know it's reliable intel?"

"It came from Aries 7. We received a coded message, and the identity was confirmed."

All of our informants had code names, so no one except Noah knew their true identities. Aries 7 had been a trusted source for years and had never steered us wrong. I desperately hoped this was the first time the information was incorrect. But the chance was next to none.

Mason trudged over to Noah, handed him a folded paper, then dropped into a vacant chair.

Noah read the message, his resigned expression indicating he believed it to be accurate. He folded the note, then closed his eyes and exhaled. "Aries 7 has confirmed Oz's death during interrogation. To the best of our informant's knowledge, Oz gave up no information. He died protecting us."

There wasn't enough air in the room. I couldn't get oxygen into my lungs. Mason announcing Oz's death was one thing, but to hear Noah confirm it made it final. Oz was gone. Something inside me cracked and burst open, a dark, poisonous rage so powerful that I struggled to contain it.

Pain.

Destruction.

Blood.

The thoughts were overwhelming. I gripped the arms of my chair, my knuckles taut and white. It took every ounce of strength I possessed to restrain myself, and my body trembled from the effort.

Brynn placed her hand on my thigh. "Asher?"

And just like that, the urge to harm someone passed at her touch and the sound of her voice.

"Are you all right?" Her eyes were wide and concerned.

Sweat covered my face, and my shirt clung to my body. "Fine. Just shocked. And sorry."

"I had my doubts about Oz, but I never wished him dead."

I squeezed her shoulder. "I know."

Died during interrogation. Which meant he was probably tortured then murdered. Another senseless killing by The Colony. And if what Noah said was true, if I was connected to whatever A36 was, Oz had been mistaken for me. Maybe even died in my place.

Paige sat opposite me a couple seats further down, hands clasped on top of the table. Her eyes were unseeing, staring into space. I doubted she even felt the tears tracking down her face.

Around the room, some had reactions similar to Paige, while others swore vengeance. The Colony would pay for killing one of our own. Which reignited my enraged thoughts from moments ago.

Noah held up a hand once more, and the room gradually quieted. "I'll get further confirmation, of course, but I feel it's safe to assume Oz is gone." He paused and gripped the table, steeling himself. "To honor Oz's sacrifice and his memory, we'll have a brief memorial tomorrow. But first, we have another mission to plan for tomorrow night. You're dismissed."

. . . . .

Weeks passed. We needed a new team member and had tried out several on practice missions, but so far, no one really clicked with us. I would have loved to poach someone from Luciana's team. All three of them were well-trained, and we'd worked together for so long, they were familiar with our habits. She'd picked up on my intentions and told me to stay in my lane and quit sniffing around her people.

Even though Oz had been on my team the shortest amount of time, he'd fit in well and caught on to our short hand speech and lingo quickly. The new prospects we'd tried out on practice missions had been utter failures. If they'd been live missions, we'd all be dead. Maybe it was because we were still mourning Oz, but still... nothing felt right.

Paige especially had taken Oz's death hard. She'd seemed off, out of step over the past few weeks. "You know I loved him in my own way, just not the way he wanted. Oz was a friend, Ash. In a weird way, I'll miss him pestering me after missions and following me around the compound. But I think I'll miss watching him play with the children most of all."

Since we hadn't filled the vacancy on our team yet, we'd only functioned as backup for other missions. I wasn't comfortable going out unless the four of us moved as one unit and felt we could trust each other. That wasn't something that would happen overnight, but I'd know the right person when I met him or her. Even with Oz's initial difficulties, I'd had a good feeling about him after he'd asked for another chance. He'd just fit.

Brynn and I were drenched in sweat, taking jabs at each other in our weekly sparring session. Noah came in, crinkled his nose from the smell, then stepped back a couple feet from the ring. We broke and joined him. Brynn wiped her arm and flicked the sweat in Noah's direction.

He gracefully dodged it. "You guys reek. But I have good news. I may have found you a replacement. Declan came in about a week ago. Said he'd been with Barton's sector for a little over a year, then traveled to this area when he'd gotten word some of his family might be around here. He's been out of the field for the couple months it took him to get here, but I think he's ready. You should go meet him."

Brynn looked at me and shrugged.

"Might as well." I removed my sparring gloves. "No one else seems to be working out. Maybe some new blood is the answer. We'll get cleaned up and meet you in training."

Brynn tossed me a towel. "Sure hope this one works out. I'm ready to get back out there."

·   ·   ·   ·   ·

Noah was right. After watching Declan, there was no doubt in my mind he was ready to be put back in the field. He was fast, accurate, and had quick reflexes. Although the way the other female recruits, and some of the males, looked at him made me wonder if he'd be a distraction. Not for Paige, but maybe Brynn? Declan was a few inches shorter than me, had a muscular build, startling blue eyes, and dark, wavy hair.

My gaze slid in her direction to gauge her reaction and I said, "Well?"

Brynn considered Declan, tracking his movements about the training course. "He's a pretty boy, but he's got the skill set."

I grinned. "Prettier than me?"

Brynn stood on her tiptoes, nuzzled my neck, and then whispered in my ear. "No one's prettier than you."

And then I was distracted. Focus, Ash.

Maybe he wasn't as accurate a shot as Paige or me, or quite as good at hand to hand combat as Brynn, but Declan could hold his own in both areas. His level of comfort with every task was obvious.

Noah waved him over and introduced us. "Ash has an opening on his team."

I held out my hand, and Declan shook it. "Nice work out there. I'd like you to meet the rest of the team and do a practice mission. Are you up for it?"

His answering easy smile revealed perfectly straight teeth. "Absolutely. Just tell me when."

"We'll schedule it for tomorrow."

"Looking forward to it."

Noah walked with Declan back toward the course. I had a good feeling about this. He could be our missing piece. I turned to leave, when I noticed Brynn wasn't beside me. She stood in the same spot, head cocked sideways, gaze tracking Declan.

Maybe he was a distraction for her, after all.

• • • • •

Brynn was the only holdout on my team. "I'm not convinced."

She and I stretched out on our bed, her head resting on my stomach. I was ready to add Declan to the team, but she was still reluctant. He'd run through five practice missions with us, and they were practically seamless. Sure, there were small issues here and there, but it was just a matter of learning our quirks and how we did things. Paige had given an enthusiastic thumbs up. But Brynn wasn't on board.

"What is it? You can't argue against his tactical skills. He's no marksman, but he's not middle of the pack, either. He had your back more than once during the practice missions. On the personal side, he seems pretty cool, and even I can see he's nice to look at."

Brynn stared at the ceiling and chewed on her thumb nail. "I can't put my finger on it, but the vibe is weird. On the surface? Yeah, he's more than qualified."

I reached up and gently pulled her hand away from her mouth. She'd chew her nail down to the quick unless I intervened. "Noah, Paige, and I are comfortable with him. Maybe you will be, too, after a few missions." I smirked. "I love you, babe, but you have to admit, you tend to keep people at a distance for a long time before letting them in. If you ever do."

She pretended to be indignant. "Yeah, well I'm just discriminating. Not everyone is worthy, you know."

I cupped her cheek and brought her lips to mine for a slow, sweet kiss. "I'm certainly glad you think I am."

She gave the smile that lit up my world. A smile only I was privy to. "I know your heart, Ash Solomon. And you're more than worthy."

ASHER

"I received some strange information today, and I'm not sure how to tell you, or what it could mean, brother."

Noah and I sat on opposite sides of a table in his room enjoying some rare downtime. I'd convinced him to close his latest book and challenged him to a game of chess. And I was beating him. Again. Even better, the latest supply run had brought in the rare treat of beef, and in between moves, we wolfed down a couple cheeseburgers each, grease and melted cheese running down our hands.

Our first assignment with Declan two nights ago had been a success. Honestly, it couldn't have gone better. The guy was a perfect fit for our team. Despite how smoothly things had gone, Brynn still held back from fully accepting him. After the mission, she'd taken off on her bike, anxious to have some time by herself to rock climb and destress. Her solo trips were a regular occurrence, and Noah and I looked forward to our brother/best friend time together.

Before Brynn left, she'd again reminded Noah about contacting Barton to check up on Declan and see if he was being up front regarding his reason for leaving. Noah had a lot on his plate right now but promised to get around to it. He was still checking into the A36 business Mason mentioned and wondered if it was connected to Oz's death.

"Strange how? And since when haven't you known how to tell me something?" I wiped my hand on the side of my pants and picked up my queen.

"It's about your house."

My hand froze mid move. "My family's house?"

Noah's voice was quiet. "Yes. A young teenage girl with wheat-blonde, wavy hair has been seen entering the house. She may be staying there."

My heart stuttered. "How young?"

"About the age Elsa would be if she'd lived."

My queen dropped to the board, scattering the other pieces and effectively ending the game. "How do you know what's going on at my house?"

He rubbed the back of his neck. "On the off chance your parents or sisters ever returned, Patrick had your house checked on a routine basis. After he and Mom were gone, I continued to have it monitored by Insurgents in that area. I didn't tell you because I knew you'd get your hopes up."

"But now there's a reason to hope."

Noah paused for a long moment. "Possibly. They've tried to make contact with the girl, but she's skittish and keeps evading them."

The first couple years after my family disappeared, I'd clung to the childish hope that they'd return some day, and everything would be as it was. When I'd forced myself to face reality, that dream had to be tucked away so I could move on with my life. Now, maybe it was time to resurrect that glimmer of hope.

"We have to go there."

Noah nodded. "I know. I'm already packed, and we'll leave when Brynn gets back tomorrow."

12

ASHER

Even with the driving split among the three of us—each of us taking at least
five-hour shifts to total more than fifteen hours per stretch—the trip back
to my house took more than two days. Noah hated being away from the
compound for any length of time, but he and Brynn were the logical choices
to go with me and he'd left a very competent Paige in charge. She'd
immediately started prepping a new mission, and I'm pretty sure I detected
a hint of jealousy in Noah's eyes at how easily Paige had fallen into the role
of Controller.

We'd spent the night at one of the Insurgent safe houses set deep in the
woods far from the main roads. With any sort of travel, reaching your
destination was never guaranteed—especially with soldiers patrolling most
areas. Xander, a former operative who'd worked under Patrick, ran the safe
house, and it was nice to catch up and reminisce with him. He'd also brought
us up to date on the activities of other Insurgent sectors. Although Noah
communicated with them on a semi-regular basis, Xander interacted with
them more often since he took in freed captives from several sectors.

To the casual observer, the house looked like any other abandoned cabin
you'd find in the woods. In its better days, it might have served as a weekend
retreat for a family, a place where they could enjoy the tranquil lake a short
distance away, hiking trails, and other outdoor activities. Even in its prime,
it didn't come close to the upscale homes behind the gates of The Colony.
The weathered, neglected look was a façade. If someone wandered through

the area and found themselves at the front door, they'd be greeted by Xander, who appeared to be the only occupant. Beneath the cabin was an expansive facility that could house over three hundred rescued hostages and the Insurgents who assisted in returning them to their families or finding them another home.

Only through the help of collaborators and anonymous sources who donated large sums of money were we able to operate facilities like this. Their support was invaluable, and I couldn't imagine what would happen to the rescued hostages without it.

Sleep had eluded me the night before. We'd camped out, and I'd spent most of the night pulling Brynn as close as possible, her back warm and comforting against my chest while she slept. At least she'd be with me if this trip ended in disappointment. If I fell, I knew she'd be there to catch me, the same way I'd been there for her after her parents' deaths.

Watching Patrick and Anna die had been as devastating as losing my own parents all over again. But no matter the pain, I'd set my own grief aside to support Brynn and Noah. After witnessing his parents' deaths, Noah had to relive it by breaking the news to his sister when we'd arrived back at the compound that night. When I'd offered to take his place to spare him even more pain, he'd insisted it had to be him.

Noah requested privacy when he spoke with Brynn, something that didn't bother me at all. As much as the Wallaces were my family, Noah and Brynn were blood relatives and siblings, and I hadn't felt excluded. But I still waited outside the door for her. Her agonized screams and wails of deep sorrow and pain clawed at my insides. I felt them as if they were my own. If there was some way I could have borne the hurt for her, I gladly would have shouldered it.

Brynn threw open the door, and I stood silently, unsure if she wanted to be with me, Noah, or alone. Her grief-filled eyes met mine, and I'd never seen her so lost. I opened my arms, and she flung herself into them, burying her face in my chest. Noah stood watching us, tears rolling down his cheeks, and I held one of my arms out toward him. He lurched over, and the three of us stood that way for several long minutes mourning the loss of Patrick and Anna, good people who had welcomed me into their home, loved me as their own, and saved countless lives as co-founders of the Insurgents.

I stayed with Brynn throughout that night. That was when her room became our room. The next morning, I'd quietly packed my sparse belongings in the space I shared with Noah, and he nodded in understanding. No explanations had been necessary.

They'd dealt with grief in their own ways. Noah was determined to take over for Patrick and continue his legacy of holding the record for most rescues among the Insurgent sectors. In hindsight, I realized preparing Noah to assume leadership had been Patrick's intention all along. Maybe just not quite as soon. Neither Brynn nor I had the temperament for it. We both excelled as operatives, but Brynn could be abrasive, although I'd never say that to her face, and I had difficulty accepting failure of any kind. Noah was able to separate his emotions from mission parameters. His ability to look ahead, anticipate possible roadblocks or problems, and make allowances for them served him well in a leadership capacity.

Brynn had taken a different route. She'd thrown herself into missions, volunteering for anything that came her way. Exhaustion made her reckless and a danger to herself and her team. Noah told her to back off, but she'd refused to listen. He'd finally had to pull rank and, as her Controller, threaten to pull her out of the field and reassign her to a desk job permanently. Being chained to a desk and staring at a computer screen was Brynn's worst nightmare. But the threat finally did the trick.

I'd learned my lesson about trying to change or protect Brynn, so I'd stayed out of her way. My interference would only have pushed her away, and I hadn't wanted to live through that again.

My whole body hummed with equal portions of hope and dread as we drew closer to my home. A childlike part of me buried deep inside clung to the thought that by some miracle, my family would be there. The Asher who knew hope was trampled or crushed more often than not forced me to face reality and avoid reopening wounds that had scarcely begun to heal.

After the day my family disappeared, I'd never gone back to my house—not even for any of my things. Patrick had returned to search for my parents and sisters, but of course they weren't there. He'd only brought back my clothes and some other things he thought I'd want. Entering an empty house haunted with happy memories of a family I no longer had wasn't something I wanted to do. To my knowledge, Patrick had locked the doors and only checked back once a month or so, on the slim chance any of them had returned. I supposed the house stood empty and unchanged, just as we'd left it that morning so long ago.

Patrick and Anna, along with other Insurgents, had searched for my parents and sisters for weeks, with no luck. The group had still been small enough to meet in in our basement, which also housed my dad's lab. It was dangerous to ask questions of the wrong people—the result could be soldiers knocking on your door and hauling you off. If word leaked out people were sniffing around, their families were also at risk.

Noah was driving when we turned onto the rutted dirt driveway. It was twilight and completely peaceful outside. With the windows rolled down, the early evening sounds of crickets filled the air, and the glow of fireflies twinkled against the trees. A child's laughter floated on the warm night air, and for a moment, I imagined it was Elsa's tinkling voice as she ran through the yard. If by some miracle the girl seen at this house was her, the little girl voice would be long gone. Elsa would be a young woman and I'd have missed her growing up. Sadness engulfed me at the thought.

Trees formed a canopy across the driveway, and shrubbery had grown wild for the past several years with no one to tend to them. I was surprised Noah remembered where to turn. Weeds grew over the tire tracks made by my family years ago and stood nearly as high as the tires on our Jeep.

The smell was the same. I inhaled deeply and closed my eyes. Crushed leaves, fresh apples, and the heavy floral scent from Mom's magnolia trees. I could almost pretend I was eight-years-old again, sprinting through the forest with my sisters, not a care in the world. We'd planned adventures with Noah and Brynn instead of missions to harvest sites.

Images flicked through my mind, one after the other. Picnics in the backyard with watermelon from our garden. Late evenings catching lightning bugs, and Cami begging Mom to let us keep them as pets. Cold winter days building snowmen.

Camping trips where Dad taught us to hunt, fish, and live off the land. Defense classes that enabled us to protect ourselves. Hiking trips that strengthened our muscles. Endless code drills.

Now I understood. He'd been preparing us to survive.

The Jeep bounced over a deep rut, and I snapped back to the present. The canopy of trees gave way to a larger yard where our house was nestled. Brynn reached from the back seat and squeezed my shoulder, lending me support. She knew how I felt and how difficult being back here was for me.

Our house was barely recognizable. It hadn't been tended to since the day Patrick and Anna had packed us up and moved to the compound. Straggled weeds grew rampant from Mom's formerly well-maintained flower gardens bordering the porch. Weather-worn shutters hung sideways from shattered windows, and some were missing completely. Crooked steps with missing boards led to a sagging porch.

I felt as hollow as the shell of a house staring back at me. Neither of us had a family to warm its insides. So many heartwarming memories were made here, and now it was nothing more than a dark, empty building. I wondered if it missed us. If it questioned what became of us, and why we left it to rot a little bit each day, uncared for and alone.

Noah stopped the Jeep at the front porch, but I couldn't bring myself to get out just yet. Everywhere I looked, ghosts flitted about, and remnants of conversations I'd had with my sisters and parents played in my head.

I thought about how close I was to the last place I'd seen Cami and Elsa. My eight-year-old self felt like we'd run for miles that day before Cami twisted her ankle. Now, I knew it was only a short half mile jog. Part of me felt like it would be disrespectful to their memory if I didn't at least visit the outcropping where I'd left them. Another part was deeply disappointed, because I knew I lacked the strength to do it.

What was wrong with me? One of my sisters could have come home looking for me. Elsa could be inside right now. I catapulted from the Jeep. "Elsa!"

What was left of the graveled driveway crunched beneath our boots as the three of us hurried toward the rickety steps, a couple of which were completely rotted through. I imagined the dark area beneath the porch now housed small wildlife.

Skipping over the broken steps, I strode the last few steps to the front door. Patrick said he'd locked it the last time he was here, but that had been years ago. Anything could have happened since then. Soldiers could have returned. Travelers passing through might have broken in and taken shelter.

Elsa could have remembered the spare key hidden beneath the rock in Mom's garden and let herself in.

The knob turned easily, then the door swung inward on creaky hinges. Faint rustling indicated small animals had also set up camp inside the abandoned dwelling. My hand stretched out behind me, and Brynn instinctively knew I was reaching for her. She gripped it and walked through the door with me. Noah followed behind. I flicked on the light switch, with a distant hope the electricity still worked. No such luck.

Noah rifled through the bag slung over his shoulder then passed out flashlights. I probably could have moved through the house with my eyes closed, but considering all the detritus on the floor, a flashlight was the safer option.

The room was a disaster. Furniture was overturned and broken. Empty food cans lay strewn about the floor. Remnants of a campfire took the place of Dad's chair. It was a miracle the house hadn't burned to the ground. Even after the passage of time, it still felt like a violation. Uninvited strangers had entered our home and torn it apart, tossing our belongings about like trash.

"Elsa, are you here? It's Ash." My only response was the faint skitter of rodent feet across the floor.

"Why don't you two search the house, and I'll look outside," Brynn said.

Noah shook his head. "No, we stay together. The local sector hasn't mentioned Colony soldiers in the area, but I don't want to take any chances."

I shone my flashlight in the direction of the kitchen. "Let's finish checking this floor, then we'll go upstairs to our bedrooms."

Stepping over broken furniture, corroded area rugs, and crumpled pages ripped from books, we wound our way through the obstacle course of the first floor before treading carefully up the stairs. Cami and Elsa had shared a bedroom, and if Elsa had truly come home, maybe she'd taken shelter there.

I'd prepared myself for disappointment—expected it even. Still, the ache in my chest grew as we searched room after empty room. When I found no trace of her in our parents' bedroom, I leaned against the wall and closed my eyes, hands bunched into fists at my side.

Brynn slipped her arms around my waist and leaned into me. "I'm sorry, Ash," she murmured.

I held her tightly and pressed my face to her hair.

"We've still got the basement and grounds to check," Noah said.

"It's just Dad's lab and the laundry room down there, but you're right. We still need to check it."

We retraced our steps through the first floor toward the basement stairs at the back of the house. The door leading down to the lab was wide open, the darkness like a gaping maw. Being inside, these steps shouldn't have been as dilapidated as those outside, but the last thing we needed was one of us to be injured falling through them.

I tested the first couple, and they seemed solid, so we continued our descent. At the bottom, I swept the flashlight around the room. Many happy afternoons were spent down here watching Dad work. I used to think maybe I'd follow in his footsteps and be a scientist when I was an adult. Now, the lab counter was cluttered with broken beakers and metal containers. Overturned bookcases and piles of shattered petri dishes and test tubes littered the floor. The senseless destruction was a far cry from Dad's orderly and clean workspace. Mom used to joke about how we could eat off any surface down here.

My boots crunched the broken glass as I approached Dad's desk. Or what was left of it. Drawers had been tossed across the room, their contents leaving a haphazard trail behind them. Most of his files were kept on the computer, but the chance any of them had survived were slim to none. Bits and pieces of it were scattered across the floor.

Noah gathered the fragments he could find and examined them. "Dad mentioned Colony soldiers had destroyed Garret's lab the day he was taken. If their only objective was to bring in your family, why would they have torn the place apart?"

I shrugged. "I didn't know they'd done this. After that day, I never wanted to come back here."

"The hard drive is missing. Kind of curious, don't you think? Like they expected to find something in Garret's files." He rummaged through other papers and lab equipment, but his efforts turned up nothing. "What about backups? Surely Garrett had files copied somewhere else in case the computer crashed."

Brynn huffed. "Or was stolen by soldier lackeys."

"Dad was a community doctor and a scientist. Why would The Colony need his files? It doesn't make any sense." But I knew for a fact Dad kept backups. After a storm had almost knocked out his computer, he'd repeated many times over the importance of backing up files, in addition to having a backup in case plan A fell through. "He uploaded things to a secure site. After all this time, do you think his files would still be there?"

Noah shrugged. "All we can do is try. I'm sure it has a password on it. Do you have any idea what it would be? Some combination of you, Cami, or Elsa's names? Birthdates?"

Crap. Dad had never shared passwords with me. My shoulders drooped as the door slammed shut on that prospect. "I have no idea where he uploaded anything, let alone passwords. I know he told us never to make them anything personal, so that rules out anything related to his children." Another dead end. We'd come all this way for nothing. Even without searching the grounds, I knew with an unexplained certainty Elsa wasn't here. The sighting had merely been some random girl who'd fit a vague description of her passing through.

"I'm not giving up yet." Noah stepped carefully around the room, nudging broken pieces of lab equipment and papers with his foot. He didn't really expect to find anything, but this was Noah's process—performing mundane activities while he considered ideas and memories, discarded them if they weren't important and connecting the dots from one incident to another if they were. At least, that's the way he'd explained it to us. Momentous epiphanies involving field missions had occurred to him while showering. I hoped he'd be blessed with another one while we were here.

Noah stopped, and his head rose slowly, his eyes fixed on something directly below my face. He strode in my direction, his head tilting to the side the closer he got. When he stopped directly in front of me, his hand rose to my neck and pulled the necklace I always wore from beneath my shirt. "Your father gave this to you." It was a statement rather than a question.

"Yeah. It was in our go bag in an envelope with my name on it. He said to never lose it. It's the only thing of his I have, and you've seen it hundreds of times."

"I'm not sure I've ever really seen it." His eyes narrowed as he turned the pendant over and examined the back of it. "Can you take it off?"

I lifted the chain over my head then dropped it into Noah's outstretched hand. "Brynn, shine your light over here, please." The medallion glittered in the light Brynn held, while Noah flipped it from front to back, running his fingertips gently over its surface. He stopped abruptly, and a smile slid across his face. "I was right."

My brows drew together. "About what? What did you find?" My pulse quickened as Noah pressed the tip of his fingernail into a nearly invisible crevice at the side of the medallion. A tiny disc, smaller than his fingernail pressed into the crevice, slid into view. All these years I'd worn Dad's necklace without knowing something was concealed inside it.

"Whatever is on here, it's important enough that Garrett didn't want it to fall into The Colony's hands. If I'm right, this might lead us to the connection between them and your Dad. Maybe you'll finally get some answers about what happened to your family, Ash."

I felt the vibration in my chest first. Noah and Brynn were focused on the disc and didn't seem to hear it yet. But I'd know that sound anywhere. It was carved into my memories from my last morning at this house nearly a decade ago. The *thumpa-thumpa-thumpa* of the blades haunted my nightmares. "Chopper."

A beat passed, then understanding flashed in their eyes.

"They're coming!" Brynn yelled.

With careful precision and the steady hands of a surgeon, Noah replaced the disc into my necklace and draped it over my neck. We bolted toward the basement stairs, took them two or three at a time, then sprang across the living room and leaped off the porch to the rutted driveway. Peaceful twilight skies had given way to a summer rain, which could work in our favor.

Colony soldiers were still a couple miles out, which gave us a narrow window of time to get the hell out of here. Brynn jumped headfirst through the door, and I pushed her into the backseat. Noah scrambled into the driver's seat then started the engine. The Jeep jerked forward, leaving a spray of gravel behind us.

Brynn searched the sky from the back window.

"Any sign of them?" I asked.

"Not yet," she yelled over the sound of rain pelting the windshield and the whine of the engine.

Overgrown, canopied trees provided cover for us as the Jeep bounced over the rutted dirt driveway. Noah steered onto the main road, slid into a right turn, then pushed the vehicle to its maximum safe speed. Headlights were off, but we knew these roads well after growing up here. I watched the rain bounce off the windshield as we sped past the familiar landscape.

"I have eyes on them." Brynn called from the back seat. "Looks like they're landing at your house, Ash."

"When they don't find us there, they'll search the highways. We need to get off the road and hole up somewhere."

Noah squinted through the darkened windshield. "I'm headed to the Bentley farm. Their barn was still standing when they abandoned the property."

The deserted farm came into view a couple miles later, and when we reached the barn, Brynn and I leaped out of the Jeep. Rusted hinges creaked from years of disuse as we swung the doors open. Noah pulled inside then turned off the engine. We closed the doors behind him.

Brynn pulled the flashlight from her bag and surveyed our surroundings. "I don't even want to think about how many snakes have taken up residence here." Multiple opponents twice her size, and she didn't blink. Throw a snake in her path, and Brynn screamed like she'd been tossed in the middle of a horror movie. It was a miracle she ever camped out.

To avoid the aforementioned reptiles, Brynn and I crawled back into the Jeep with Noah.

"Why would The Colony come here now?" Brynn gripped the backs of the seats and pushed her head up between Noah and me.

"Maybe it's just routine surveillance?" I didn't really believe it even as the words left my mouth.

Noah sat sideways and leaned his head back against the window. "It can't be a coincidence. I get a report of a young girl matching Elsa's description being observed at the house, then less than an hour after we arrive, soldiers show up? They were waiting for us to make an appearance."

A long moment passed before Brynn spoke. "Someone fed us this information knowing we'd check it out."

"Further proof of a connection between your dad and The Colony, Ash. Maybe they thought you'd lead them to something?"

I let out a long sigh. "Strange things are happening, brother, and I think there's a lot we weren't told. Which makes me awfully anxious to see what's on that disc." What if my parents weren't who I thought they were? I had so little of them left, and I couldn't bear the thought of tarnishing the images I clung to so tightly. Knowing they'd hidden things from me churned up some uncomfortable feelings. Maybe it was wrong, but my short years with them were a part of my life I didn't want to dismantle and investigate. I wanted to keep those idyllic memories of my family preserved and intact.

13

ASHER

Even though I was about ninety-nine percent certain Elsa had never been sighted at my house, I couldn't have lived with myself if we hadn't followed up on it. And without seeing my dad's lab, we might never have found the computer chip in my necklace.

We spent the night in the barn and made sure The Colony soldiers had cleared out before returning to Xander's safe house. Seeing what was on that chip was a priority, but dread and uncertainty were doing a pretty good job of wedging their way into the compartment of family memories I'd locked away. Knowing the truth could be within my reach, that it had been with me all of these years, hanging around my neck, unnerved me. Why hadn't Dad mentioned the chip in the letter with the necklace?

With the lack of sleep the night before and then the long drive back to the safe house this morning, we were exhausted, but anxious for answers. Xander loaned us his laptop and offered us his office for privacy.

Noah riddled me with more questions. "Garrett never said anything to you about this chip?"

I shoved my hands through my hair and sighed heavily. "It didn't really come up while he was sending his three children away and tearing apart our family."

The next few minutes could change everything. What if my father had lied to me all those years?

"Sorry, brother. No. I remember Dad wearing it, but he must have put it in the bag sometime before that day. Maybe it's a duplicate, but he never mentioned it was anything special."

Noah nodded then spun around in his chair and inserted the chip into the reader. My hand reached for Brynn's as a directory of files appeared on the screen. I scanned the names of the folders. Most of them seemed to be related to projects Dad had worked on—some with long, complicated medical names—and didn't mean anything to me. Until Noah paged down, revealing another folder, much larger than the rest.

It was labeled 'Asher'.

My brow furrowed. None of the other files had Cami or Elsa's names on them—I'd paid close attention when Noah paged through them. But there was my name on a folder nearly three times the size of anything else on Dad's chip.

Noah turned and looked up at me. "Are you ready?"

"Open it." A strange sense of calm flowed over me. Somewhere in the past several minutes, dread and uncertainty had given way to curiosity and the need for answers. Time to drag the skeletons out of the closet.

Noah clicked, and within the folder were several smaller files dating back to when I was two-years-old. Maybe they simply corresponded to my treatment dates when I was sick. He clicked on the one with the earliest date. It contained measurements of my height, weight, respiration—all routine readings taken at a doctor's appointment. My height was at the one hundred fiftieth percentile for others in my age group. Not a surprise. I'd always been tall for my age, which also explained why my weight was in a higher percentile.

"With the exception of your increased height and weight, everything looks normal." Noah continued opening files and scanning them, reading faster than I could keep up. Brynn squeezed my hand, almost as if she was lending me her strength.

Noah muttered a curse and frowned.

"What?" I asked.

"I know you were sick, but there's nothing here that mentions you being treated for a specific condition. Garrett took loads of blood samples and measurements, but I can't find a listing of administered drugs or any special types of therapy. Do you know exactly what he treated you for?"

Brynn's brows drew together when she looked up at me, her confusion mirroring my own. "I think it was some kind of leukemia. I was pretty young, so I don't remember all the complicated medical terms."

Noah continued scrutinizing the files, opening one after the other and comparing them. He shook his head. "No. That's impossible. I'm no doctor, but your white blood cell counts are too low for leukemia. Yours were normal, and Garrett mentions nothing about leukemia or any other type of cancer."

This didn't make sense. My parents had told me I'd been very sick, and with Dad being a physician and scientist, he'd treated me himself. There'd been no need for hospitals. "Maybe I have the diagnosis wrong, but I have memories of him treating me. Even after I was better, Dad still drew blood samples regularly to monitor my condition and make sure there was no recurrence."

Noah scrolled through more files. "Asher." His voice was quiet and questioning.

I leaned over his shoulder to see what he was referring to. At the bottom of the screen was a folder labeled "Subject A36".

A36.

The same term Mason heard Colony soldiers mention on the night he and Oz were ambushed and Oz was taken. Why would my father have a file by that name? Had Noah been right, and there truly was some kind of connection between my father and The Colony? My blood turned to ice. Brynn gripped my hand even tighter.

Noah opened it. Inside were numerous files with various dates, the earliest on my birth date. Something in my stomach twisted, and my breathing quickened. I had no possible way of knowing what was in these files, and yet somehow I knew with certainty its contents would alter the course of my life. Maybe change everything I'd believed about myself.

Noah clicked on the earliest one.

Paragraphs full of medical jargon filled the screen, but that's not what caught my attention. Beside one of the paragraphs was a familiar picture of a newborn baby wrapped in a blue blanket. Beneath the picture were the words Subject A36.

I inhaled sharply. There was a reason the photo was so familiar. This same picture had resided in a frame on my mom's dresser. I felt disconnected from my body. My vision narrowed to a tunnel. At the end of it was that file staring back at me, mocking me for believing everything my parents had told me all these years.

I was Subject A36.

"That's me," I murmured.

Noah looked up at me. "Are you sure?"

"Positive. Mom had that same picture on her dresser." I drew in a shaky breath and exhaled. "Okay. So I'm Subject A36. My parents lied to me my whole life. But what does this mean?" My voice wavered. Anger, doubt, confusion, and fear were a whirlwind coursing through me.

Brynn brought a hand to my cheek and gently turned my face to hers. "Sit down with me. Let Noah read the file and figure out what's going on, okay?"

I nodded and allowed her to lead me to a tattered floral print couch in the corner. I sat down heavily, propped my elbows on my knees, and dropped my head in my hands. Sitting felt better. My limbs felt like limp noodles and standing had become difficult. Brynn placed one hand on my arm and draped the other over my shoulders. Her warmth made me realize how cold I was. Down to my marrow cold. But my palms were sweaty, and my stomach churned.

Was I Asher Solomon or Subject A36? Why was The Colony searching for A36? And why did my father have information about it?

Noah continued scrolling through the files. He was silent and didn't give any indication one way or the other about what he read. Brynn rubbed soft circles on my back.

Vague memories danced through my mind, spinning back over conversations we'd had. How Dad explained I was sick while I denied feeling that way. How I'd tried reading over his shoulder sometimes when he entered data on his computer, curious about his work, and he'd scold me. How I'd never been allowed in his lab unless he'd required my presence or was there to supervise me. How, after I'd been cured, I'd disobeyed him, hidden behind one of the shelves, and observed the way his features twisted in anguish when he'd studied my blood under a microscope.

I'd assumed the disease had made a recurrence, but I'd never gotten sick again. Now I wondered what it was he saw.

Finally, Noah spun his chair to face us. Brynn's hand stopped moving.

"Well?" My voice was coarse. Anxious.

Noah hesitated before answering. And that spoke volumes. So did the pools of sympathy in his eyes. It was bad—possibly worse than I'd believed. He stood, closed the distance between us, and sat on the chair to my right. It was obvious he was reluctant to tell me what he'd discovered.

"Just say it. It's got to be better than what I'm imagining." But Noah's expression told me it wasn't.

His voice was gentle, but firm. "Your dad used to work for The Colony as a scientist. He was assigned to a highly sensitive, top secret program.

Several years into the project, he left and took part of it with him. His name wasn't Garrett Solomon. He assumed that identity after he ran."

My anxiety level dropped a few notches. Yes, I was shocked to learn my father had worked for The Colony, not to mention under a different name, but that's something I'd process later. For some reason, he'd escaped. That had to be worth something. "Well, that explains why they were looking for him, right? Why the soldiers came to our house? If he stole something from them, I'm sure he had a good reason. And I'm sure they wanted it back."

Noah rubbed his stubble-dusted jaw and met Brynn's gaze. I could see him communicating silently with her as siblings do. And I knew my dad working for The Colony wasn't the only thing he'd discovered.

He cleared his throat. "Ash, you need to brace yourself, because what I have to tell you will significantly impact your life. And it's going to hurt like hell."

I was standing on a precipice. A solid wall against my back pushed me forward, inch by inch, closer to the edge. I had nowhere else to go. Moving forward was the only option. But I knew what Noah was about to tell me would push me past the point of no return. Over the precipice.

Brynn's hold on me tightened. "Just say it."

"You were what Garrett stole when he left."

My brow furrowed in confusion. "Me?"

"You were... created in the lab where your father worked." His voice hitched. "Built to the specifications of The Colony."

I slid over the precipice, falling weightless. Nothing above or below to anchor me. And then a sudden, horrific realization washed over me. "Wait. Are you saying I was made from genes stripped from innocent people? The people we rescue and set free?"

Noah's voice was soft and gentle. "No. Not from people. You were genetically altered in the lab before you were... born. Garrett and another scientist ran hundreds of trials before their success with you."

I blinked. Genetically-altered. I was created in a lab. Not born. What had been done to me? And why? "What made me a success?"

Noah shifted uncomfortably in his chair. "Well, first of all, you lived. Most of the test subjects died before they were born. With all the DNA enhancements, the majority of the specimens didn't survive."

Anger exploded to the surface of my perfect storm of emotions. "Specimen? Is that what I am now?"

"Ash, look at me." Brynn turned my head to face her. "That's not what he meant. You're still you. Nothing changes that."

Noah reached over and gripped my knee. "No, brother. Of course not. When I say specimens, I'm referring to what was still in the petri dish."

I closed my eyes and drew in a shaky breath. Something sat heavy in the pit of my stomach. Things were moving too fast. Did this mean I wasn't human? Noah mentioned DNA alterations. "What kind of alterations?"

"The Colony wanted certain qualities enhanced. Speed, physical build, stamina, strength, strategic thinking, coordination, intelligence. And those are just a few. It also explains why you've never needed much sleep and have always healed so rapidly." Noah's gaze dropped to the floor.

None of those traits were negative things. So I'd been better at sports than other kids my age. A little taller and stronger. Broader in the shoulders. Big deal. That meant there was more to it.

Noah's lips pressed together tightly, and he avoided looking me in the eyes. He was holding something back. Something he was clearly reluctant to tell me. "What else?"

He scrubbed his hands over his face before continuing. "They also wanted certain traits to be suppressed or stripped. Your humanity—empathy, sympathy, kindness. The ability to feel or express love."

If that was what The Colony wanted, then they'd failed miserably. Clearly, I was capable of feeling love. I'd loved my family and experienced a devastating loss when they were taken. I loved Brynn so completely, I didn't possess the words to describe it. She was the best part of me. Although not blood-related, Noah was my brother in every possible way. "But I feel all those things, so they failed with me."

"He's right. None of that describes Ash." Brynn's voice was disbelieving, and her arm tightened protectively around my shoulders.

"Garrett gets the credit for that. He stole you from the lab and hid you from them all those years. When he said you were sick, in a way you were, Ash. What had been done to you, the plans for your future... it was beyond cruel. I never would have believed it if it wasn't in Garrett's personal files."

I was barely breathing. Maybe I'd stopped minutes ago, I couldn't remember.

"You were built to be an assassin, to follow orders blindly and without question. Never to be allowed to think for yourself or make any decisions regarding your life. Not even what you could eat for dinner. When Garrett was "treating" you, he was attempting to change your DNA back to its original form. He wanted to give you a chance to be the boy you were meant to be, not the monster he'd been instructed to create. He and your mom changed their names, went into hiding, and tried to give you as normal a life as possible."

I slumped down and dropped my head to the back of the couch. Everything I'd believed about myself, my family, our life—all a lie. And then, like a bolt of lightning, it hit me, and I felt the resounding jolt in every cell of my body.

They weren't my family.

My "father" was my maker.

Images fluttered through my mind. Cami, Elsa, and I playing in our favorite tree. Mom tucking me into bed and kissing me goodnight. Dad teaching me to fish, the pride on his face when I'd taken to it so easily.

So many memories.

So many deceptions.

Cami and Elsa weren't my sisters. Mom and Dad weren't my parents. If I hadn't been breathing before, I was making up for it now. My chest rose and fell rapidly. I was hyperventilating. Brynn's and Noah's voices called to me through a long tunnel, far away. But I was already gone.

14

ASHER

"Asher, wake up." Through the darkness that engulfed me, I heard her. The voice that soothed my anger, broke through the horror of my nightmares, reassured me when I was overcome with guilt, and murmured words of love meant only for me.

My consciousness strained toward Brynn. But if I woke, it meant facing what I'd learned about myself. The reality of what I was. The family I'd lost all over again.

A cool hand pushed hair away from my forehead, and I tilted my head toward her touch. I didn't want to wake up. But staying here in the darkness was the coward's way out. I was stronger than this.

My eyes fluttered open to see Brynn staring down at me with an expression of concern. "Hey," she whispered. "How do you feel?"

I winced when I angled toward her. "My head hurts." Now that I'd acknowledged it, the throbbing grew worse.

"You slammed your head against the wall when you were hyperventilating. But I'm pretty sure the wall sustained more damage. I always said your head was hard." The corner of Brynn's mouth tugged into a half smile.

"Help me sit up." She grabbed my hand and pulled, while I pushed my way to a sitting position. Noah was bent over the computer again. I hoped he hadn't come across any more epiphanies. What he'd learned today was more than I could handle, and my shoulders ached from the weight of it. Now that I thought about it, my whole body hurt.

What was I?

"Noah?" I asked.

He swiveled in the chair to face me. "Are you all right?"

"I've been better." I turned my face away from Brynn. Where I'd experienced emotion overload earlier, now there was nothing. Emptiness. Numbness. I should have been drowning in crashing waves of emotions. In my case, they were turned off. Maybe I was in shock. Didn't the mind shut down the body when the trauma was too great?

Then I remembered that was what The Colony had wanted.

Brynn kneeled on the floor in front of me and clutched both my hands in hers. Always attuned to my emotional state, she'd felt me slipping away. I should have expected this. Her voice was fierce and determined. "None of this changes anything. Not between us. Ever. Do you understand me? You're Asher Solomon. Garrett and Trina were your parents. Cami and Elsa were your sisters. I'm your family." Her eyes bored into mine, her last words a whisper. "I know your heart."

"Goes for me, too, Ash," Noah added. "No matter what, you're my brother."

Brynn's deep brown eyes held no hint of doubt, only love, support, and reassurance. What I always saw when I looked at her. My whole world had been shaken and turned inside out over the last hour. I was reeling from the shocking revelations of my origin, my intended purpose, and the realization that I had no family. But as I looked into Brynn's eyes, I saw her faith in me, saw her opinion of me was resolute. Constant. And I wondered what I'd ever done to deserve her.

I nodded and kissed her knuckles before squeezing her hands tight in mine. Brynn and Noah loved me, and that was the only certainty in my life right now.

After sitting up straight, I turned to Noah. "So, Dad—er, Garrett—repaired the genetic alterations and now I'm just some normal guy?"

Noah hesitated. More bad news was about to be dumped on the load that already threatened to collapse me. "He did what he could. Once your DNA was altered, some of it was difficult to reverse. Garrett effectively suppressed some of the genetic effects, but basically, they're still lurking inside you."

Unnatural things lurking in my genetic makeup. Traits that didn't need to be unleashed in the world.

"Ash, you clearly have the capacity to love, sympathize, and empathize. All of that you learned from your family. But shutting off those emotions and becoming an unfeeling assassin?"

I flinched at the term.

Noah's expression softened. "That's still inside of you. Some of your less desirable genetic traits couldn't be reversed. There's a lot of complicated medical jargon I can't explain, mostly because I don't completely understand it myself, but I got the gist. Picture it this way. Garrett couldn't remove the Colony-coveted traits, so he essentially patched over them. The problem is he had no way of knowing if the patch was permanent or temporary."

"Because they killed him." That explained why he regularly drew blood samples to see if anything had changed. To see if the monster inside me was making its existence known. "Are you saying I could become the killer I was designed to be?"

"His research was limited, because nothing like this had ever been attempted. He had no other studies to refer to. But Garrett's opinion was that you'd still be you unless something triggered those buried instincts to bring them to the surface."

My brow furrowed. "Triggered the instincts? Like what?"

"He wasn't sure. He monitored you closely when you were a child, looking for any indication you'd lost your ability to empathize or let your anger get out of control. But nothing ever happened. You were just an average—well, not *average*—but a kid who preferred to be outside more than inside and wanted to climb trees and build forts." He grinned sheepishly. "The non-average parts were the physical enhancements. You were like us in all the ways that count, but physically, you were more advanced than the rest of us."

So, this was something like a Dr. Jekyll and Mr. Hyde scenario. Somewhere inside of me, a killer slept quietly, biding his time until some unknown event provoked his awakening. If he awoke, did that mean he killed indiscriminately? Was I a danger to the people I loved? I experienced a brief flash of waking in the morning to Brynn's lifeless body beside me, not remembering what had happened. And I was covered in her blood.

I jerked backward instinctively, putting some distance between us.

"What?" Brynn asked. "What is it?"

I could only gape at her, unable to get the image of her sightless eyes staring back at me out of my mind.

"Asher?"

I looked at Noah, horror stricken. "So what's inside could be released at any time by some unknown event—a smell, an action, a word—who knows what could cause it. And I could turn on any of you. Even kill you."

He leaned forward and placed his hand on my thigh. "You're my brother. I know if it came down to it, you'd gladly give your life for me or Brynn. No matter what you were built to be, we're not afraid of you."

Brynn's expression was resolute and stern. "Absolutely not. Even with the enhancements, extras, or whatever they gave you, I know the truth. You'd never do anything to hurt us."

I shook my head slowly and whispered. "You can't know that."

Brynn moved closer to me and gripped my shoulders. "Yes, I can. I'd bet my life on it. Don't you dare pull away from me. I won't let you. Not now, not ever. You need us. And I need you."

How could I have doubted she'd think anything else? But my impulse was to protect her. If being around me put Brynn in danger, then I needed to leave. And I knew exactly what she'd have to say about that. *It's a stupid, useless decision, and you have no right to make that choice for me, Asher Solomon.* Running away would only put her at greater risk because she'd come after me. And I'd do the same thing. If the tables were turned and she chose to leave, it would utterly destroy me. No way would I put her through that. I was grateful she and Noah were willing to stand by my side and support me through this because she was right. I needed them.

I pulled her toward me, kissed her forehead, then murmured, "Thank you."

We sat with our foreheads touching for several moments, until Noah cleared his throat. I pulled away from Brynn and looked at him. "So, what happens how? What do we do with this information?"

"We know why The Colony wants you. Why they searched for Garrett all those years, and why it was imperative you escape. Beyond that, I really don't know, brother."

His statement was a punch to my gut. If it weren't for me, would my family still be alive? Would The Colony have left them alone? My sisters could have grown up. My parents could have had many more years together. But because of what was done to me, they were all dead.

And that's something I'd have to live with the rest of my life.

15

ASHER

On the outside, I appeared to be the same person, but it was a part I'd been playing for over seventeen years. It was effortless. Inside, I was a complete mess. A whirling vortex of doubt, insecurity, and questions. But most of all, fear. No matter what Brynn said to reassure me, the vision of her mangled body in our bed refused to be driven from my mind.

Knowing my parents had hidden things from me churned up some uncomfortable feelings. Maybe it was wrong, but my short years with them were a part of my life I didn't want to dismantle and investigate. I wanted to keep those idyllic memories of my family preserved and intact. My younger self had blind faith in Dad's order to abandon my sisters that day, even though I may not have agreed with him. Parents kept their children safe. Sure, I'd questioned his instructions to continue on without them, but trusted he had good reasons behind his decision. As the years went by and I matured, the logic for leaving Cami and Elsa never presented itself. Questioning that action felt like a disloyalty to my father, so I'd stored it away and avoided examining it too closely.

Now, I knew why. All these years, guilt had turned my focus to what my family had faced after I'd run. Had the soldiers taken my parents and sisters? Killed them in our front yard? Stripped their coveted genes for those who could pay the price? When Patrick and Anna searched for them the next day, there was no trace of their bodies nor any indication they'd been killed on site. No blood, no bodies. Nothing.

With The Colony searching for me, my presence at the compound put everyone in danger. My friends and family—I couldn't bear it if they were injured, or worse, because of me. Especially knowing I was the cause of my parents' deaths.

I closed my eyes and heard Dad's wavering voice going over the instructions for the first time. His eyes were intense with frantic desperation. It was obvious even considering being separated from his children caused him crushing pain. He and mom had loved us all so much. Family was the most important thing to them, along with our safety. That's why he'd insisted on the drills. He'd known someday we'd be found, so our time together was limited and precious.

He'd promised to come back for us. I'd learned that promises were like a beacon in a storm—things to cling to and place our hopes in but could be easily destroyed by the chaos surrounding them.

After we'd returned to the compound, I'd spilled everything to Brynn while lying in bed that night. Our room was our safe zone, and in there, we only spoke the truth to each other. After our time apart, we'd made promises. No secrets, no pretending. No trying to change each other. That time without her was a prison of my own making, a place I never wanted to visit again. Now, there was only honesty. No matter what. Life was too short to live any other way.

We lay on our sides facing each other, legs and arms intertwined.

"Tell me." Her voice was soft, and she smelled of vanilla soap from her shower earlier in the evening.

"I don't know who I am."

"You're Asher Solomon, the same person you've always been."

"They weren't my family."

"By blood, no. But we both know blood doesn't make a family. Sometimes we make our own. Family means the people we want to spend our lives with, through good times and bad. You were their son and brother, Ash, in every way that matters. Biology didn't factor into Garrett's decision. He stole you away because he loved you."

"My parents lied to me."

"They lied to protect you. You were a little boy who couldn't possibly comprehend what was done to you. When you were old enough to understand, Garrett would have told you the truth. I know you believe that. When he knew he was out of time and wouldn't be there for you, he gave you the necklace."

"I'm afraid. I keep seeing a vision of you dead in our bed. I wake up, and you're cold and mutilated beside me. I killed you without realizing it." My body trembled at the mention of it, fear coursing through me.

"That would never happen. No matter what they built you to be, that's not who you are. You're not a mindless robot who follows orders. They didn't want you to feel emotions or any kind of human connection. But you do. I know how much you love me. At your core, you're incapable of hurting me."

"I don't know what I am."

"First of all, you're not a *what*. You're a *who*. A man who frees people who have no hope and face certain death. Someone who has a short temper when it comes to new recruits because your priority is teaching them how to stay alive. An inspiration to every person on your team with your determination, bravery, and integrity. The best friend of my brother, someone he's always been able to count on for support, advice, and counsel." She pulled me closer, so there was no space between us as she contoured herself to my body. "The man who loves me harder than I ever thought possible and who I love back just as fiercely. That's who you are, Asher. Don't ever forget it."

•　　•　　•　　•　　•

Pin cushions and I had a lot in common. Noah had taken Dr. Cothran into his confidence and asked her to draw blood and study my DNA. And she'd studied. A lot. Noah wanted to compare Garrett's last recorded observations to see if there had been any significant changes.

Walking softly around the compound had become my norm, and I feared unexpected loud noises or any added stress might trigger whatever lay dormant below the surface. I pictured a grenade inside me, and if I moved a certain way or jiggled just right, the pin would fall out and everyone around me would be caught up in the explosion.

Brynn reassured me, reminding me after all these years and all these missions, through the strenuous physical activity and the dangerous situations, someone dropping a pan in the kitchen wasn't likely to provoke any life-threatening situations.

I wasn't convinced.

When we were younger, Noah and I had found Patrick's old comic books in the basement. In one of the series, anger caused Dr. Bruce Banner to turn into the Hulk. If anger was my trigger, we could be in for a heap of trouble.

I was the first to admit my temper could get the best of me sometimes and had spiked some lofty levels more than once. My impatience with new recruits had left them cowering in corners after training sessions with me, but there had been no loss of lives or limbs. Bruised egos and hurt feelings? Plenty. I never cared about that, though. They needed to be prepared, and I took my job seriously. If I didn't train them well, their lives were in jeopardy.

I never dreamed I was the danger.

So, I strove to keep my emotions in check. Anger hadn't triggered anything before, but it seemed a logical conclusion that it could. Would, eventually. Seemed logical to me, anyway. Of course I went out of my way to suppress any negative emotions.

After living with the same group of people for so long, especially in close quarters, the change in my behavior didn't go unnoticed. It was unavoidable—particularly my new, never-before-seen sunshine and rainbows attitude.

"What's up with you, Asher?" Elijah slid into the seat across from me and placed his dinner tray in front of him. Wonderful. I enjoyed his company, but he was occasionally too inquisitive for his own good. And apparently offended by silence. Elijah never stopped talking.

From the table behind him, barks of laughter rang out. As usual, Declan was surrounded by a group of admirers hanging on his every word. He was the new favorite play toy around here and seemed to enjoy being in the spotlight. It didn't appear to be arrogance that caused him to draw attention to himself, it was more that he genuinely liked being around people and had an easygoing personality. People gravitated to that.

I dropped my gaze back to my plate and stabbed at my pasta.

"Asher?"

"Nothing. Just thinking about tonight's supply run."

"It's just that you've been so... nice over the past few days. Did you lose a bet to Brynn again?"

Several months back, Brynn had bet me I couldn't go a day without yelling at a new recruit. I'd lost in two short hours. To pay up, I'd had to take over her training classes for six weeks. It had been sheer torture for me.

"You're usually not so accommodating to other people."

I dropped my fork to the tray, pushed back from the table, and folded my arms over my chest. Elijah wasn't going to shut up. I reminded myself yet again to be calm and keep a lid on my irritation. "No, I didn't lose a bet. Maybe I'm just taking a new approach to life. Not letting the small stuff get to me."

While he chewed, a gleam sparked in his eye. "Would this new approach encourage you to do some extra training sessions with me? Have mercy, Ash. I'm a charity case. You know my goal is field op."

I struggled not to roll my eyes. We'd had this conversation multiple times. Elijah wasn't cut out to be in the field, and no amount of training was going to change that. He simply didn't possess the instincts. No matter how many times he'd fired a gun, he still anticipated the noise and jerked reflexively. When he flinched, it threw off his aim. He was a danger to himself and others. Who knew when a shot would go wide or when he'd react too quickly and shoot one of our own people.

"So, what's the topic of conversation today, guys?" Declan slid into the seat beside Elijah and helped himself to a French fry on Elijah's tray, dousing it in ketchup before shoving it in his mouth. He looked questioningly between my exasperated expression and Elijah's pleading one.

"Nothing big. I'm just begging Ash to help me achieve my dreams." Elijah smacked Declan's hand as he went in for another fry.

"So, just your basic small talk, then. Why do you look so annoyed, Ash?"

I scrubbed my hands over my face, then clasped them behind my head and leaned back in the chair. "Elijah wants to become a field operative."

Declan looked between us. "And this... displeases you?"

"No, it doesn't displease me," I snapped. "How did you get in this conversation anyway, Declan?"

He shrugged. "Just being a concerned citizen."

"Look, Elijah, you know where I stand on you transferring. You're more valuable to us as a computer tech. Breaking into security systems is a walk in the park for you, and you've saved us more times than I can count."

His fork clattered against the metal tray. "I'm tired of staying behind the scenes. I'm just the nerdy computer guy. Everyone treats me like their goofy little brother, but no one really takes me seriously. I think I could be just as valuable in the field. I could help, Ash. After extra time with you, I'm sure I could pass the physical exam and improve my shooting accuracy. Please."

Elijah's pleading expression resembled a puppy seeking affection, and turning him down would be like kicking that poor, innocent dog. I'd trained enough recruits to know some people would never have what it took to make a successful field operative. Sure, building muscle and stamina would help pass the physical requirements. Weapons handling and defense training could be learned. Strategic decision-making could be taught.

But not intuition. That voice inside that told you to turn left instead of right. To take cover a second before a shot zipped past your head. That a sniper was on the roof, even though your eyes told you differently. That your opponent would shift left instead of right, giving you an advantage.

Those instincts were part of us since birth, ingrained in us. Kept us alive. I couldn't live with myself if I sent an incompetent recruit into the field and he got himself or others killed.

I had to kick the puppy.

Leaning forward on the table, I placed my hands in front of me. "Elijah, you're aware I don't think the field is the best use of your talents. We all depend on you and your technical expertise. No one else here can do what you do, at least not at your level. I hope you realize how important you are to the success of our missions. When we rescue people from harvest facilities, a lot of that is because of you. Being in the field isn't the only way to help."

Elijah's expression slid from hopeful to crushed, and the light faded from his eyes. He shoved his chair away from the table and readied to leave.

Declan inserted himself into the conversation again. The guy just couldn't help himself. "Come on, Ash. What could it hurt to help Elijah? You can't predict when knowing how to shoot a gun could save your life or someone else's, right? It's a good idea to learn."

He met Elijah's gaze and nodded almost imperceptibly, like they were brothers-in-arms with a common goal. Seriously? The two of them were ganging up on me. The thought crossed my mind they might even have planned this. Maybe Declan had a point. What could it hurt giving Elijah some extra training? At best, he'd improve his accuracy by double digits. I doubted that was a possibility, but at least he'd become more comfortable with a gun. It would also distract me from all the A36 business.

"I'd help, too." Declan looked as hopeful as Elijah, and I knew I was beaten.

I huffed out a breath. "Fine. While I still don't agree that the field is for you, Noah and I agreed it wouldn't hurt to train you further with weapons. Everyone here, no matter their position, should be able to handle a gun. You never know what could happen."

And just like that, Elijah's face lit up again, and he high-fived Declan. If Elijah really was a puppy, he'd be jumping all over me, licking my face. I was relieved that wasn't the case.

"Well, it's not the answer I'd hoped for, but I'll take what I can get. Thanks, Ash. You, too, Declan. I really appreciate it."

"You're welcome," I said. "Ready to start?"

"What... now?"

"I've got extra time before the supply run, and like you said, I'm accommodating. Declan, you free?"

"Ready to roll."

Elijah shoved half a sandwich in his mouth, Declan grabbed a handful of fries, then both trailed behind me out the door.

ASHER

Working with Elijah had been advantageous for both of us. Teaching him to shoot gave my mind something else to concentrate on—you know, other than having been manufactured in a test tube and programmed to kill indiscriminately. To his credit, after just a few hours, Elijah made great strides. He'd never be a marksman, but was a decent shot at close range.

Keeping busy prevented me from dwelling on less pleasant things, which was why I was in the briefing room with Noah, my team, and Beta team. We were scheduled to depart in six hours.

Noah's comm unit crackled. He pulled it from his pocket.

"Noah?" The voice was frantic and rushed.

"Go ahead."

"We've got problems. The outer barrier has been breached, and spotters sighted several incoming vehicles. It's confirmed they're not ours."

My adrenaline level shot from normal to off the charts in a second, and I leaped to my feet. The outer barrier was only ten miles away. Occasionally, other vehicles breached the boundary we liked to keep between us and the outside world, but typically they passed us by, unaware that a branch of the nearly-deserted road they were on led to our compound. If it was Colony soldiers, we didn't have much time. They'd found us.

"How many vehicles?" Noah asked.

His radio crackled again. "Ten trucks. And I picked up five helicopters on radar."

Noah stared into space, his eyes unfocused. I knew the decision he warred with, and it's something we'd planned for, a protocol Patrick had put in place but hoped would never be necessary.

He took a deep breath. "Evacuation Protocol. Send it out immediately."

We'd drilled the Evacuation Protocol on a regular basis in the event our compound was infiltrated and we were forced to fight or withdraw. First Patrick, and then Noah, made sure we were prepared if the time ever came.

And that time was here.

All residents were assigned a job. Every single person. Tech people uploaded any sensitive information to Central, then destroyed the hard drives and remaining equipment. Drivers brought around transport vehicles to the loading dock. Medical prepared any patients for travel and packed medical stock. The rest of us met in the weapon supply room, armed ourselves, and defended the compound long enough to get everyone else to safety. If any rescued were on site, they were evacuated first. Essential supplies were packed and sent with the first wave of evacuees.

The Protocol echoed over the speakers throughout the compound. Through the closed door I heard scuffling and heavy footsteps as people scattered to their assigned stations. My gaze shot to Brynn.

Not all of us would escape this.

Some of us would die.

I wouldn't fail my family again. No one would be left behind this time.

Elijah shot out of his chair. "I just did the daily upload an hour ago, so we won't lose much. I'll grab the supply packs." He rushed from the room.

Despite the impending danger of invasion, Noah looked at Brynn and me with a calm expression that belied what I'm sure he felt underneath. On the outside, he was the picture of a reassured, confident leader, fully prepared to handle this type of situation. He wouldn't be with us. His job was to inform Central of our situation, communicate updates and location coordinates, and get everyone to the safe house. "Stay safe."

Brynn nodded. "See you on the other side, brother."

Brynn and I sprinted through the doorway, turned left down the hallway, then took the stairs two at a time. The common area was a hive of activity as people raced to pack equipment and get to their assigned places. To Noah's credit, no one seemed to be frozen in panic or confused. I'd accused him of drilling us excessively, but he'd insisted we couldn't be overprepared. And tonight proved he was right. I never should have doubted him.

The two of us slid past others moving purposefully. We passed several operatives already armed with weapons more powerful than the handguns we usually carried. We dodged others exiting the armory and shouldered our way through. Mason, Jonah, Declan, and Paige already had the well-stocked cabinets open and moved seamlessly, handing each operative guns, grenades, and extra ammo as they passed through the line. Brynn and I grabbed ours then headed to our designated stations.

The ear-splitting alarm had been turned off, but the protocol was still in effect until Noah called a code clear. An electronic voice rang out overhead. "Automatic locks engaging." With the exception of the door leading to the loading dock, every other entry or exit point to the compound was locked. The doors were thick, heavy steel, reinforced with metal bars as an added measure of security. If the soldiers wanted in, we'd make it as difficult as possible. Explosive charges were set just inside the doors on the outside chance they made it through.

Teams were assigned to multiple areas. Each door was covered. Operatives were stationed outside the compound, and snipers were hidden in trees and on the roof. Others guarded the loading dock during the evacuation, and then accompanied the transport vehicles.

Brynn and I were among those assigned to the door at the loading dock. Our orders were to make sure our people were evacuated safely and keep the area clear of soldiers.

Adrenaline coursed through my veins, but my mind and body were calm. I was ready for this. In the back of my mind, the fear of Brynn being hurt niggled at me, straining at its bonds to take control. I slammed the door on it before it could wriggle its way free. Letting that fear overtake me would put not only myself, but everyone around me in danger because it would prevent me from doing my job. If I failed, people died. It was as simple as that.

If the soldiers showed up at the front door, there were only three ways they could get to the loading dock area.

The single road leading to the dock, which was doubtful, since it was heavily guarded.

Fight their way through the numerous operatives inside the compound.

By chopper. Which was also questionable. We'd shoot it down before it landed.

Brynn took her place by the door leading into the compound. Jonah, Declan, and Paige joined us after weapons distribution and dispersed into the transport area to their assigned locations. I stood several feet from the loading dock, where I could see both the incoming road and the lines of evacuees being loaded into the vehicles. I'd also have a visual if a chopper was headed our way.

It was a crisp, cool night, but the normal nighttime sounds were drowned out by radios crackling, operatives calling out evacuation instructions, confused rescuees asking questions, and scared children crying. No hooting owls, no chirping crickets. Even the fireflies had bugged out.

Overhead, chopper blades thundered in the distance. They'd gotten here quick. I doubted they'd be able to land. The operatives on the roof were armed with bazookas.

Evacuees still streamed down the stairs to the graveled lot then were herded onto the transports. We'd just hit a harvest facility last night and hadn't gotten the rescued to a safe house yet. They'd been scheduled to leave tomorrow morning. Over a hundred men, women, and children had been housed here, not counting the residents of the compound, and were the first to be evacuated.

Thanks to Patrick's and Noah's plans, the organization was flawless. The transports were quickly filled, armed operatives jumped on the running boards, then the vans sped through the gate. Five had departed already, and more were almost ready to go.

An explosion lit up the sky. I ducked instinctively, shielding some of the rescued in line, then turned toward the sound. One chopper down, four more to go. The sound of gunfire echoed through the night air, and voices shouted. Whether Insurgents or Colony soldiers, I couldn't be sure, but this fight had started.

Tears streamed down the faces of some of the evacuees. There were clearly terrified, but our operatives hurried them along and kept the panic to a minimum. More kudos to Noah.

Two more explosions reverberated through the night, but neither was from a chopper being hit. My stomach sank. They must have been from the doors. Soldiers attempting to blast their way in. Those doors wouldn't withstand more than a couple of heavy hits. The steel was thick but not infallible.

And if they'd made it to the doors, we had operatives down outside the compound.

A panicked, out of breath voice sounded in the comm unit in my ear. "Breach at the front door! Repeat, the front door is breached. Soldiers are in the compo—" It cut off abruptly, and I knew we'd lost more people.

And then a thought struck me so suddenly, I nearly staggered from the shock. I'd assumed the soldiers were here to destroy our compound, kill the operatives who freed their hostages, and capture any "donors" they could get their hands on. But what if that was only the secondary objective? Just a bonus that came along with the primary goal?

Maybe their real target was A36.

If that was the case, all these people—friends I'd fought with side by side and lived with for years—were dying because of me. And they didn't even know it. Besides the three of us, Noah had only taken Dr. Cothran into his confidence.

"Move quickly! The faster you get on the transport, the sooner we can get you to safety."

Gunfire was closer. Through my comm, I heard tense, but controlled operatives voicing updates on their areas and coordinating attacks. Our own explosives planted at the entrance doors had taken out numerous soldiers, but more poured in behind them.

Three more transports to load, and then two left for the rest of us. If soldiers were already in the building, we'd never get the vans loaded in time.

I made the decision. "Mason, you and Declan stay and cover the transports. The rest of us are moving in to stall the soldiers and give the vans time to get away." Jonah, Brynn, Paige, a few operatives from another team, and I rushed into the compound, taking turns covering each other as we advanced toward the sounds of gunfire and shouting.

I checked in with Luciana stationed toward the front of the compound. "Luci, sitrep."

She was winded and sounded like she was moving fast. "We're retreating to the common area and shutting the doors behind us. Half of my team is down. They're not killing us unless their lives are threatened. Only wounding."

What? Not killing us? That didn't make any sense at all. Maybe I'd misunderstood. "Luci, repeat."

"I think they're planning to take some of us for harvest, Ash. It's the only thing that makes sense."

I was stunned. But it did make sense, of course. Preserving us for harvest. Stripping our best qualities and selling them to the highest bidder. We'd die the slow death we'd saved their hostages from. I could see how The Colony would think that was fitting in a morbid kind of way.

"Move to the common area," I told my team. "Watch each other's backs. They want to kill us by harvesting, not in a gunfight. Take out as many as you can." In this fight, my only concern was the preservation of the lives of my own people.

Outside the entrance to the common area, we heard Luciana getting what was left of her team in position. With it being a two-story room, the best shooters were placed on the catwalk overhead. The eight of us entered and joined her team, spreading out in position.

Behind the double steel doors came the shouts of the soldiers. I could only assume they'd blow this door as they had the others. We were prepared—shooters on the catwalk, operatives flanking each side of the path leading from the doorway, others taking cover behind computer desks.

I flanked the right side of the door. Brynn was directly across from me, Jonah behind her. My gaze met Brynn's, and she gave a small nod. That tiny gesture spoke volumes—she was ready, we could do this, she had my back, she loved me, and we'd come through this alive.

An explosion rocked the room. Vibrations from the floor beneath me traveled up my legs and almost knocked me off my feet. Desks toppled over, and glass from overhead lights rained down upon us. My ears rang, and a high-pitched tone replaced the sounds of shouting around me. The steel doors buckled but remained intact. Probably not for long, though. The soldiers wouldn't stop until they gained entry. I crouched in anticipation.

A second explosion blew the doors off the hinges, then soldiers streamed through.

We opened fire. Several of the first soldiers who entered the room cried out as they were hit by the shooters on the catwalk. Those who entered behind them ascertained the shooters' location and focused their efforts in that direction.

Even with all of us shooting, the soldiers continued to pour through the destroyed steel doors in waves. We'd take out five, and ten more would replace them. They just kept coming.

With three precise shots, I killed three guards firing on Luciana and her team. I dropped to the floor, crawled forward, ducked behind an overturned desk. One of our people lay unmoving on the floor, but I couldn't tell if he was dead or only wounded. Like me, the remaining Insurgents had taken cover behind overturned furniture. Alex and Jada from Luciana's team were down, and Jonah and Brynn moved in their direction to provide support.

Soldiers fanned out as they poured into the room, their plan to surround us, but I wasn't having any of that. "Watch the fringes!" I concentrated on trimming their numbers. On my right, Paige focused on those who were trying to flank us, while I set my sights on the onslaught of soldiers storming into the room. Seriously, were they cloned? I'd swear we'd already put down hundreds of them.

Jonah and Brynn were nearly pinned down while they covered Alex and Jada. My instinct was to leap over the bodies, overturned desks, and anything else that stood between Brynn and me, but I knew she was capable of taking care of herself. She'd made that crystal clear dozens of times. Jonah was also a good shot, calm and focused under pressure.

Brynn crouched low and twisted to her left. As I turned my attention to the enemy in front of me, I detected movement in my peripheral vision. A soldier had taken cover behind some equipment a short distance away from Brynn and had her in his sights. Before I could call out a warning or take aim, a shot came from behind me. A cloud of blood burst from his left eye, and he dropped hard.

I spun around to see Elijah standing, gun in hand, an easy target for anyone looking.

I lunged for his arm and pulled him to the floor.

His eyes bulged. "Ash, I got him."

"You have my eternal gratitude, Elijah, but you need to leave. Get to a transport while you still can. Stay low. I'll cover you until you get to the door."

He nodded, then crawled through the overturned desks and destroyed equipment. I'd been right about his instincts—it was a miracle no one had taken him out. But Elijah was there when I'd needed him most. He made it to the exit, and I could only hope he got to the van safely.

Paige had seriously thinned the numbers on her side, and I gestured for her to cover the door, then turned my efforts in Brynn's direction. What I saw next seemed to be in slow motion. Brynn and Jonah faced forward, backs to the wall, but somehow, a soldier had maneuvered his way behind them and advanced in their direction. Unless my teammates had eyes in the back of their heads, there was no way they'd see him. My blood turned to ice.

Even as I took the shot, I screamed at her. "Brynn, down!" She immediately dropped, but not before I saw a spray of blood. She'd been hit. Wounded and down, Alex and Jada still fired on the targets in front of them. Jonah immediately spun in Brynn's direction and faced the soldier I'd clipped in the shoulder.

Their shots rang out simultaneously. Jonah toppled over backwards. The soldier staggered back against the wall, clutching his chest. Now that I had a clear shot, I finished what Jonah had started.

I'd already suffered the loss of far too many people. It was more pain than any one person should have to experience in a lifetime. Brynn was my heart. I wouldn't let this happen again. I wouldn't fail her like I'd failed my sisters.

I caught movement in my right peripheral vision, felt a sting in my shoulder. My body whipped sideways, but I knew I wasn't in any immediate danger. It was only a flesh wound. Paige took care of him, and I turned my attention back to Brynn. I had to get to her. Not knowing how badly she was injured whipped my panic into a frenzy.

Out of nowhere, shots rang out from every direction, but they weren't from us. A fresh wave of soldiers stormed through the door. We didn't have the numbers. No way could we handle this. I signaled for Luciana, Paige, and the other few remaining to head to the loading dock. I had to get to Brynn.

I glanced over my shoulder in Brynn's direction and was met with a surprise. Declan moved toward her, gun in hand. Relief flooded through me. He'd reach her sooner than I would and could get her to safety.

Assuming she was still alive—a thought that threatened to stop my heart.

Declan stood over Brynn, who still showed no signs of movement, and waved his hand at the seven remaining soldiers behind him, directing them to flank the doorway leading to the hall.

He wasn't firing on them.

They listened and obeyed him.

The overwhelming number of reinforcements who'd sent my team retreating withdrew through the same door they'd entered and waited in the hall.

What was happening?

Declan stared down at Brynn, then reached up and pulled strands of his dark hair forward around the left side of his neck.

Everything crashed into me at once. Brynn's feeling that something was off with Declan and her hesitancy in welcoming him as a team member. The way he'd slid so comfortably into our team, almost as if he'd known our ways and quirks. How Noah had never gotten around to checking out his story with Barton. All the times I'd seen someone else make the same gesture out of habit, to cover the burns on his neck with locks of hair. Only the burns were no longer there, and the straight blond hair was now dark and curly. Declan's familiarity of names throughout the organization, his knowledge of Insurgents, his easy-going manner... he'd fit in so easily, the urgency to check up on him had fallen to the wayside.

"Oz."

"No."

I jerked my gaze to the right at Paige's utterance. I should have known she wouldn't leave me here without backup. Her head shook slowly in denial. "It can't be. Oz is dead. We mourned him."

Oz's new startling blue eyes, raised chin, and haughty expression mocked me. Even his voice was deeper. We'd been unaware we were pawns in his game, and he'd beaten us. Badly. The only person he hadn't completely fooled lay unmoving at his feet. Fear stole my breath. Brynn was at Oz's mercy. I had to play this right, or I'd lose her. Maybe forever.

"Oz."

"I have to admit, Ash, I was skeptical when Dr. Everly sent me back here. I was sure you'd know it was me. But none of you was even suspicious. I fooled you all." He gestured towards Brynn. "Except for her. Brynn was never on my side."

"Why would you do this?" Paige asked. "Why would you turn on your friends? We mourned you."

His eyes widened in disbelief. "Why? For you, Paige. I did this for you. I mean, look at me." Gun still in hand, he held both arms out to the side. "The scars are gone, I'm a bundle of hard muscle, and, well, I'm gorgeous. When Everly wanted the location of Ash and our compound, I saw my opportunity to become someone you'd want to be with."

"You did this for me?" Paige's voice quivered with incredulity. "Oz, you became a good friend, but I told you that's all I'd ever feel for you. Do you think I'm so shallow that changing your appearance would make me feel differently?"

He stared at her, silent. Unmoving.

Her voice grew stronger. "You've become everything I despise. Didn't you ever wonder why I looked like this? If these genes were handed down to me from my parents? They weren't. My parents chose this appearance. This appearance isn't natural. They never asked me what I wanted. I had no choice, no input about my own life. They *bought* these looks from genes stripped from innocent children, mothers, fathers."

Her tone grew harsher, her words vibrating with anger. "Once I was old enough to understand what they'd done, I walked away and never looked back. That's why I fight, Oz. I despise people like them and everything they represent. You thought I'd love you?" She scoffed. "I loathe you and what you've done."

Judging by Oz's wide eyes and gaping mouth, we experienced the same earth-shattering shock. Paige's revelation explained everything—why she worked double the number of shifts as other operatives, why she spent so much time with the children, comforting them and playing with them. She'd devoted her life to the Insurgents to make amends for what her family had done. For the people who'd lost their lives making Paige into the ethereal beauty she was.

We may have shared the same shock, but the crushing disappointment was all Oz's. Within a few short moments, his outlandish dream of Paige welcoming him with open arms and declarations of love had disintegrated. His face fell with the realization. Oz had traded his honor and integrity for something as superficial as physical appearance. I'd sorely misjudged him.

His gaze dropped to Brynn.

My heart sank. If Oz thought Paige was all he had to lose, it was the gravest mistake he'd ever make. If he harmed Brynn in any way, I'd kill him. No questions asked.

"Don't do anything stupid, Oz," I warned.

"It's a little late for that, Ash. Weeks ago, I made a stupid decision, and look where it got me. If I don't carry through on the promises I made, these soldiers will drop me where I stand. At least this way, I have a chance of staying alive a little longer."

He bent down, draped Brynn's arm over his body, then pulled her up. Her head lolled against his shoulder, but I still couldn't tell if she was unconscious or dead. Blood seeped through her shirt and dripped from an unseen wound.

"Put her down," I growled. My hands clenched into fists.

Oz gestured with his head to the soldiers flanking the corridor, guns held at the ready. "I really don't think you're in a position to be making demands."

"Oz, please," Paige begged as he walked to the doorway. "You've already brought the soldiers here. You're responsible for the deaths of so many of our people, some of them your friends. Don't make it worse. Just put Brynn down and leave. She needs medical attention."

"And I'm sure she'll get it where she's going. Having Brynn in their possession means controlling Ash. He's the objective. I'm just the delivery boy." With two guards at his side, Oz headed toward the corridor leading to the front of the compound.

Paige threw a questioning glance in my direction. She didn't know about A36.

I couldn't allow this to happen. If Oz took Brynn, I might never see her again. Who knew what unconscionable things The Colony would do to her? The thought of her being strapped down, helpless, and begging for her life while her genes were harvested enraged and terrified me. Her fate wouldn't be the same as Cami's and Elsa's. I'd do everything possible to stop it from happening. I chased after him. "Take me. Leave Brynn, and you can have me."

Oz stopped, turned toward me, then barked out a laugh. "Yeah, they said you'd try that move. But who's to say once you got on the helicopter you wouldn't spazz out, or whatever they think you can do, and kill everyone on board? Once Brynn is behind the gates of The Colony, they own you. And when you come for her and the gates lock behind you, you'll truly be under their control. You'll never be allowed to leave."

I looked at Brynn's motionless body still being supported by Oz. She had to still be alive. I'd feel it if she wasn't. If her life ended, part of me would go into the darkness with her, and surely I'd feel the infinite emptiness within myself if she left this world.

I needed to know with certainty. "Oz, please. If you ever considered me a friend, please, tell me. Is Brynn still alive?" My voice broke on the last words.

For a brief moment, a flash of pity crossed his face, but it disappeared so quickly, I might have imagined it. "I could tell you, Ash. I could easily put your mind at rest or destroy your life with a simple yes or no." He cocked his head and arched a brow. "But I guess you'll have to find out for yourself when you come after her. See you. Soon." He pivoted and continued trekking toward the corridor. With the added few inches of height and several more pounds of muscle, Brynn's extra weight was only a minor inconvenience for Oz.

He couldn't leave this compound with her. I had no way of knowing if The Colony would truly provide medical care for Brynn, or if they'd kill her before I could get there. Assuming she was even alive to need help.

"No!" I screamed. I hurdled the detritus between us as I dashed in her direction. Paige crouched behind a desk and laid down cover for me. Bullets whizzed past, but I knew if I was hit again, it would be superficial. The Colony needed me.

Soldiers surged forward to block my path to Oz and Brynn. Oz threw a glance over his shoulder and smirked at me. If I got my hands on him, he'd regret that expression with the final breaths he took.

He was only steps from the door, Brynn's head bobbing lifelessly as he whisked her through the room.

Desperation thrust me forward, muscles taut and straining as I leaped over the obstacles that stood between us while dodging bullets.

They were taking her from me.

Taking away my family.

Again.

This.

Couldn't.

Happen.

A familiar wave coursed through my body, that feeling of something bursting open inside me I'd experienced when we'd thought Oz dead. I'd restrained it before, but now I let it take control. It was eager to be released. Lightning spiked to every extremity and internal organ. It fired through my brain. My senses immediately heightened, and I became hyperaware of my surroundings. What had lain dormant for years, the identity my father ruthlessly worked on suppressing despite what I was created to be, came thundering forth. His presence made itself known as he internally raged at the injustice being committed.

A36 immediately assessed the situation, the threats that stood between me and my objective. Then he determined the most efficient ways to dispose of them.

Oz and Brynn were thirty feet away from me, fifteen feet from the door. Three guards flanked my right, two more were on my left. Two followed Brynn and Oz.

My muscles kicked into overdrive, my body moved of its own accord with reflexes and instincts that seemed natural.

I jerked the gun from the first soldier's hands and hit her face with the butt of it in three rapid fire shots. Bone showed through her skin before she dropped.

Whipping around to my right, I shot number two in the chest.

Number three charged at me. I wrapped my right hand around the front of his throat, and as his momentum carried him forward, I lifted him and slammed his body to the floor, smashing the back of his skull. Blood and brain matter splattered in arcs as his eyes stared sightlessly.

Number four stood gaping at me, his face horror-stricken. I rose from the ground, closed the distance between us, then snapped his neck with enough force that his head was nearly severed from his body.

Since they'd been instructed not to kill me, this wasn't even a challenge. My pulse rate had barely risen.

I crouched down, unsheathed a knife attached to the hip of the soldier whose neck I'd broken, spun around, and sliced into the abdomen of the fifth target behind me, disemboweling her.

Then I stood and scanned the room.

Paige stared at me, her face pale. She looked hesitant, but not afraid. "Ash, what just happened?"

I didn't have time to answer her question. There was no sign of Oz, Brynn, or the two guards with them. I launched myself over the remaining two desks in my path, then sprinted toward the front door. Reaching Brynn was my only focus. Anyone who attempted to stop me would be eliminated.

A helicopter engine started up, the sound vibrating deep into my chest. I pushed myself even harder, dodging and leaping over bodies littering the floor. Killing those guards had barely spiked my heart rate, but the thought of losing Brynn sent it skyrocketing. I shot through the front door and onto the gravel lot just in time to see the helicopter rising from the ground. Brynn lay on the floor of the chopper. Several of her braids dangled out the open door, swinging like pendulums.

"No!" I roared.

I sprinted toward the chopper fast enough that Oz's expression underwent a rapid change from victorious to wary. It was more than fifteen feet off the ground now, far too high for me to reach.

And yet... something inside spurred me on, confident the jump was within my ability.

Spying an abandoned Jeep ten feet ahead of me, I leaped to the hood, catapulted myself off it, and hurtled through the air toward the helicopter. Both hands thrusted out in front of me, and I willed myself to stretch farther toward the rung of the chopper.

Oz watched in horror, even as he backed away from the edge of the open door.

My left hand grasped metal, and I struggled to gain a firm grip. Sweat made my palms slick, and just as my hand lost its hold, my right swung around and found purchase, saving me from a long fall. The sudden addition of well over two hundred pounds to one side of the helicopter caused it to tilt sideways. Oz cursed in alarm as he held onto a bench with one hand and clutched Brynn's leg with the other.

One of the soldiers who'd helped him escape crouched down and aimed the butt of his gun in my direction. Before he made contact with my head, I reached up and grabbed the end of it, yanking hard. The gun, with the soldier still attached, sailed over my head, falling to the ground below.

The chopper spun in a circle as the pilot struggled to maintain control. Wind whipped my hair around my face, and my muscles strained as I pulled myself up. Swinging my legs to the side, I gained enough momentum to get one foot on the rung. Almost there. Oz would fail in his mission to deliver Brynn to The Colony.

My head popped over the edge of the open door and I froze. The remaining soldier held a gun to Brynn's head. Oz's voice rang out over the whirring of the blades. "Let go, Ash, or I swear, if she's still alive, I'll end her life right now."

No. Brynn was so close, I could almost touch her. Within my reach. I quickly calculated my options. I was fast and could easily heave myself into the chopper. Killing the guard and Oz would take only seconds and was an act I'd perform with pleasure. But I wasn't faster than a bullet. If Brynn was still alive, a bullet tearing through her brain would mean certain death. If I allowed Oz to take her, she stood a chance of surviving. If it was true The Colony wanted Brynn in order to control me, I was at their mercy. Some way, I'd bring her back. Or die trying. There was only one choice.

I shouted to make sure Oz heard every word of the promise I made. It was one I'd never break. "The next time we meet, I'll kill you." With one last glance at Brynn, her eyes closed and braids curtaining half her face, I let go.

The last thing I saw was Oz saluting me with one finger.

17

ASHER

"What were you thinking, Ash? Are you all right?" Paige rushed over to where I lay crumpled on the ground, assessing my injuries.

My enhanced DNA let me survive a fall that would have killed most people, or at least severely injured them. From what I could tell, I'd only suffered a few gashes and minor cuts that, based on my history, would heal by morning.

"I'll live."

She crouched down and slung one of my arms over her shoulder, helping me to my feet and into the compound. Or what was left of it. I took in the destruction of the place I'd called home for the past several years. Small fires burned from the blasts that blew out the doors. Equipment littered the floor, along with shards of glass. Sizeable holes in the walls revealed the still silent forest outside.

And bodies. So many bodies. Some lying with limbs bent at awkward angles after falling from the catwalk above, others unnaturally pale after bleeding out from wounds, and many unidentifiable after being caught up in the explosions. The coppery smell of so much blood was nearly overpowering. Loss of so many lives—even enemy lives—should have saddened me, no matter that most were taken in self-defense. Many of the victims were friends. Others were fathers, mothers, husbands, wives, sisters, brothers—more than just soldiers following orders.

I surveyed the carnage I was personally responsible for, the five soldiers I'd murdered in brutal and violent ways. After so much needless killing of innocent people by The Colony, families ripped apart and children who'd never grow up, I'd always been intent on preserving as many lives as possible. Breaking the cycle. Killing was my last resort.

Sadness, repulsion, remorse, guilt—all emotions I should be experiencing right now. But, instead I felt... nothing. The space inside me that normally housed those feelings was an empty void. Maybe it was shock over the uncertainty of Brynn's status—whether she was dead or alive and her fate upon reaching The Colony. Maybe. I fervently hoped that was the case, and not the other possibility.

This was my new norm. A36 felt no empathy for others. Killing was merely the means to an end.

"Ash, what happened to you?" Paige's voice wavered, was nearly a whisper. "What you did... I understand it. Oz was taking Brynn. You were desperate. But what I saw wasn't you. You moved so fast. And jumping onto that helicopter? That should have been impossible." Her eyes were wide in awe.

But I saw the sliver of fear alongside it.

"I promise to tell you everything, but right now, our priority is to make sure everyone got out then meet Noah at the safe house." Turning to face her, I grasped both of her upper arms. "No matter what you saw, Paige, I promise you're safe with me. I'd never hurt you."

She nodded, but despite my reassurances, she still looked wary.

I honestly couldn't blame her.

•　　•　　•　　•　　•

The rocking motion of the transport truck was nearly hypnotizing, and I stared into space at nothing. I felt the gazes of the other surviving operatives on me. Word had spread rapidly about my actions. Some looked at me in wonder and admiration, others in terror and uncertainty. Most sat as far away as possible. Only Paige stayed close.

Before we'd left, I'd cleaned up as best I could. Judging by the stares around me, it hadn't made much difference. My face was streaked with blood—not my own—and my hair was matted with it. As I'd washed, the water turned red with the blood of my victims. But it had no effect on me. I felt nothing but stabbing disappointment over Oz getting away and barely-contained fear for Brynn.

The transport slowed. Gravel crunched underneath the tires. We'd arrived at the safe house, and I knew Noah was waiting. Before I could stand, the door at the back of the truck flew open, and his head popped in, counting the number of survivors. He spoke words of reassurance to the operatives as they exited the truck, but his gaze roamed over the tops of their heads.

He searched for his sister.

I rose, and Noah's eyes widened in shock. He took me in from head to toe—from matted hair to blood-stiffened clothes. I probably looked like a serial killer after a killing spree, which technically wasn't far from the truth.

"Ash, what the hell happened to you? Is Brynn on the other transport?"

Paige cast a sidelong glance at me. On the way here, we'd discussed how Noah should be told. No matter what we said, he'd undoubtedly blame himself. But Oz had fooled all of us. There's no way Noah could have known things would turn out this way.

I draped an arm around his shoulder and steered him toward the house. "Let's go inside."

Noah's body stiffened, and his relieved expression quickly gave way to panic. He shoved my arm away. "Brynn's not..." Voice catching, he couldn't finish the sentence. "Tell me."

"I'm almost certain Brynn's alive," I said gently, leading him inside to an unoccupied room. Worry for Noah and his reaction to Brynn's kidnapping was the only thing keeping me focused right now. Underneath, I felt the stirrings of A36. He wanted anyone and everyone responsible to pay. Preferably with blood. So far, I'd been able to keep him leashed, but who knew how long that would last.

I sat with Noah and relayed the events that led to Brynn being delivered to The Colony. Once I finished, he ran his hands over his closely cropped hair and hung his head low.

"I'm so sorry I couldn't save her, Noah. I tried but couldn't take the chance Oz wouldn't kill her." I swallowed hard. "It's my fault she's gone. But I swear on my life I'll bring her back."

Noah stood and slammed his fists against the wall. "So stupid. How could I have been so stupid?" He kicked the chair he'd been sitting in across the floor. It slammed into the wall. Flakes of plaster floated to the floor.

Paige had stayed in the other room to give us privacy, but after the loud bang, she peeked around the corner, brows raised in question.

I shook my head.

Noah leaned against the wall across the room, arms crossed over his chest. "It's not your fault, Ash. This is all on me. All I had to do was make one call to verify Declan's identity. But I was too busy. He seemed to pick up names and procedures so fast, it made his transition easy. He was working out, so verification slipped to the wayside." He gently shook his head while fixing his gaze on the floor. "And she even reminded me about it. Brynn told me something seemed off with Declan and asked if I'd contacted Barton yet. She *knew*. And if I'd taken my head out of my ass and listened to her, my sister would still be here."

"Noah, it's not—"

He let out a cry of anguish. "And the compound. If I'd checked in with Barton, I would have known about Declan, and our compound would never have been attacked. All those lives are on me, Ash. Every one of those deaths is my fault because of my own idiotic assumption." He was still for a long moment, but I heard him say quietly, "Our father would be so disappointed in me."

The death toll could have been worse. In the event an operative was taken or missing, it was policy to designate a new evacuation safe house. When Mason had returned to the compound without Oz, Noah changed the location before we'd begun questioning Mason. The Colony wouldn't find us here. At least there was one piece of information we knew Oz hadn't turned over.

I crossed the room, gripped both his shoulders, then tilted my head down to catch his gaze. "If I hadn't left my fingerprint on that ball during the mission, none of this would have happened. Oz turned on us, and the attack on the compound was imminent. Even if you'd discovered he was lying about being in Barton's sector, he'd given the information to The Colony long before he walked through our doors again. We could talk about blame all day long, but that doesn't do anything to help Brynn."

He nodded, but ducked his head again.

I inhaled deeply, then blew out a rush of air. "There's something I didn't tell you."

Noah's head shot up.

"Whatever they created me to be—A36, a mindless assassin—it happened. It must have been the fear and rage of losing Brynn that freed him. I murdered several guards in cold blood trying to get to her and felt nothing. I leaped feet into the air onto a helicopter trying to save her and was forced to fall back to the ground so they wouldn't kill her. Didn't get more than a few scratches. Paige witnessed all of it, and she knows everything. We talked about it on the way here."

I dropped my hands from his shoulders to study his reaction.

Noah took a step backward and looked at me cautiously. "How do you feel now?"

"Maybe it's the patch or whatever Dad did to my DNA, but my feelings for everyone else—Brynn, you, my friends—are all intact."

"So, you can suppress it?"

"For now, anyway. I'm in control, not A36." My nose twitched. I desperately needed a shower. The smell of blood enveloped me and took me right back to the compound. Maybe that smell would never completely go away. It was my penance for murdering those soldiers. I wondered if this detached demeanor, or whatever was blocking the feelings of guilt and remorse, would dissolve and all the emotions I should be experiencing would come crashing over me like an avalanche of grief.

But my focus was needed elsewhere. Heartless as it sounded, it happened, it was over, and there was nothing I could do about it. "We'll get her back."

"That goes without saying. Any ideas?"

"I'm what The Colony wants. They only took Brynn to control me. As long as they have her, I'll do anything they ask."

Noah huffed. "Guess we have Oz, Declan, or whoever he is, to thank for sharing that information. If they'd captured you and brought you in, there was still no guarantee you'd play by their rules. But as long as they have Brynn..."

I cut him off. "They knew if I boarded that helicopter, I'd kill everyone on it. By taking Brynn and leaving me here, they own me."

"They know you'll come for her."

"We can't risk sending anyone else. If it means turning myself over to them before they release Brynn, I'll do it. Anything for her. But once I know she's safe, I plan to even the score with Oz. If something happens to me, promise me you'll take care of him."

Noah's expression turned dark and threatening. "You know I will."

Whether by my hand or Noah's, Oz would pay dearly for what he'd done. No matter the deal he'd made with The Colony in exchange for his idea of perfection or a better life, Oz's future wasn't bright—or very long. I planned on snuffing it out the first opportunity that came around.

Noah stared into the distance and rubbed his chin. "I've been thinking about what happened. When you turned on those soldiers A36 knew enough not to harm our own people."

I nodded. "I felt no aggression at all toward them. It was still me, with the exception of efficient and violent killing. Only a super enhanced version."

He spoke slowly. "Once we get to their headquarters, if there is some way you could engage A36, maybe to sneak past their guards, do you think there's a chance we could bring Brynn out?"

"What do you mean "we"?"

Noah looked at me like I'd just asked him the stupidest question he'd ever heard. "I'm going."

"Absolutely not. They only want me. It's bad enough they have Brynn, but you can't just turn yourself over to them, too. You need to stay here and run things."

"Paige can work with Central on that. We both know how capable she is. Even if they release Brynn, someone needs to be there when she gets out." He rubbed his hands over his face, then shoved them in the pockets of his leather coat. "You know once they get their hands on you, there's no way they'll release you. You'll never get out. You won't be coming back here."

I shrugged. "Maybe, maybe not. A36 could probably make it out of there if worse comes to worst. Besides, I don't care what happens to me. I just need to know Brynn will be safe." I swallowed hard. "And if I don't make it, you have to promise not to let her do anything stupid, okay? She'll want to stay with me, but I won't let her."

His expression was solemn as he gripped my forearm. "I promise, brother. Even if I have to put her in restraints."

Despite the seriousness of the moment, I grinned. "My money's still on her."

18

DR. EVERLY

Ackerman had radioed ahead with good news—the girl who was so important to A36 was in our possession. It seemed Declan had made good on his promise. Ackerman had been furious after I'd made the deal with Oz, that he'd hand over Brynn, essentially giving us A36, in exchange for some genetic enhancements. He'd been sure the second Oz was given his freedom, he'd go straight to the Insurgents and warn them.

But I'd had a feeling about the boy. With his facial scarring, I gambled he'd be interested in repairing the skin damage. And after the job the soldier had done on his face, the boy had needed a full genetic panel alteration to look normal again. Needed it desperately. Oz hadn't needed time to mull it over—he'd jumped at the opportunity. He'd given the location of the Insurgent compound as well as pertinent details about A36. And he remained ignorant of the magnitude of his actions.

Oz became Declan and played the Insurgents for fools. Even those who'd known him for several years had no idea of his true identity. Although childless by choice all these years, I felt a maternal pride at his success in duping them and delivering the girl to me.

When we'd attacked the compound, the goal hadn't been to extract A36—it was taking what mattered most to him. If Ackerman's soldiers had tried to bring him in, I had no doubt A36 would have slaughtered everyone on that helicopter, save Brynn, then disappear for another decade or more. This way, he'd come for the girl and be mine to control. Problem solved.

Reputation restored. Career back on track. I'd find my way back to favor with the director and then make up the lost time on Project Adam and the secondary purpose of A36. My whole body tingled with excitement.

All these years I'd waited, and now everything I wanted was within reach. That little rescued donor brat who'd dropped his ball had been the best thing to happen to me in nearly ten years. Because of him, the parasite that had burrowed into my bones, crushed my soul, and stolen every ounce of happiness when August Rickman disappeared with Subject A36 released its hold on me. For fifteen years, finding A36 had been my sole purpose in life. Ten years ago, I'd thought my search was over when August and his family had turned up on a secluded farm hiding under the name of Solomon. I just hadn't counted on him being so prepared and clever enough to hide A36 from me yet again. Twice, I'd underestimated him.

Together August and I had worked on Project Adam and become world renown in our field. It was ground-breaking genetic engineering. Career-changing. At the start, we were met with one failure after another. Multiple batches of specimens had to be eliminated for various reasons—some at the engineering stage, others after being born. Nevertheless, we continued with our efforts. A36 was one of six specimens in his batch. Three of them expired hours or days after birth. A36 initially had some minor health difficulties, but August had taken a special interest in him and tweaked some features. Or so he'd told me at the time.

Over the next two years, the other specimens from the batch expired, and it became evident A36 was something special. He exceeded expectations in both physical and intellectual challenges. A36 became our benchmark and would be the model for all future endeavors.

The night before we were to begin cultivation of another batch, August disappeared. And he'd taken A36 with him. It wasn't quite the shock it should have been. I'd noticed the changes in him after the birth of his daughter. He'd softened and lacked the ability to distance himself from the specimens. No matter—I'd continue Project Adam.

But August had outwitted me. All records of A36, both computer and handwritten, had been destroyed. Every note, scribble, sample—any trace of evidence connected to A36—gone. It was clear he'd been planning his escape for some time.

The director was furious. After nearly a decade of work, the perfect specimen had been created—something that would ensure our future and way of life—and it had been lost on my watch.

I'd reassured him Project Adam would continue, but no matter what I'd tried—every combination, every tweak, every new enhancement—duplicating A36's genetic profile had been beyond my capability.

A36 was the sole survivor of Project Adam.

August had won.

Until now.

I paced the floor in my office, anxious for Ackerman to return and move on to the next phase of this plan. Which would essentially require waiting for A36 to show up on my doorstep and beg to be let in.

My comm unit buzzed. "Ma'am, Colonel Ackerman and his team have returned."

"Excellent. Tell him I'll be waiting in the medical unit."

• • • • •

The girl—Declan said her name was Brynn—was still unconscious and being readied for surgery. She'd suffered a shoulder wound and required an operation to remove the bullet. I'd let the surgeon know his career, and most likely his life, depended on this girl surviving, no matter the difficulty of the procedure.

I studied Brynn as she was being prepped. Her body was slim, her muscles toned. Her dark skin had warm orange undertones, and her thick hair was long and luxurious. The locks were clearly strong and healthy. They were tied back in long braids gathered at the base of her neck and showed no signs of breakage. She really was quite striking.

According to Declan, she and A36 had been together for several years and shared an unusually deep bond. He'd also mentioned Brynn was a fierce soldier, someone to be reckoned with. I'd gotten the distinct impression he was afraid of her and didn't wish to be around when she woke.

Brynn was rolled off to surgery, leaving Ackerman and me alone in the room.

"Your prediction of A36 was correct. He activated."

"Given his history of losing his loved ones and his connection to the girl, the stress of losing her seemed a logical trigger to launch him from a well-trained, intimidating Insurgent back to his base level. With further training, just think what he'll be able to accomplish."

Ackerman grimaced. "A survivor went back and retrieved video footage from one of the six he killed. I've never seen anything like it." Now that I looked more closely, I noticed how pale he was. For a man who'd spent years in battle, he resembled a shell-shocked civilian. "The way he tore through my soldiers... It was like they weren't even human. Or he wasn't. He destroyed them in the span of a couple minutes."

For the second time tonight, I felt a hint of maternal pride. I'd helped create A36, and it sounded as if he was everything I'd hoped for.

"That level of violence? It was barbaric. Blood was everywhere."

"What did you expect, Ackerman? I prepped you on what he'd be capable of. None of this should come as a surprise to you."

He shook his head slightly, eyes wide, but unseeing. "But those soldiers. The sheer brutality..."

I huffed out a breath and waved my hand. "Collateral damage. They were a means to an end. We have the girl, and A36 will follow. What we need to worry about is how we'll contain the subject once he's on the premises."

Ackerman cocked his head and blinked, like he couldn't believe what he was seeing. "You're the devil."

I grinned. "Not quite, but close. Who did you think you were working with, Ackerman?"

· · · · ·

"She's certainly not the most docile captive we've held here." Ackerman and I observed Brynn through the one-way mirror. Her surgery was a success—the bullet had been removed, the wound sutured, her body treated to ward off infection. Now, she just needed time to heal and she'd be fine. But that seemed easier said than done.

Since she'd regained consciousness, Brynn had caused nothing but problems. She refused to remain still and had ripped her stitches out more than once. Until she'd been threatened with sedation. Then she'd thrown food trays, IV poles, and anything else she could get her hands on at anyone who approached her bed. We'd finally had to put her in restraints—which had required the efforts of six soldiers. Impressive.

At least it took care of her physical abuse of the staff.

However, it did nothing for the threats and curses she hurled at everyone who entered her room, and I'd have loved nothing better than to strap a muzzle on her. The only time she was quiet was when she ate or eventually tired herself so much that she fell into an exhausted sleep.

The girl was a fighter, and I grudgingly admired that about her.

"Have you spoken with her yet?" Ackerman attempted to cover a smirk when a male nurse walked away in tears after checking Brynn's vitals. Apparently, I wasn't the only one who held some admiration for her spirit.

"I'd planned to let her tire herself out on the afternoon shift, then make my entrance. She's been demanding to see someone in charge and offering rewards to anyone who would deliver Declan to her."

Ackerman chuckled. "So she did wake up long enough to see him. Feel her out to see if there's any chance of her switching sides. She could probably teach some of my soldiers a thing or two."

I glanced sideways at him. "She could probably teach you a few things also, Ackerman."

He glowered in my direction before spinning on his heel and leaving the room. I turned my focus back to Brynn. Her attention darted about the room as she tested the strength of her restraints. Like a caged wild animal, she constantly assessed her environment, searching for anything that could be used to her advantage. This one needed to be under constant observation. If given an opportunity, she'd attempt an escape and would probably end the lives of anyone who got in her way. When she'd served her purpose and was no longer useful, Brynn had some valuable qualities that would fetch a high market price. Buyers would line up for her genes.

Once she was alone again, I left the observation side of the mirror and entered her room.

Her eyes narrowed as she sized me up, from the tips of my toes to the top of my head, then recognition lit her eyes. "About time they sent someone in charge. Didn't expect it to be a civilian."

"What makes you think I'm in charge?"

Brynn lunged in my direction, which was only inches due to the restraints, but I involuntarily flinched and stepped backwards.

She barked out a laugh. "That's why. You're not tiptoeing around me like the medical staff, but you're also not a soldier. That haughty expression and air of superiority are dead giveaways. Your reaction tells me you have no physical combat training." She loud whispered, "And you're scared of me."

I raised my chin and looked down my nose at her. It angered me that she'd sensed my fear. My heart raced, and sweat trickled down the back of my neck.

She grinned, as if she knew exactly the effect she had on me.

That only angered me more.

"Why am I here?" Brynn demanded. She displayed no respect for my authority, and I was determined that she not have the upper hand.

"Let me make this clear for you. I'm in command here. You don't question me or my actions. Your life has been spared for one reason. Once you've served your purpose, your genes will be harvested then your body disposed of." I offered her a cold smile. "So I'd advise you to play nicely. Depending on your actions, I can make your remaining time easy or extraordinarily difficult and painful."

She shrugged. "It makes no difference to me. Do your worst."

Although outwardly calm, inside I was seething. This girl could try the patience of a saint. Keeping her alive long enough for A36 to arrive might prove challenging. "You're here because of Subject A36."

Her eyes widened only minimally in recognition before she dropped the blinds of disinterest once again. "A36? Is that supposed to mean something to me?"

"Come now, Brynn. Let's not have secrets between us. You know exactly who I'm talking about." I sat at the foot of her bed. With restraints, there was no way she could harm me, and I wanted to cover my earlier mistake by letting her know she didn't intimidate me.

She seethed and made no attempt to hide her hostility toward me. If she somehow managed to escape the restraints, I knew I'd have only seconds to live.

"Why don't you tell me a bit about A36? Maybe it will jog my memory."

"Considering you've known him nearly all your life, and more intimately in the past couple of years, I doubt you need any reminding. But I bet you didn't know this was his birthplace. A lab on the other side of this very building. Something else that might interest you is, along with August—who you know as Garrett—I'm one of his makers. A36 was the result of years of trial and error. We learned from our mistakes, and the outcome was a perfect specimen."

Brynn's eyes sparkled with fury, and it gave me a sense of satisfaction. After all the trouble she'd caused in her short time here, her rage and discomfort were the least of my worries.

"He was created to deal with our enemies in very... unique ways. No emotion, no connections, no regrets."

"No humanity." Brynn spat out those words as if it were a bad thing. She was too young to understand now, but perhaps when she was older and had gained more life experience—or had something worth protecting—she'd come to understand the value of that quality. No emotions to cloud judgement. The ability to remove obstacles in a matter of minutes.

"He's the ideal weapon. And a very expensive one. A36 was given advantages in nearly every area—strength, intelligence, reasoning, physical characteristics, healing. He was perfect in every way." I patted her leg. "You're not in love with a person, Brynn. You're in love with an ideal. One, ironically, you've been fighting against for years."

"You disgust me." She pulled hard on her bindings, and a sliver of doubt about their efficacy wedged its way into my chest. "Trying to turn a little boy into a monster to do your bidding. Garrett was the best thing to ever happen to Ash. He knew this was an inhumane way to be treated and a monstrous thing to do to a person. Garrett gave him a home, a family, and taught him how to love. To feel empathy."

My mood darkened like a cloud blotting out the sun. "August destroyed years of struggle and work. He turned A36 into something... ordinary. When he returns home, my team and I will undo the damage and restore A36 to his original form. After that, the years spent with his "family" will mean nothing, nor will the people who once mattered to him."

"Comes home? This isn't Ash's home, and it never will be."

I chuckled, somewhat amused at her ignorance. "You still don't understand. When A36 comes for you, and he will very soon, the only way he'll ever leave this facility is when he's instructed to. He's the sole reason you're still alive. With Declan's help, we captured you because we knew you were the easiest way to ensure A36 complied with our demands."

The cords of her neck stood out, and she fought fiercely against the restraints. Leaping to my feet, I put some distance between us. I clasped my trembling hands behind my back.

"You're nothing but a filthy piece of—"

"Now Brynn, there's no need for name calling. I'd originally thought we'd have no need of you once we have A36. Perhaps we'd strip some of your genes for marketing. But now..." I felt more satisfaction than a cat with a full belly napping in a sunbeam. "As long as you're alive, there's no doubt A36 will do anything he's asked. And we intend to ask much of him. You see, he will never leave this facility unless we command it. But you will never leave this room."

I spun around and strode toward the exit. As the door closed behind me, Brynn let out a stream of curses, followed by a scream of frustration, fear, and hurt.

Yes, this was going to work out nicely.

19

ASHER

Without the luxury of a helicopter, it would be a two day drive for Noah and me to reach the walls of The Colony. I didn't want him to come with me. Brynn's life was already in jeopardy, and I couldn't put anyone else in that position because of me. I'd tried reasoning, begging, and pleading with him to stay at the safe house. When that didn't work, I'd threatened and intimidated, but to no avail.

Noah had made his decision, and he refused to be swayed.

Since there was no question I'd be coming for Brynn, they could easily have sent a chopper for me. I wouldn't have fought them—because the sooner I could get to her, the better. But I was sure the delay in seeing her was meant to torture me. I was crazy with worry. The thought of her being in any kind of pain—or that she may already be dead—threatened to break me. If I knew for certain she was already gone, I'd probably end myself before we even arrived at the gates to prevent The Colony from getting their claws in me. So, even though I'd planned to do this alone and not endanger anyone else, I was grateful Noah would be there for support.

I drove us along a narrow, rutted road that wound through the sparsely populated countryside. Because of harvesting, communities and residences were few and far between within a hundred-mile perimeter of The Colony. Those Outliers that weren't captured had moved to obscure, safer places farther away or they lived off the land in dense forests and kept their heads down. No matter where they landed, it was a gamble. Due to demand, soldiers had widened their nets and were scouting areas that had never before seen harvesting.

The Jeep was old, and our ride was far from smooth. It didn't help that there were no windows, it hadn't rained in weeks, and rust-colored dust coated the inside of the vehicle. And us.

"You can't go all the way to the gates. If they know you're with me, you'll wind up a prisoner with Brynn, assuming she's..." My breath hitched before I could even finish the sentence.

"Just stop," Noah said. "We've been through this. If you allow yourself to wallow in negative thoughts about Brynn, you could engage. And who knows what the result of that would be. You didn't harm anyone you knew last time, but how do we know you wouldn't take out your aggression on me with no one else around?"

I nodded. Deep breaths, Ash. But inhaling too deeply just drew more road dust into my lungs. It was a miracle I hadn't been overcome by coughing fits already. "I'll leave you with the Jeep at least ten miles out and walk the rest of the way. Stay out of sight. Maybe later you'll be able to enter the gates and hide somewhere while you wait for Brynn. At least get close. She needs someone to get her to safety as soon as possible."

He sighed heavily. "It's not ideal, but it's probably the best option. Leaving you to do this yourself isn't what I want."

We hit a pothole, and Noah's body slammed into the metal door on the passenger side. That was sure to leave a nasty bruise. Most people—all people—had to deal with things like that.

But not me.

My accelerated healing process would make any bruises I got, if I even got any, disappear in less than a day. Once, I'd fallen out of a tree and broken my arm pretty badly. It mended completely in less than two weeks. Cami had complained long and loud about that, because she'd been in a cast for six weeks after breaking her leg.

I ate enormous quantities of food and never gained any weight. My metabolism rate must be through the roof. Mom always fed me substantial snacks between meals. I'd just thought I was an average growing boy until Noah pointed out I ate more than he and Brynn combined. It also explained my lack of need for a normal eight hours of sleep per night. That had definitely been a benefit over the years.

Thinking about my childhood occupied my thoughts while Noah had slept earlier. Looking back, so many things clicked into place. I'd also realized just how much my parents had loved me. How much they'd sacrificed for me. Dad wasn't just my maker. He'd risked not only his career, but also his life when he'd whisked me away from the lab. Mom's, too. And my sisters'. My parents—and they were my parents—had done everything they could to ensure I had a good life. They'd even created the story of my illness to reverse the devastating effects of my genetic programming. At least those that Dad could, as clearly there was evidence something still lived on in me. Dad hadn't been able to suppress everything, but he had given me the tools and skill set to experience normal emotions. To express love for others. I'd be thankful to them for the rest of my life.

However long that would be.

"We're getting close, and I need to eat before we go any further. Who knows what will happen once I enter the gates. If I'm going to get Brynn out of there, I'll need to keep up my strength." I pulled off the road into a clearing, then parked behind a grouping of bushes in case anyone we didn't want to run into just yet traveled the same road.

Noah got out of the Jeep and stretched his limbs after sitting for the past several hours. "Well, I saw some cows in a pasture a few miles back. One might keep you full for a little while. Too bad we don't have a way to cook it." He smirked.

"Very funny. But steak sure would be good. Can't remember the last time I tasted it." With the supplies we received from the collaborators, fresh meat wasn't plentiful, and anything frozen was out of the question.

Noah went around to the back of the Jeep and pulled out the equipment we'd packed.

I shoved my hands in my pockets and leaned against the vehicle. "This is where I'll leave you. We can make camp here, and I'll leave tonight when it's dark."

Noah's expression was somber. I felt the same way, knowing this was most likely the last time I'd ever see him. Once I knew Brynn was safe, I'd end my own life before allowing them to control me, experiment on me, or whatever treatment they had in mind. I refused to be their puppet.

"Promise me you'll do everything in your power to get away from there."

Promises. I'd made promises to Cami and Elsa so many years ago and hadn't been able to keep them. I didn't want to do the same thing to Noah. "I haven't been able to keep my promises, no matter how much I intend to. All I can say is that I'll do what I can to stay alive and make sure Brynn is freed. I'd give my life for either of you."

Noah clasped my upper arm and pulled me into a hug. "I know you would, brother. But I'd really rather it not come to that."

Over a campfire that night, Noah and I reminisced about treasure hunts from our younger days, stupid stunts we'd pulled on Brynn—and how she'd gotten revenge on us—and shared our favorite memories of our parents. Neither of us wanted to say goodnight because it felt more like goodbye. Noah stayed awake as long as he could, but exhaustion finally triumphed, and he fell asleep while leaning against an overturned tree. I gently lowered him to the ground, pulled a blanket around his shoulders, and looked at the man who'd always been more of a brother than a friend. I sincerely hoped this wasn't the last time I'd see him.

I slung my bag of meager supplies over my shoulder then made my way to the main road. Ten miles, give or take a couple, stood between me and the gates of the city. They already knew I was coming, so I didn't feel the need to stay hidden. If breaking in undetected had been an option, I'd have given it my best shot, but no doubt they had every soldier on alert.

It was a beautiful, clear night, and thousands of stars twinkled overhead. I took it all in—the gentle wind that blew the leaves of the trees lining the road, owls hooting in the distance, and rushing water from the nearby river. Who knew the next time I'd be able to experience it on my own as a free man. Or even be outdoors. Once I turned myself in, I'd likely be strapped to a table, poked, prodded, and experimented on.

Strangely enough, I wasn't nervous—not for what would happen to me. While Brynn was their captive, The Colony held certain parts of my anatomy in a vise. Brynn would tell me not to follow their instructions, to give them nothing. But she knew that wasn't an option, and if the tables were turned, it would be the same for her.

She breathed, I breathed. She bled, I bled.

ASHER

About five miles out, I felt a rumble in my chest before hearing the motors. Then a fleet of helicopters and caravan of trucks came into view. Was this really necessary? Seemed like overkill to me. Bright spotlights from the sky and headlights on the ground blinded me, and I held up my hands to shield my eyes. I stopped moving as the trucks encircled me, blocking any attempts I might have made to escape.

Escape wasn't my priority.

"Subject A36, get down on your knees and place your hands behind your head." The voice came from overhead. They weren't taking any chances with me, and I fully expected to be hit with a tranquilizer any second. I metabolized sedatives at a much higher rate than normal humans, something I'd assume they'd take into account. Maybe not. When I'd needed surgery to remove a bullet a couple of years ago, I'd awakened on the operating table and caused a panic for everyone. Especially the anesthesiologist.

I dropped my bag to the ground, slowly lowered to my knees, and placed my hands behind my head. Heavily-armed soldiers, weapons drawn, approached me from every vehicle. One of them, who I assumed drew the short straw, inched toward me, iron restraints in his hand. "If you make the slightest move, we have orders to shoot to kill."

I cocked an eyebrow. "You expect me to believe that? If I die, you'll be dead before you can blink."

The iron restraints clanged together as his hands trembled.

"But don't worry. I don't intend on hurting anyone. Yet." I grinned.

My words didn't calm his jitters. As he drew closer, I could smell the fear coming off him in waves. I'd never really given much thought about fear having a smell. It was distinct, like blood, but not coppery. Acrid like sweat, but with an undercurrent of something wild. Kind of gamey. I guessed that's how predators sniffed out their prey.

And I was built to be a predator.

With backup from five other soldiers roughly ten feet away and probably snipers in the helicopters hovering overhead, the frightened man removed my hands from behind my head then placed both my wrists in iron shackles. They were connected by heavy chains to matching cuffs around my neck and ankles.

After I was secured, one of the choppers landed. I was carried aboard, then chained to an iron loop on the floor of the helicopter. Soldiers escorting me never lowered their weapons. They weren't taking any chances. I still wasn't ruling out the tranquilizer gun and chuckled to myself when I thought about lunging toward them—which might inspire a few to jump out of the chopper, figuring their chances of survival were higher than if they stayed on board to face me.

I rested my head back against the wall of the chopper and closed my eyes. Might as well rest while I could. By my estimation, we were only a few miles out, and in a matter of minutes, we were descending.

We landed on the roof of The Colony headquarters. Encumbered by multiple restraints, and with no one brave enough to offer assistance, I rolled out of the chopper as best I could, then stood. Another group of guards moved toward us the second my feet hit the landing pad. My gaze fell upon a short woman, her dark hair secured in a tight bun at the nape of her neck. I judged her age to be around the same as my father's, if he'd lived. She smiled gleefully, as if she'd won the lottery.

I guessed that lottery would be me.

DR. EVERLY

A36 stumbled as he crawled from the helicopter and moved toward me. He was surrounded by heavily armed guards, but I held no illusion any of us was safe. Even in chains, his every movement was threatening. Calculating. Escape wasn't possible, but he'd undoubtedly use them as a weapon and kill anyone within reach.

Finding A36 had been my sole purpose for well over a decade, and seeing him in chains before me, finally under my control, was the choicest reward for all my hard work and dedication. I hadn't experienced this kind of euphoria since the day August and I had at long last achieved success with a viable specimen.

And here it was in the flesh after all these years.

An unusual kind of pride came over me while I observed him. Despite the added weight of the chains, A36 stood tall and held his head high. And he glowered at me with undisguised hatred. I wouldn't have expected anything less and was anxious to see him in action. It would be a pinnacle in my career. Soon, I'd be able to undo all the alterations August had made to transform him into Asher Solomon and witness his return to who he was created to be.

A36 came to a stop in front of me. His steel gray eyes sparkled with rage. "I'm Dr. Everly."

"I don't care," he growled. "Where is Brynn?"

Given his lack of respect, I was loath to provide him the information. But I needed him to be cooperative, so I gave in. "She's being taken care of. She underwent surgery to remove a bullet and is recovering. Perhaps you'd like to see her later?"

A36 tried to hide the expression on his face, but I understood that until this moment, he hadn't known if Brynn had survived her injuries or if we'd killed her. And he'd come anyway. For love, I guessed, and felt a whiff of disgust. Hopefully, August hadn't altered him beyond repair.

"She's the only reason I'm here. Now that you have me, release her."

I was in charge, a fact that would soon be made clear, and under no circumstances would I negotiate with him. "That's not possible. I created you, and you're under my command now. Your former life is over. Welcome home, A36."

22

ASHER

Brynn was alive. My knees threatened to buckle upon hearing the news. I let out a breath I hadn't realized I was holding, along with all the stress and uncertainty I'd been carrying since she was taken.

I knew nothing about Everly, other than she'd apparently worked with my father. With her beady little eyes, obvious superiority complex, and implied ownership of me, she inspired a special kind of revulsion in me. I'd love nothing better than to rip that bun off the back off her head and shove it in places that would make her extremely uncomfortable.

Could I really trust her to be truthful with me? Not likely, especially where Brynn was concerned. Yet I knew she told me the truth and Brynn was alive.

I needed to get to her, make sure she was being treated well.

Tell her goodbye.

The thought was enough to cleave my soul in half, but now wasn't the time to show any weakness. Instincts told me Everly would rip out my jugular if it was exposed. Any ripping out of jugulars would be done by me. If it came to that.

And I very much wanted to rip out hers, and anyone else's who was responsible for holding Brynn here. Which also reminded me how much I was looking forward to seeing Oz. Declan. Whatever the hell his name was. I'd plan something special for him.

"Prove to me Brynn is alive. Until I see her, you'll get nothing from me."

Everly raised a brow and smirked. "You're not free to make decisions, A36. You'll learn that soon enough. But for now, I'll let you see her to reassure you I always keep my word."

Right. She expected me to believe that?

"You won't be getting very far wearing those chains." She signaled to someone behind me. "We'll replace them with a shock collar. If you make any sudden movements or give us the slightest indication of violence directed toward me or anyone here, I won't hesitate to activate it."

They wanted to put a shock collar on me. Like a dog. I shouldn't have been surprised. To The Colony, I was nothing but a pawn. Someone to carry out their orders. Not a human with free will. The only decision I'd be permitted was how to kill. Not if. Not when.

"Keep in mind, A36, that if you're terminated, Brynn will follow. We'd have no reason to keep her alive."

I barked out a laugh. "Come on, Everly. We both know you can't kill me. You've been searching for me over a decade and didn't go to all this effort just to kill me less than an hour after bringing me in."

Her expression darkened. "Perhaps we won't kill you, A36—yet. But I won't hesitate to punish Brynn for any unwanted behavior on your part. Are we clear?"

Her words were like a knife to my chest. Brynn couldn't be allowed to suffer any more because of me. Guilt coiled in my gut knowing she'd been captured for no other reason than how we felt about each other. Threatening to harm her was a form of manipulation guaranteed to work on me.

It hit me like a bolt of lightning. Brynn's chances of walking out of here were slim to none. Equal to my own. I'd been an idiot to assume otherwise. Maybe my intelligence wasn't heightened as much as Everly thought.

She raised her brows in question.

I gritted my teeth and squared my jaw. "Yes. We're clear."

Everly smiled sweetly in reply.

It didn't fool me. Behind it was a barracuda who'd strike down anyone who stood in her way.

Once the chains were removed, my body felt much lighter. For those few moments before the shock collar was fastened in place, I thought about how easy it would be to snap Everly's neck. What a satisfying sound it would make.

"If you're ready, you can follow me down the hallway." She spun then entered the double doors leading into the building from the landing pad.

I followed her, my pulse racing at the thought of seeing Brynn. I didn't hold much hope that Everly would actually let me talk to her. But I needed to see her.

Everly and I, along with a small army of guards, entered an elevator and then descended several floors. I took the opportunity to observe her closer. Not a hair out of place. No fly-aways, no stray gray hairs to mar the perfect inky black-colored bun. Her attire was very professional. A well-tailored dress under a crisp, white lab coat. She paid a lot of attention to detail, and I doubted much slipped past her.

Except when my dad had stolen me away from here right under her nose.

His undetected deceit and the mountain of problems it surely caused her put a smile on my face.

"Smiling, A36? What could you possibly have to be happy about right now?"

"A couple things, actually. Thinking about how you must have looked after discovering my father and I had disappeared from this laboratory."

She couldn't stop the fleeting scowl. Once her face was again an expressionless mask, she asked, "And the other?"

My smile broadened. "Planning the way I'll end your life. So many options to choose from."

She swallowed hard and turned her attention back to the digital display on the control panel.

I'd unnerved her. That was good. Despite the soldiers acting as a layer of protection between us, and the shock collar, I still frightened her.

The elevator stopped on the twenty-fourth floor then the door opened to a sterile, white hallway. Everly's heels clacked on the tile. Several doors lined the corridor, and past those was a long desk inhabited by people dressed in scrubs. This must have been a medical unit. I felt their curious stares on me, probably wondering what prompted all the security.

Shortly after passing the desk, Everly pulled out a badge then held it up to a scanner on the side of the door. When the red light on the panel changed to green, the door slid open.

Guards trailing behind me, I followed her into a sparsely decorated room with rows of chairs facing what looked like a large, rectangular mirror. The walls were padded, muffling the sound in what looked to be an observation room. And I had a pretty good idea who they'd been observing.

Everly flicked a switch beside the mirror. It became a window looking into a room with medical equipment and an IV stand surrounding a bed.

Lying in the bed with restraints on her wrists and feet was Brynn. My Brynn. And she was very much alive.

Despite Everly's claims, deep down I hadn't trusted that Brynn had survived until I'd seen her. The sound was on, and I heard her yell at a woman who'd come in to check her vitals. Her words weren't meant for polite company. The restraints clanged against the metal bed railing as she fought against them. I couldn't help but smile. In all the years I'd known her, no matter how dire the situation, Brynn had never given up fighting.

When I was around ten-years-old, Brynn, Noah, and I had discovered a cave we'd never explored. It was quite large and airy with cavernous ceilings, and we'd followed it into the mountain for a good distance, voting on which path we'd take every time we came to a fork. The problem was, none of us kept track of our turns. After two hours trying to find our way out, we'd admitted to being hopelessly lost. Noah and I were tired, frustrated, and wanted to sit and rest. We'd been alternating use of our flashlights, but still, it was just a matter of time before the batteries went dead. Sitting in pitch blackness was kind of freaky, but leaving a light on would waste valuable battery life. Brynn had pulled us up from the rocks we'd been seated on, declared us damsels in distress, then said if it wasn't for her, we'd both rot away inside the cave giving the rats, or whatever else dwelled there, a veritable feast.

She'd instructed both of us to keep our mouths shut—no more giving opinions on which direction we should take—and to follow her. After a few wrong turns, she'd led us back to the entrance. Her sense of direction had been much better than mine or Noah's.

Watching her now, not letting up even the slightest, hurling curses toward the observation window without knowing if anyone even watched, I loved her so hard I could barely breathe. My strong, confident, beautiful fighter.

"Your girl hasn't made life very pleasant for our staff."

I huffed. "Why should she? You shot her, brought her here against her will, and you're holding her prisoner. Did you think she'd get down on her knees and offer you eternal gratitude?"

"We saved her life."

"You tried to take her life."

Brynn's threats halted abruptly. Her eyes widened, and she looked directly at me through the glass. I knew it was impossible for her to see me. Still, I felt the connection between us, and it pulled at something deep inside me.

"Ash?" Her voice was soft. "Asher, are you here?" she asked louder.

"I'm here," I replied under my breath. Tears prickled at my eyes, but I refused to let Everly see them and turned my head to the side without taking my gaze from Brynn's.

"Don't listen to what they say. Don't let them make you into something you're not, do you hear me? You're not what they created. You're so much more than that. Remember who you are."

"I remember," I whispered. And I did. I knew exactly who I was deep inside. But I also knew what I might have to become to ensure Brynn's safety. And possibly Noah's. When Brynn wasn't released, he'd search for her. He could get himself captured. That was last thing I needed. Both of the people I loved most in precarious situations because of me.

"Charming," Everly said. Judging by her expression, it was the opposite of what she meant. "Now you've seen her. You know she's alive. She'll stay that way as long as you comply with my wishes and submit to testing." She turned to one of the guards. "Notify them to administer the sedative and keep her under heavy sedation until further notice."

Brynn's door opened. A nurse holding a syringe, along with four guards, approached the bedside. Upon seeing the needle, Brynn struggled valiantly, and even with restraints, the guards fought to hold her down until the nurse emptied the contents of the syringe into the IV bag.

I called out her name. Wanted to hurl myself through the glass to help her. Instinct erupted inside me like it had during the attack at the compound right before I'd activated. I breathed deeply in an attempt to stave it off, but it had no effect.

Everly saw what was happening, and turned off the mirror.

My heart raced. Sweat dripped down my back. All I could think about was hurting anyone who stood between me and Brynn. A scream ripped through my chest, and the guards around me shrank back in fear.

Maybe this was what needed to happen. Release A36 and...

A jolt shot through me and set every nerve ending on fire. My skin was melting off. Every muscle spasmed in pain. I dropped to the floor. My head slammed against the tile.

Darkness.

23

ASHER

A thousand drums played in my head. Mallets beat a rhythm against the walls of my brain. Cymbals crashed for added effect. I groaned in pain as I tried to lift my eyelids. Whatever I was lying on was unyielding and offered no comfort to my aching body.

Memories of how I'd gotten here flashed through my mind. Surrendering myself. Everly. Brynn in restraints, sensing I was here. Brynn pinned down against her will and sedated.

A36 making an appearance.

Everly, true to her word, had shocked me. During missions, I'd received mild shocks from electric fences, but the aftereffects of this were considerably more painful. I felt like I'd been electrocuted with live wires.

After peeling my eyelids open, I took in my surroundings. I was engulfed in a sea of whiteness. White ceiling, white walls, white floor. No windows, other than the observation mirror at the foot of my bed. Cameras were located on the ceiling in all four corners of the room. Reinforced restraints attached to my wrists and ankles severely limited any movement. When I tested their strength, movement was barely noticeable. Another strap ran across my chest. While unconscious, I'd been dressed in loose-fitting white pants and a shirt. What was with all the white? Was this whole city devoid of color?

Thankfully, the shock collar had been removed.

I had no idea how long I'd been unconscious—minutes, hours, maybe days. They'd probably sedated me. Remembering how Brynn had screamed and fought off the guards clenched my heart, and I squeezed my eyes shut against the memory. How was I going to get her out of this?

My empty stomach rumbled. How long had it been since I'd eaten? They'd have to feed me, right? Without food, I couldn't do anything for them.

The door to my left slid open, then Everly strode inside. She'd changed clothes, but still wore the same type of tailored dress beneath a starched white lab coat. With nothing else in the room except my bed, she had no choice but to stand.

She looked down at me, her lip curling in disgust. "That could have become an unfortunate situation, A36. At least now we know the collar is effective at putting you down."

"Is Brynn all right? If you hurt her, I swear I'll..."

"You'll do what?" She nearly laughed, and anger tore through me. "There's nothing you can do. From where I stand, you're completely helpless." Everly enjoyed this, and her eyes sparkled in triumph.

I clenched my fists. "I won't always be this way. At some point, you'll have to undo the restraints."

"And the collar goes back on before you're released."

I breathed heavily, frustrated at my inability to do anything. Adrenaline pumped through my body, and I felt the urge to move, expend energy, do... something. Being pinned down like this was maddening. Claustrophobic, in a way. I closed my eyes and attempted to slow my breathing. Losing control didn't help my situation, and I needed to focus. Moments later, I breathed normally again. "Brynn?"

"She's fine, for now. As I said, you cooperate with me, and she'll be taken care of. The second you step one toe out of line, she'll suffer the consequences." Everly leaned over the bed, her face inches from mine. "And I'll make you watch."

My hands clenched into fists, and I gritted my teeth. Anger clouded my vision.

Everly stepped back and watched me thoughtfully. "You know, after August and his wife were captured, they underwent extensive interrogation for weeks. Torture, too. I personally held a gun to your mother's head, confident August wouldn't let her die. She'd pleaded with him not to tell me anything. And he didn't. I'd underestimated their depth of feeling and need to protect you, and neither gave up any information. With his wife's dead body cooling in the chair she'd been tied to, August begged me to see reason and abandon my search for you and my work on Project Adam. To let you live your life, unaware of what you really were.

"Before I turned the gun on August, I vowed to never stop searching. Project Adam is my life's work, the legacy I'll leave behind. It's too bad he couldn't have lived to see what he'd helped create."

She'd killed them. Both of my parents. They'd died protecting me. And Everly had just described it to me in such a cold, unfeeling manner. She might as well have been explaining something she read in a book.

Control lost, I roared in anger and strained against my bonds. Everly stumbled backwards, startled by the ferocity of my reaction. I'd kill her. I swore a silent oath that somehow, I'd end her life. Painfully.

"Enough!" she screamed. "If you want to ensure Brynn's safety, these outbursts will stop immediately. Perhaps I'll put the collar on her when you're not using it just to ensure your compliance."

Her threat to harm Brynn was enough to shut me up, but my chest still heaved with anger. Everly might be able to control me physically—for the moment—but she couldn't control my thoughts.

But she could read them. "I know you'd love nothing more than to break out of those restraints and tear me limb from limb. But soon, I'll be the most important person in your world. You'll do anything I ask. And Brynn? You'll cast her aside like she's nothing but a plaything you've outgrown. You start desensitization therapy tomorrow." Her eyes gleamed in anticipation, then she turned and left the room, the door swishing closed behind her.

Never. No matter what Everly did to me or put me through, my feelings for Brynn would never change. She was my anchor. I heard her words as clearly as if she'd been in the room with me, whispering them in my ear.

Remember who you are.

• • • • •

Nourishment wasn't a problem. Everly made sure I was fed well, and often. But when I wasn't being fed, I was tortured.

Although I needed little sleep, I wasn't permitted any. Loud music blasted in my room at all hours, and strobe lights flashed intermittently. If I managed to drift off, the sound of blasting horns immediately woke me. At this point, I had no idea how long I'd been sleep deprived.

Desensitization therapy was brutal, horrific, and soul-wrenching. I was strapped to a chair, eyes taped open, and shown videos of bloody, gory killings. Adults, teenagers, children, all were brutally slaughtered. Knives, guns, beheadings, disembowelment—those were only a few of the methods I witnessed.

I was no stranger to violence, but hours of watching such heinous atrocities, combined with little to no sleep, had an adverse effect on me. Which I'm sure was Everly's plan all along. They wanted to numb me, deaden my reaction to even the most abhorrent massacres. I was also being pumped with caffeine. With every meal, I was given caffeine pills and forced to drink caffeinated beverages several times per day.

I wasn't sure what was real anymore and suffered from waking dreams. Or maybe they were hallucinations. Was there really a difference?

Some were comforting and brought me peace. I was back at the compound prepping for a mission. Noah and I were playing chess, ragging on each other. I was stretched out on our bed, my head on Brynn's stomach as she read to me. I ate wild strawberries with Cami and Elsa in the patch beside our house, hands sticky and red juice running down our chins.

Others were terrifying. Brynn brutally attacked by soldiers while I was forced to watch, restrained and unable to help her. Noah on his knees, a gun held to his head. Cami and Elsa captured, and being led into a harvest site. My parents being tortured after not giving information on my whereabouts—which was true. A fact too devastating to think about right now.

Once per day—I think that's how often it was, as time was a swirling mass of liquid I could no longer quantify—I was allowed to see Brynn. At first, it was through a camera feed, but I told Everly that was unacceptable. How did I know it wasn't recorded at an earlier time? I needed to see her through the observation window again to be certain she was alive, and I refused to eat until I saw her. Everly begrudgingly agreed.

Those few moments I was given with her, even though we couldn't speak or touch, even though she had no idea I was there, were what held me together. Seeing her fed my soul. Knowing she was still fighting gave me the strength to keep going, to endure all this for her in the meager hope she'd eventually be set free.

Brynn helped me to remember. To reach through all the atrocities I was shown hour after hour and grab onto something real. Just knowing she was here in this building gave me added strength.

But this cycle couldn't go on forever.

24

DR. EVERLY

A36's resistance was stronger than I'd anticipated. After days of desensitization therapy and sleep deprivation, his mindset was still more "Ash" than the predator he was born to be. Brynn was holding him back. Seeing her maintained and reinforced his connection to the person August had helped foster. Threatening to stop the visits had no effect on A36. He would shut down completely, refusing to eat or talk. Even the shock collar didn't work. He'd rather endanger his own life than not see Brynn every day.

That connection had to be severed.

When August and I had altered A36's genome, we'd enhanced the physical and mental characteristics needed to become a successful assassin. Heightened emotion wasn't required, so those characteristics had been dampened. Essentially removed from the equation. From the samples we'd obtained of A36, I'd studied the adjustments August had made. And he'd made them just in time. Physical traits—eye color, height, build, hair color—could be changed at any time with gene stripping and alteration. Mental and emotional characteristics were more difficult to alter after a person was born, but August had found a way. He'd essentially patched over A36's emotional deficits, allowing him to experience normal emotions. By now, it was too late to make any corrections in A36's genome.

But I wondered if the patch could be removed.

Genetically altering A36 again wasn't feasible. So, what could I do to break the bond between him and Brynn? Clearly, their connection was strong and deep. They were young and in love. Strong and deep needed to be replaced by doubt and mistrust. A36 needed to feel abandoned with nowhere left to turn. Cut off from his support system. Once that happened, he'd flounder and search for a safe harbor in a storm.

I intended to be that safe harbor.

The answer was obvious. I couldn't believe it had taken so long to occur to me. I pressed a button on my comm unit.

"Yes, Dr. Everly?"

"Send someone up from the technology department immediately."

"Yes, Ma'am."

I knew exactly how to start chipping away at that bond.

25

ASHER

I wanted to give up. Exhaustion had crept into every bone and crevice in my body. I hurt in places I never knew existed. The lights and loud music in my room had a new pattern. Three days ago, or at least I think that was how long it had been, it all stopped, and I nearly burst into tears from relief. Blessed silence. Peace. My mind shut down almost immediately, and I fell into the deep sleep my body craved. After no more than five minutes, the lights and music started up again.

I knew it was possible for people to die from sleep deprivation, but Everly seemed to know exactly where the danger zone was. She never let me venture past that boundary, but I surely existed on the brink of it. I was allowed the bare minimum that prevented me from crossing over.

The video footage had gotten more violent and tragic. And I could feel it working on me. When I'd killed the soldiers who'd helped Declan take Brynn, I'd felt nothing. And that hadn't changed. Watching innocent people be tortured and killed was a different story. Over the first week or so, I'd felt horror and empathy for the victims and wanted so badly to turn away. But that hadn't been an option. I couldn't close my eyes, either. I tried to convince myself it wasn't real. Told myself the victims were only actors and no one could be that cruel to another human being. Anything to maintain my sanity.

But the heinous actions looked so real. And Everly assured me they were.

Now, it was just another routine video filled with innocent victims being snuffed out in brutal ways. They could show me all the killings they wanted. I might no longer react to them, but that didn't make me want to imitate the actions.

Still, I wasn't the same person who'd walked in here days ago. I was slowly disintegrating, my humanity being carved away one piece at a time. Everly was determined to override everything Dad had done to make me normal. She was trying to destroy the Asher part of me and all the values instilled by my parents, Patrick, and Anna. In short, everything good and decent about me. If that happened, only A36 would remain. Without seeing Brynn every day, I was afraid I'd slip away for good.

Today, when I'd thought I was being taken to the observation room, shock collar and restraints intact, the guards led me somewhere else. Everly stood waiting, but looked... very somber. Almost sad. She stood with her hands clasped in front of her. My nearly constant state of haziness immediately dissipated, and my heart sank.

"Why are we here? Is something wrong with Brynn?"

"Brynn is fine. I hate to be the bearer of bad news, but something has come to our attention. The video feed in Brynn's room was missing some time over the past several days, an hour or so each day. We assumed it was merely a glitch in the system. Today, our tech department recovered the missing hours." She sighed heavily. "I'm sorry to say it wasn't a glitch, but someone who'd turned off the system while they were with Brynn."

My stomach clenched. I didn't like where this was headed. If someone had turned off the feed, it was because they didn't want anyone to see what was happening. They might be hurting her in a thousand different ways. If she was sedated, they could be taking advantage of her in ways I didn't want to consider. I closed my eyes, sick to my stomach, repulsed at the thought of someone touching her when she was unable to defend herself or give her consent. Because if she were conscious, there's no way she'd let anyone near her.

Everly ducked her head and wrung her hands. "It's... a delicate situation."

"Take me to her. Now. If she's been hurt in any way, I..."

She shook her head. "No, A36. You misunderstand. She hasn't been hurt. She... well, I'll let you see for yourself."

I was wheeled over to a monitor, and Everly turned on the feed. "This was from four nights ago."

It showed Brynn sleeping. A dim lamp in the corner provided the only illumination in the room, but it was still bright enough to confirm it was her in the bed. A ray of light fell across her slumbering body as someone opened the door and entered quietly. It was a tall man who looked to be around my age. As he drew closer to Brynn's bed, she turned over and saw him.

I stiffened, waiting for her reaction. But it wasn't what I'd expected.

She smiled at him in greeting. Not the kind of smile you'd give to someone holding you captive. Not even the kind you'd give a friend. It was the type you gave to a person you were much closer to. The kind of smile she'd only given me. When he reached the bed, he released her from the restraints. Brynn was only luring him in. The second she was free, she'd overtake him and try to escape.

But that's not what happened. Her arms reached up and slid behind his neck, pulling him closer. When he leaned over and kissed her, it was obvious she enjoyed it. She kissed him back. Passionately.

My world turned sideways. My heart stopped.

"I'm so sorry you have to see this, A36. I debated even showing it to you."

The man slipped into bed with Brynn. My Brynn. Their actions weren't the awkward motions of a couple with each other for the first time. Their movements were fluid and familiar.

My breath came too fast. My heart beat too hard.

No. She'd never do this to me. Honesty and trust were the most important things to our relationship. We meant too much to each other, and Brynn didn't trust people this soon. She loved me. This had to be a mistake.

As I watched, the man removed his shirt then helped Brynn pull her own over her head. I couldn't bear another second. To see her with another man, to watch them touching each other in the way that we'd touched only each other...

"Turn it off."

"Are you sure? Don't you want confirmation—"

"I said turn it off!" The room spun. I felt too warm. My stomach churned, and I bent over and vomited.

Everly grabbed a towel and wiped my mouth. I wished my hands were free to push her away. I didn't want her anywhere near me.

"I'm sure this comes as a shock to you, A36. Your reaction is entirely understandable. To think Brynn would be so deceitful and break your trust that way after such a short time apart. The clip you just saw was from a few days ago, and hours were missing from subsequent days after that, so I can just imagine what they must show."

"Take me to her."

She seemed confused. "You want to see her? You realize it would still only be from the observation room."

"I don't care. I need to see her." I still needed confirmation she was alive. Somewhere in the back of my mind, I wondered if she'd been killed trying to escape and Everly had created all this drama to ensure I wouldn't want to see Brynn again.

I was taken to the observation room that had been a safe haven for me during these past weeks. Brynn had been a lifeline, the tether to my sanity and identity. But now my whole world had crashed down around me. She'd betrayed me and everything we'd ever meant to each other. Another wave of nausea came over me, and I gulped air in an attempt to ward it off.

Everly flicked the switch, then I saw Brynn. She was curled on her side gazing out the window. Sun streamed through the glass, casting a bronze glow over her body. It reminded me of the day I'd found her lying on the dead tree trunk in the forest. That was the first day she'd become something more than a sister to me. The first day "we" had started.

The images I'd seen on the video played back in my head. Things that had happened on the bed she was now lying on. The smile she'd given the man, a smile she'd reserved only for me—that was something I'd never get out of my head.

Brynn's eyes were red-rimmed and puffy. Was she sad because she couldn't see him during the day? Had she forgotten about me? About us?

How could I believe in myself if she no longer did?

Everly jarred me from my thoughts. "It's best you know the truth about Brynn. It's clear she's moved on, and her feelings weren't as strong for you as you thought. Sometimes we put our trust in the wrong people. It's a hard lesson to learn."

Put our trust in the wrong people.

Everly's words struck a chord with me, deep down past the blurry haze of exhaustion clouding my mind. I latched onto that spark of rationality and clung tightly.

Trust.

Trusting the wrong people.

I'd known Brynn most of my life, and in all those years, she'd never given me a reason not to trust her. Integrity was everything to her in both personal relationships and working relationships. Being able to depend on your team members, trusting them to have your back—that was vital to Insurgents. Without it, we'd be dead in the field.

We'd known other couples at the compound who'd gone through the drama of cheating and dishonesty. Sure, we were teenagers, and sometimes drama came with the territory. But what we did—rescuing people who otherwise had no hope and giving them back their lives—was so much bigger than petty relationship woes.

Brynn and I had discussed it, and we both knew what we felt for each other was more than casual, more than a way of biding time until something new and shiny caught our eye. Our commitment wasn't something we took lightly. We'd given our hearts to each other, trusting they'd be cherished and protected.

And I knew.

Brynn would never hurt me. That was a certainty, just as the sun would rise in the east tomorrow morning. I hadn't placed my trust in the wrong person.

But Everly was doing her best to convince me to.

I turned my gaze away from Brynn to Everly. On the surface, she'd made a decent effort to look sympathetic. But now that I knew she was lying, the excitement and hope lying just beneath the surface of her façade were easy to detect. She knew Brynn was the lifeline I clung to, a reminder of who I was. For Everly to have the weapon she'd created, she had to drive a hard wedge between Brynn and me and break our connection.

"For one brief moment—very brief—you almost had me doubting Brynn. You really thought doctoring some video would be enough to destroy what we've built and nurtured over the past decade? Try again." The corner of my mouth turned up in a challenging smirk. "I dare you."

The sympathetic mask she'd donned fell away, replaced by unbridled rage. I hoped she'd let out a roar of frustration. At least it would be a genuine emotion instead of the false ones she created to manipulate me.

"Come on, Everly. Let it out. It can't be healthy to hold all that anger in."

Judging by the look on her face, if thoughts were daggers, I'd be dead already. "Get him out of here," she seethed. "Take A36 back to his room immediately."

Before they led me out, I threw one last glance back toward Brynn. She hadn't moved, was still lying on her side, staring out the window. But she uttered one word that made my heart swell. "Ash."

When the door closed behind me, Everly took my advice. Her furious cry followed me down the hallway.

26

ASHER

Five days went by, with no communication from Everly. No visits to the observation window to see Brynn. I'd had no human contact at all. The strobe lights and blasting music had ceased, and I slept, when my mind would allow me to, uninterrupted. I wasn't even restrained. My meals were slid through a slot in my door regularly, three times a day. Not even medical staff entered my room.

Weeks had passed since I'd spoken to Brynn, touched her. Seeing her was all I'd had to hold onto. Although I couldn't see anyone through the window, I was certain I was still being observed, so I begged and pleaded to be taken to her or at least for someone to tell me how she was. Blood from my hands streaked the door and observation window after I'd pounded on them for hours, multiple times per day, to no avail.

Brynn had been wounded and held hostage because of me.

I had no idea what became of Noah after I'd been taken into The Colony. He'd planned to wait for Brynn then take her home. Obviously, that wasn't going to happen.

I'd never felt so helpless in my life.

On the sixth day, Everly came to the observation window early in the morning. I'd been doing pushups, sit-ups—anything to keep my mind occupied and stave off the boredom. Fluorescent lights lit up the window, and there she was, accompanied by two guards. Lab coat so crisp it could slice through skin. A bun so tight, I wondered if she could even blink. The blood stains on the window framed either side of her face.

I leaped from the floor and charged toward her, stopping when my face was only inches from hers. My fists pounded the glass. "Take me to Brynn!"

She was unflinching and eyed me coldly. "Whatever misconceptions you're harboring, you are not in control here, A36. Make no mistake, you and Brynn survive at my discretion. I hold your fates in my hands. I've allowed you to see Brynn on the condition that you comply with my wishes. After over two weeks, it's clear that technique isn't working."

I didn't like the direction this was headed. My heart pounded, and I dreaded what she'd say next.

"Your bond with her is preventing you from performing your duties. Therefore, it needs to be severed. Beginning today, you'll receive weekly updates on Brynn. No visits. You submit to our testing and training, and she'll be cared for. Step out of line, and maybe she'll miss a few meals or be used for experimental testing. Brynn's a feisty girl with several physical characteristics on the preferred list. Harvesting is a strong possibility." Everly arched a brow and pursed her lips in amusement.

Rage exploded through my body. It ripped through my veins, seeking an outlet. I wanted to kill Everly. Rip off her the limbs. Gouge her eyes with my thumbs while she begged for mercy.

I backed up until I hit the wall on the other side of the room and could go no further.

Everly tilted her head to the side in question.

Pushing off the wall, I shot across the room and hurled myself into the glass. And then did it again. And again. Between the adrenaline and rage, my body was numb. I'd feel the pain later.

Everly chuckled at first, then laughed at my futile efforts. Until my fifth attempt when the glass cracked into a spiderweb pattern. Eyes widening in horror, her laughs turned into shrill cries commanding the guards to stop me.

But they couldn't.

And now I was the one laughing.

Instinctively, they raised their guns, but bullets couldn't penetrate the window. Because I'd been locked in my room for the past five days, I wasn't wearing the shock collar. No one would come in after me. They couldn't kill me and didn't want to put their own lives at risk.

Two more hits, and the spiderweb expanded even further. In the center, a tiny hole appeared as fragments of glass fell away. One more, and I should be through.

Everly screamed into her comm device, but I didn't listen to what she was saying. I was solely focused on breaking through the window. I backed against the wall again, readying my body for another go, when I heard a hissing sound. My eyes darted around the room that held only my bed, then up to the air conditioning vents. They spewed a light blue substance.

She was gassing me. I'd be unconscious in seconds.

But not before I had one more go at the window. I squared my jaw and clenched my fists, then sprinted toward the window for the last time. When my shoulder made contact, shards of glass pierced my skin. The warmth of blood gushed down my arm.

But I was through.

The hole was wide enough for my injured arm. I reached in toward Everly. Stretched my fingers in her direction. I knew I'd never reach her, but my injuries were worth it just to see the terror on her face. A strange tingling started at my feet then spread through my body. Only moments before I passed out.

I dragged my arm back through the jagged glass, now red with my blood, as pieces fell to the floor. Peering through the hole, I glowered at Everly. My voice was low and guttural, full of hatred, but I managed to get the words out before collapsing. "*You* survive at *my* discretion."

•　　•　　•　　•　　•

I woke in the infirmary, and the first thing I saw was Everly.

My limbs twitched. I was ready to spring out of bed, but the restraints were back in place. A dull ache blanketed my shoulders. After hitting the window so many times, I'd expected more pain. Times like this, I was grateful for my accelerated healing ability. Cuts on my hand and arm from where I'd shoved them through the hole in the glass were bandaged, but I suspected if the dressing were removed, there would be few marks and no scarring.

"Further outbursts from you will not be tolerated. Is that clear, A36? Brynn's meals will be withheld today because of your actions. As I'm sure you're aware, a person can go without food for extended periods. But if we start withholding water? Her days are numbered."

I turned my head away from her. Tears pricked my eyelids, and I blinked them away. Brynn suffered even more because of me. I'd acted without thinking and let A36's instincts take control. My girl was fierce and strong and could handle more than most people. But when I thought of her alone in her room, hunger clawing at her stomach and thirst wracking her throat, I wondered if she'd lose hope—and maybe her faith in me. A weight settled on my chest, and fear gripped my heart when another thought occurred.

Did she regret tying herself to me?

I grudgingly admitted capturing Brynn in order to control me had been a smart play. When it became apparent they weren't releasing her once I'd turned myself in, which I now understood had never been an option, I'd thought my enhanced abilities would afford protection for both of us. In the back of my mind, I'd truly believed if I pretended to play by the rules, I'd break both of us out in a matter of days.

What a fool I'd been. I'd grossly overestimated my position.

Now I knew. I was Everly's puppet, and she held the strings. To keep Brynn alive and avoid her enduring any more hardships, my only option was to do exactly what Everly commanded.

No matter if it compromised everything I believed and stood for. No matter if it meant selling my soul.

I turned my head and met Everly's gaze. Her eyes danced in victory. She knew she'd won.

Jaw clenched, voice dripping with sarcasm—no one said I had to be nice—I spoke. "When do we start?"

27

ASHER

"No! Your orders are to clear the building. Take the shot without hesitation." Everly's face was splotched red with anger. For the past few days, I'd been thrust into multiple simulations and given orders. According to her, I'd failed miserably. I'd succumbed to testing and had been poked, prodded, and studied to no end. I felt like a specimen under a microscope. Nonstop weapons training—which was pointless, considering my background. Sparring with any opponent brave enough to climb in the ring with me, although all of them were following orders and forced to. Physical training to maintain my genetically-enhanced physique.

It was awful. But the simulations were the worst.

I gripped the practice gun so tightly, my knuckles were white. "He was a civilian, not a hostile. There was no reason to kill him."

"That's not your decision to make. I give orders. You follow them. It's that simple." Everly spoke through gritted teeth. Her frustration with me had reached new heights today. Several hairs had sprung free from her perfectly coiffed bun. For her security, soldiers were stationed throughout the room, and as an added measure, I wore my shock collar. Like the dog I was.

"You can't expect me to shut off my brain and ignore my instincts. I'm not built that way," I shouted. My frustration was erupting.

She moved closer. Close enough that I could hurt her badly before the soldiers could react. And with every breath in my body, I wanted that. But I had Brynn to think about.

"That's exactly what I expect you to do. And yes, you were built that way. It was only after your "father" changed everything that you grew a conscience."

Everly was a monster, and she was trying to get me to join the club. Yes, I'd felt betrayed when I'd learned Dad had worked for The Colony. That he'd been my maker. But now that I'd seen this world and what had been expected of him—what was expected of me—I understood why he'd tried to hide what I was until I was old enough to understand.

"I am your brain, A36. I think for you. I give instructions, your body carries out my commands. Until you perform without hesitation, Project Adam cannot be given clearance. Right now, you're practically worthless to me. I didn't spend this many years creating you then searching for you only to fail."

I dropped the gun to the floor, which caused the soldiers to reach for their weapons, and ran my hands through my hair. "Don't you get it? I don't murder innocent people. As an Insurgent, my team didn't kill indiscriminately just because people worked for The Colony. If lives could be preserved, then they were."

A slow smile spread across her face, like she was a spider and had trapped me in her web. "But you do murder innocent people. When Declan took Brynn from your compound, you brutally killed six soldiers trying to stop him. Do you remember that?"

"That wasn't me." She cocked an eyebrow in response. "A36 killed those soldiers. He acted on his own."

"You were A36 before you were Asher Solomon. Perhaps you're using A36 to carry out Asher Solomon's deepest desires, actions so vile your conscience won't allow you to even consider they're yours."

I shook my head. "No. You're wrong. I did that for Brynn, to keep her safe. I can't become what you want."

Her eyes... softened a little? If I didn't know better, I'd think she felt a tinge of sympathy for me. "You poor boy. Maybe your intelligence genes weren't enhanced as much as we'd expected. Let me put it in simple terms. This situation is no different. You're doing this for Brynn's safety." Whatever sympathy I'd imagined had disappeared, and Everly's eyes hardened, cold as steel. "You *will* become the assassin I need, and you *will* perform your duties *without question*. Or Brynn dies. Now do you understand?" She pulled the shock collar remote from the pocket of her lab coat. "Think on that for a while, and then I'll see you back in the sparring ring later this evening."

She pushed the remote button.

Every nerve ending in my body lit up, and I dropped to the floor.

• • • • •

I jolted awake and leaped to my feet, heart racing. It slowed as I recognized the familiar surroundings of my "home" for the past several weeks. Seemed like a lifetime. To my surprise, they hadn't restrained me. Everly had used that damn shock collar on me again. I swear, my brain scrambled a little more every time she used it. My brain cells had probably decreased by half.

After falling back on the bed, I shoved my hands through my hair. Everly had threatened Brynn. Nothing new, but this time the terms were laid out in black and white. Unmistakable. I killed for The Colony, or they killed the most precious thing in the world to me. To save her life, I had to become the executioner they'd ordered all those years ago back in the lab. It went against everything I believed in, everything my parents, Patrick, and Anna had taught me. For Brynn to survive, I had to take innocent lives, follow orders mindlessly, and live with the self-hatred I'd feel.

Brynn wouldn't want me to do it. I knew that without a doubt. She'd tell me to let them kill her if it would save the lives of others. Her voice sounded in my head as if she was here in the room with me. I could almost feel her hands cupping either side of my face as she spoke softly.

Don't let them do this to you, Ash. Remember who you are. Don't worry about me. I want you to fight your way out of here, and go back to Noah. What's my life compared to all those you'll save? All the families who'll be reunited? The children who'll get to live their lives? You can't save everyone, but you can save more than one life.

I pictured the life Everly was forcing me into. Slaughtering innocents, people who'd been targeted by The Colony. Killing mothers and fathers who fought to keep soldiers from taking their children. Shutting down my conscience and losing my ability to make decisions. Trying to sleep at night, but haunted by the victims whose lives I'd ended. Maybe Everly would let me see Brynn once per month or so. If she was feeling generous.

But Brynn would be alive.

What would my life look like without her?

I could return to the Insurgents and continue to fight. Help Noah plan missions and recruit new operatives. See the grateful faces of the people I'd help save.

Go to sleep alone and wake to an empty bed every morning.

Everything I'd do, I'd do without Brynn.

I'd be a walking zombie because my heart would die with her.

I continued to turn it over in my head, running scenarios, weighing outcomes. I was in an impossible situation, asked to make an impossible decision. No matter what I chose, my life was essentially over.

28

DR. EVERLY

Not built that way? Can't kill indiscriminately? No matter how much A36 denied it, those instincts were part of him, just as much as the useless values August had taught him. He'd proven it when Declan had taken Brynn and was deceiving himself if he thought otherwise.

After my latest encounter with disappointment, I'd returned to my office to think. To plan. Turning my desk chair, I gazed out the window. This high up, the only things visible were sky, birds, and a few other towers in this complex. But it was a welcome break. I hadn't been sleeping well, and my mind hadn't stopped spinning since A36 had arrived.

My expectations hadn't been high. I'd known A36 would need readjustment before utilization of his intended purpose. I just hadn't anticipated it would be this long. His strength of character was surprising and infuriating. Thinking about August altering our perfect creation threatened to send me into a rage again. He'd ruined everything, and now restoring A36 to his default settings was left to me. But how?

I had to break him. I'd thought keeping him away from Brynn was the answer. Given more time, it probably would have been, but the luxury of time wasn't in my favor at the moment. Results were demanded. Threatening her life was my last option. It had to work. Maybe even killing her in front of him. But if I went through with it, that left me with no leverage. Threatening to kill A36 would have no effect. He'd welcome it.

And then, like lightning over a dark ocean, the solution became obvious.

29

ASHER

I paced the sparring ring, waiting for my next opponent. No one volunteered to get in the ring with me, so Everly forced three soldiers to take up the challenge. I took a swig of water then spat it in the bucket. This was child's play. The soldiers were so frightened of me, afraid of what I could do to them, they'd practically curled up in a fetal position the first time they struck the floor. I was convinced even Everly would put up more of a fight. After taking another drink of water, I rinsed my mouth then tossed the bottle to the floor.

When the soldiers had retrieved me from my room and escorted me here to meet with Everly, I'd been the picture of compliance and obedience—head down, hands clasped in front of me. To keep Brynn alive, I'd accepted Everly's terms. I played by her rules on the condition my visitation rights were restored. And not through an observation window. I wanted Brynn and me to spend time together in person. Everly informed me I was in no position to bargain, but everything depended on my performance.

The door on the other side of the room opened, and another person was shuffled in by a group of guards. I couldn't see his face, but he wasn't a willing participant. His fist caught one guard in the jaw, and a kick to a knee put down another. Through all the commotion, they struggled to bring him closer to the ring. Only the click of a gun being cocked got him under control. Being surrounded by guards, I only caught flashes of his face, but something about him looked familiar. The shape of his face. The color of his hair. Then I heard his voice.

"I did everything you asked, and this is how you reward me?"

Declan.

Oz.

He was only steps away from being tossed in the sparring ring with me. Thinking about what I'd do to him for betraying all of us, for stealing Brynn away, had kept my thoughts occupied during sleepless nights and days I was restrained for punishment. He'd traded the safety of our compound, our home, and many of the lives in it, people he'd cared about, or pretended to, for nothing more than physical enhancements. All for Paige, who'd told him she could never be more than a friend to him. And he'd become everything she despised.

When I'd last seen Declan, just before I let go of the helicopter rung and fell to the ground below, I'd promised to kill him the next time we met. Now, he was being delivered to me on a silver platter.

My dire situation was starting to look up.

Inside me, A36 roared in excitement. Redemption. Revenge. As for me, Asher, I wanted to cause Declan massive amounts of pain. To hurt as much as I did.

Before I killed him.

I felt the rage inside me as it drew back and gathered energy, much like ocean water before a tsunami. It was only a matter of time before it built to the point that it was released in a massive wave of strength, power, and rage that destroyed anything in its path.

A36 lurked just below the surface, pacing impatiently. Urging me to release him.

"You can thank me now." Everly's voice came from directly over my shoulder. She stood just outside the sparring ring. "Don't you have some unfinished business with Declan?"

In the time I'd known her, Everly's tone had only three settings—falsely empathetic, clinical and detached, or seething with anger. Now, her voice was breathy, almost—giddy. She couldn't wait to see how I'd handle this. What I'd do to Declan.

"Think about what he's done to you, how you and Brynn are here, separated, because of him."

"You're the reason we're here," I growled.

"But if not for Declan, we might still be out there looking for you. Once he understood genetic enhancement was a possibility, the information poured out of him like a river."

I wasn't stupid. I knew what Everly wanted from me and what she was goading me into. But for once, our interests were aligned. Our goals the same.

My chest heaved as my respiration rate increased. My fingers twitched in anticipation. Currents of electricity ran through my body, energy begged to be expended. I welcomed A36. He told me to sit back, relax, and enjoy the show.

The soldiers shoved Declan into the ring, then hovered along the edges with Everly, blocking any escape.

Declan's eyes were wide with fright, his movements jerky.

I stalked toward Declan, and he sunk to the floor, crawling backwards toward the corner of the ring. When he could go no further, he held up his hands in surrender. "Ash, please."

Looming over him, I sneered. "You're not even going to try and fight me? What happened to the cocky traitor who put all our lives in danger? Who deceived us all those weeks? Where is he?"

"I'm s-s-sorry."

"Sorry?"

"I didn't have a choice."

"There's always a choice. It's the option that doesn't betray your friends."

A sheen of sweat covered Declan's face. His hands trembled as he held them up in surrender. "They were going to kill me."

I grinned. "And you think your outcome with me is any different? You took Brynn from me, from Noah. Handed her over like she was nothing to you. How many times did she save your life in the field?"

Declan ducked his head, and his shoulders shook as he sobbed quietly. I closed my eyes in disgust. Behind me, Everly chuckled. This was too easy. I wanted Declan to fight, to get in my face and defend his actions to make it easier for me. To make me want to pulverize him. A36 curled my hands into fists.

Asher almost felt a twinge of sympathy for Declan. Almost.

I grabbed the collar of his shirt and jerked him up. His feet dangled a few inches above the floor. I growled, "Brynn."

While I held him with one hand, I drew my other fist back then launched it at his face. Bone grinded against bone, and I knew I'd broken his nose. Declan's head snapped back, and he howled in pain.

"Please!" He held his hands up in surrender.

Anger rocketed through me as I remembered Declan carrying a wounded Brynn through the rubble of our destroyed compound. I dropped him to the floor, kicked him over to his back, and then straddled his chest.

His shrieks turned to sobs. Blood bubbled from his nose as he breathed, and tears streamed from his eyes back into his hairline.

I could rip out his carotid artery with my teeth, and he'd bleed out in seconds. Crush his skull between my hands. Either would be agonizing, painful ways to die.

And oh so satisfying to me.

So many ways to kill a man. Maybe I'd play with him a while. I wrapped my hands around his throat and squeezed.

"Remember what Declan did, all the people he endangered." Everly cheered me on. She wanted this death and urged me to kill Declan.

I squeezed tighter.

"When he brought Brynn to us, he said he didn't care what happened to her. Or to any of you."

Declan's eyes were wide, tracked with spidery lines from burst blood vessels. His mouth was open, and he gurgled as he gasped for air. I smiled.

Then there was a whisper in my ear.

Remember who you are.

I know your heart, Asher Solomon.

I shook my head, trying to dislodge the words. Any other time, Brynn's voice would be welcomed. I'd longed to hear it while lying awake at night and every time I'd doubted myself over these long weeks.

But right now, it distracted A36 from his intent. He wanted to become what Everly expected. She wanted A36, not Ash Solomon.

Brynn reminded me who I was. As long as we were together, whether physically or not, part of my self-esteem was tied into how she perceived me. I knew how strong A36 was, and the first time he'd made an appearance, I'd wondered who was really in control. When Brynn was taken, A36 and I had shared the same objective—getting her back. We'd killed to accomplish that objective. I'd wondered what would happen when our goals weren't aligned. That time was here.

Killing Declan was a deep yearning. It took up every empty space in my body. If not for his betrayal, Brynn and I wouldn't be apart, wouldn't be here against our will. Our home wouldn't have been destroyed, and the lives of our friends and many others wouldn't have been lost.

But if I allowed A36 to kill him, I'd be that much closer to the monster Everly wanted. Gradually, A36 would gain a bigger hold over me one piece at a time. His desires would become mine. No matter how much I wanted to see Declan get his comeuppance, I had a strong notion that giving in would be a mistake I'd never come back from.

I was stronger. *I* was in control.

A36 silently howled his disapproval, but his hold receded to the background, and the plan I'd conjured last night stepped to the forefront of my mind. It was an enormous risk, but the only path I could see out of this hell.

Declan's face was red, and his eyes were beginning to roll back in his head. He was nearly gone. I released my hold, leaned forward, and whispered in his ear, "You owe me."

His nod was nearly imperceptible.

I climbed off his chest and stood.

Declan rolled to his side, clutched his neck, and gasped for air.

"What are you doing?" Everly's words were clipped in anger. "He's still alive. Finish what you started!" Her pitch was shrill, and it shot down my spine. "Kill him! This is what you were built for!"

Everly had tortured me physically for weeks. She'd forced me to watch hours upon hours of footage featuring cruel, merciless deaths of children and adults. I'd been manipulated into beating and nearly killing men and women who'd been tossed into the sparring ring with me. She'd held Brynn hostage, drugged her against her will, and withheld food and water.

As a result, I'd nearly lost myself and forgotten who I was. And I could only pray Brynn hadn't been killed days or even weeks ago.

I turned my head slowly in her direction.

"Do it!" she screamed.

"No."

Everly crawled under the ropes, strode over, and looked up at me. Anger and loathing pulsed in her eyes. "What's wrong with you? You're a failure. A disappointment. Your source of pain is lying right in front of you at your mercy, and you refuse to end it."

"I never said I refused to end my pain."

I placed my hands on either side of her face, twisted, and snapped her neck. It was over in half a second.

So many ways to kill someone.

My only regret was that it wasn't more painful for her.

30

ASHER

I took advantage of the soldiers' stunned silence. Before they could react, I moved swiftly and jerked the guns from the hands of all but one. He helped me out and tossed his to the floor in defeat.

Everly's lifeless body lay in the middle of the ring, eyes staring sightlessly, her neck at an awkward angle. She'd gotten careless over the past couple weeks. The shock collar had become an afterthought, and she'd decreased the number of guards. She'd truly believed she controlled me.

So had I—until last night.

I knew Brynn wouldn't want me to spare her life at the expense of others. That's not who she was. But if she died because of me, I'd end my own life before willingly handing it over to Everly. My actions were a gamble with Brynn's life and mine, but if she couldn't be saved, then I was determined our fates be the same.

I held a gun on the soldiers while I smashed their comm units, then I made the biggest guard give me his uniform. It was a tight fit, but I didn't plan on wearing it for long. After changing, I forced the soldiers into a closet. Before shoving Declan in with them, I pulled him to the side and spoke in a low voice. "Your life was spared for a reason. Don't made me regret my choice."

Bruises in the shape of my handprints had begun to form around his neck, and his nose was crooked and swollen. "Whatever you need, Ash. I promise." His voice sounded like sandpaper.

I pushed him in the closet with the guards, then locked the door. It was a tight squeeze, but compared to everything I'd been through, a party.

The badge I'd ripped from Everly's corpse before stuffing her in a locker got me through the door and into the hallway. I pulled the brim of my stolen hat further down over my eyes, and headed in the direction of Brynn's room. Only a few people passed me, but they were too fixated on their own agendas and destinations to pay attention to yet another guard patrolling the building.

Brynn's room was five floors above me. I was so close. My stomach was jittery at the thought of seeing her again, hearing her voice, touching her. What was I—twelve years old? It reminded me of when we'd sneaked around and made out before we'd told Patrick and Anna about us. Considering we'd been raised almost as siblings, we were unsure how they'd react to our relationship. Unless they'd figured out our secret, they'd died before we could tell them.

I kept my head down and moved swiftly. The elevator was just around the corner, but stairs were the safest option. The fewer people who saw me, the better.

With the guards in the locked closet, I figured there would be no one to raise an alarm in the next fifteen minutes or so. Maybe longer, if I was lucky. But based on prior experience, luck wasn't often on my side.

I opened the door to the stairwell then paused to listen. All was quiet. A good sign. Taking the stairs two at a time, I ascended toward Brynn's floor. My plan was somewhat open-ended. Step one had been killing Everly. Step two was to get to Brynn's room. Step three was a little fuzzy and subject to change. Reunite with Brynn, hold her in my arms for a brief moment, hopefully have an extra second or two for a kiss—and then I figured we'd fight our way out. At that point, A36 would come in handy.

Somewhere between the third and fourth flights of stairs, it occurred to me that Brynn had never seen me as A36. To her, Ash only killed people when his life, the lives of his team, or the lives of hostages were in danger. Since she'd last seen me, the parameters of acceptable kills and body counts had both increased considerably. What would she think about that? Would she see me differently?

Would she still feel the same for me?

That thought caused me to stumble, and I cracked a kneecap on the edge of a stair. I shook my head to clear those toxic thoughts from my mind. Brynn loved me. Loved all of the nooks and crannies so often filled with dark moods—guilt, frustration, confusion, and sometimes hatred. But she also loved the very best parts of me—the Ash who fiercely fought for those I cared about and the people who couldn't fight for themselves.

As long as I was in control, not A36, I had to have faith her feelings wouldn't change.

I climbed the last flight of stairs and then stopped at the landing to peer through the narrow window of the door leading to Brynn's floor. All looked normal. A few people chatted in the hallway, a handful of other employees passed through. No one seemed panicked. Nothing was out of the ordinary. No alarms sounded.

A rush of air expelled from my lungs. Maybe this would work. Brynn's room was only thirty feet to my left. So close.

I turned the door knob then stepped into the hallway. Looking like I belonged here was critical. Hesitancy would be noticed and greeted with suspicion. It also didn't help that I stood at least a head taller than most people, and my guard uniform didn't quite fit. I counted on others being too involved with their own agendas to notice.

Turning to my left, I took the first step toward Brynn. Halfway down the hall was a desk staffed with medical personnel. Most of the rooms on this floor housed patients who'd had their genes replaced with those stripped from hostages, a fact Everly had mentioned more than once. She'd found it amusing that the end products of people the Insurgents fought so hard to save were here on the same floor where Brynn had spent the past several weeks. I found it appalling, and if time allowed, I'd love nothing more than to enter these rooms, rip the patients from their beds, and throttle them. I'd tell them about the young children, parents, husbands, and wives forcibly taken from their families and then killed because of someone's vanity.

Sadly, I knew it wouldn't make a difference to those who felt entitled because of their wealth or social status.

Only fifteen more feet. So far, no alarms. The guards hadn't broken out of the closet, and Everly's hidden body wouldn't be found for a while. I hoped.

As I approached the desk, I kept my eyes straight ahead and hoped no one would be tempted to question my destination or reason for being here. Guards on this floor weren't an unusual sight. They'd accompanied Everly every time I'd been brought here to see Brynn.

Just the thought of seeing her again sent flutters through my stomach, and I nearly smiled, feeling more like a young, heartsick teenage boy rather than a seventeen-year-old who had experienced far too much loss for his age and had seen enough death for several lifetimes.

Only ten more feet.

"Sir? Can I see your badge? The system is showing an irregularity." A guard stood directly in front of me to my right, his hand resting on the gun in his side holster.

I stopped abruptly. Damn. I'd forgotten about the security system linked to all ID badges. Whenever employees passed checkpoints at various places throughout the building, their badges were scanned by overhead detectors. The information carried on microchips within the badges—employee picture, department, and position—were displayed on a security monitor. Any anomalies immediately alerted the closest security desk. Which, in this case, just happened to be located behind the medical desk.

I might have gotten away clean if the security desk was located further away, but in all the times I'd been on this floor, I'd never noticed it tucked away behind the medical personnel.

This wasn't good. He was already suspicious that the pictures didn't match. My eyes flicked to his partner, who was rising slowly from the desk and speaking into a radio with one hand, the other hand going for her gun.

They knew.

No doubt my image was in the system, and more guards were on the way.

Time to act before I was severely outnumbered.

I drew back my fist and hit him square in the jaw. Enhanced strength was a huge asset right now. His eyes rolled back as he dropped to the floor.

And then chaos erupted.

Screams from those behind the desk and in the hallway. The other guard yelling at me to stop as she lunged in my direction. An alarm blared overhead, indicating a breach.

I rushed the last few feet toward Brynn's door. In the back of my mind, I knew the guards wouldn't kill me, but that didn't mean it was off the table for Brynn. To preserve my own identity and sanity, this was my only alternative. I was all in.

The sound of the stairwell door slamming against the wall told me reinforcements were already on the floor and more would soon follow. Adrenaline shot through my body, and I reached for Everly's badge in my pocket to enter Brynn's room.

I sensed them behind me. I wouldn't make it into the room before they were on me. Pulling the gun I'd taken from the guard whose uniform I'd stolen, I turned and took out the six closest to me. I spun back toward the door and scanned Everly's badge. The door swished open.

Brynn was in her bed. Her head turned in my direction—eyes hard and chin jutted out. My girl hadn't given up fighting. The second she recognized me, her mouth fell open and her eyes widened.

Heavy footsteps behind me. Voices shouting. Gunfire would follow.

"Ash?"

Brynn was still restrained. She was an easy mark for stray bullets, or whatever they chose to shoot me with. I felt the pull to go to her and feel her in my arms again, like a tether at my core. With every cell in my body, I wanted to give into it more than anything.

But I was heavily outnumbered and only saw one way out of this. And he was more than happy to help.

"Brynn, take cover as much as you can."

She nodded, but her movements were so limited, there was nothing she could do.

I stood to the side of the door, impatient, coiled. The instant the first guard entered, I ripped the gun out of his hands. Before he could turn, I hit him in the back of the head with the butt of his weapon, and he fell to the floor. The next one got a bullet to the side of his head.

I rushed toward Brynn's bed, slid underneath, rolled to my stomach, and then aimed at the door. The next three took kill shots to the forehead. I continued shooting anyone who was stupid enough to enter until I was out of ammo. And they knew exactly when I ran out.

"Ash, what..."

The last part of her question was drowned out by four more soldiers pouring into the room.

I'd already rolled from under the bed and stood ready for them. In seconds, I'd ripped out the jugular of one, the throat of another and snapped the necks of the remaining two. Splatters of blood covered the walls and floor, and the coppery smell of it hung in the air. For now, the stream of soldiers stopped.

I knew we had only moments.

Brynn's eyes were wide. "Is it you?" Her voice held a tremor.

"It's me. I have control." The odds of getting us out of here safely were less than zero, but I had to at least hold her again. I easily ripped away her restraints.

Brynn quickly rose to her knees on the bed and wrapped her arms around my neck.

I held her against me. Buried my nose in her hair and inhaled deeply. I was home. We'd spent weeks apart, and most of that time I didn't know if she was being taken care of or was even alive. I'd endured torture and endless manipulation, staying strong for her. Now, with her in my arms, it became too much to bear. I wanted to collapse against her. Tears pricked the corners of my eyes.

A sound reached my ears. I knew exactly what it was and what I had to do.

Everything happened simultaneously.

Brynn pulled away from me to say something.

I pushed her down to the bed and shielded her with my body.

There was a subtle plink as a sniper's bullet pierced the window.

When she jerked in my arms, I knew she'd been hit.

I lifted my head to look at her. A small, red circle in the middle of her chest was enlarging by the second.

Brynn's brows drew together, and her hand reached for my face. "Ash?"

I grabbed her hand and held it against my cheek, while I watched the light go out of her eyes.

Brynn was gone. No, no, no, no. I felt my heart stop and wither inside me. All the breath left my body.

She breathed, I breathed.

She bled, I bled.

She died, I died.

There was no reason to keep fighting. I'd never let them turn me into what they wanted. I rose from the bed, gently placed her arms to her side, then I leaned over and kissed her still warm lips.

Soldiers moved outside the door, readying to come in after me. Squatting down, I picked up a gun from the floor and held it under my chin.

A rain of bullets shattered the window behind me, and I fell to the floor.

31

ASHER

I woke with a start. My body thought I was still in Brynn's room, and I needed to get to her. But I was back in my old room.

And then I was hit with crushing waves of emotion. Anger that I was still alive and wasn't given the choice to end my life. Guilt that I was still here when Brynn wasn't. But most of all, grief. Everything inside me felt broken and heavy. At the same time, I was empty. Brynn would always be with me, but right now, the spaces she'd occupied were hollow shells that threatened to collapse in on themselves.

I'd end the pain as soon as I possibly could, then follow Brynn's path.

I tried to sit up, but heavy, iron restraints held me in place. The door to my room opened, and a man wearing scrubs walked in carrying a data pad.

"How long have I been out?" Judging by the scratchiness of my voice, it had been days since I'd last used it.

No response. He took my vitals, charted them, and then left.

Hours later, the same man, along with four heavily armed guards, delivered a food tray. He uncuffed one of my hands so I could eat.

"I want to speak to someone in charge."

Still no response from anyone. I shoved my food tray to the floor.

Days passed in the same pattern. They refused to answer questions, and I shoved food trays to the floor. Or threw them at their faces. Then they fed me intravenously. They weren't about to let their investment wither away slowly and die.

By my count, it had been nine days. Nine days of agony knowing Brynn was no longer in this world. I'd vowed to Noah I'd bring her home or die trying. That vow had been broken in the worst way, and I was left alone to suffer the aftereffects.

I stared out the narrow window of my room. It wasn't much of a view, but I could see clouds and a few stars in the sky. At least I could tell if it was night or day. Not that it mattered anymore. The dim nighttime light in the corner went out, and I was plunged into darkness until the even dimmer emergency light kicked in.

Odd. Nothing like that had happened since I'd been here. Had the entire building lost power?

The door to my room opened. Someone slipped inside then closed the door behind them.

My body tensed, and I strained to make out who it was. In the time it took for the person to move from the doorway to my bed, the silhouette became very familiar.

"Brynn?" I whispered, my heart hammering against my chest. But as she drew closer, I realized this person didn't have long braids and her shoulders weren't as broad. She also lacked stealth and nearly ran into my bed.

"No, sweetheart. Not Brynn."

I knew that voice. It had comforted me after the death of my parents, stayed up with me on so many sleepless nights, and cheered me on with every challenge I faced. But it couldn't be. She'd died years ago.

"Anna?" My voice broke.

As she moved closer, the emergency light gave shape to her features. She had a few more wrinkles and some strands of gray running through her hair, but it was Anna. Her eyes glistened. "My boy. What have they done to you? I've missed you so much." Her cool hand stroked my cheek and pushed the hair away from my forehead.

"How are you here? Am I dreaming?"

She shook her head and sat on the edge of my bed. "I'm real, and you're not dreaming."

My hands itched to be free so I could touch her. "But we saw you die, you and Patrick—"

"You saw Patrick die." Her voice hitched. "But I made it. The Colony patched me up and brought me here. Said they could use my medical skills."

"Please, Anna, you've got to undo my restraints." My voice was hoarse with tears. Anna was alive, and she was here.

"We don't have long. I called in a lot of favors to get this time with you."

The second my hands were free, I pulled her into a hug. She still smelled the same, and it brought me home, where I'd been safe and loved after my own parents were taken. A sob escaped me. "They killed her. Brynn is gone."

She pulled away from me, and brushed tears off my cheeks. "No, sweetheart. Brynn's alive."

I shook my head. "But I saw her. She died in my arms."

"She was wounded badly, but is recovering. I saw her just an hour ago. I'm calling in a lot of favors this evening. After you killed Everly, security tripled. It's a miracle I'm here now."

Brynn was alive. The thought stole the breath from my body and sent heat radiating through my chest, spreading into every limb. I was alive again.

"I also found Noah. An undercover Insurgent recognized him in the city, and we made contact." She beamed with joy at having found her family again.

"I have so many questions about my parents, what you knew about me—"

"I know, Ash, and I'll answer all of them, but getting the three of us out of here comes first."

I ducked my head sheepishly. "Um... we're together, you know. Brynn and I."

Anna tilted her head to the side and smiled knowingly. "I knew how you felt about each other before you did. The two of you were sadly mistaken if you thought Patrick and I didn't know. You wasted time and effort with all that sneaking around." She leaned in and kissed my cheek. "And I couldn't be happier about it. Brynn needs a strong partner, and she's certainly found one in you."

"Why didn't you let us know you were alive?"

"If you'd known I was still alive, you would have tried to rescue me."

"In a heartbeat." I squeezed her hand.

She nodded. "And the odds were against it. I'd never put you in that kind of danger. I couldn't bear it if something happened to any of my children."

My heart warmed, knowing she still thought of me as her own.

"Ash, there are residents here who can help us. Not everyone is loyal to The Colony, and they've helped smuggle people out of here before. It won't be without its challenges, though."

"You know what I am and what I can do."

She cupped my cheek with her hand. "Yes, sweetheart, I do, but that's something I'd never ask of you. That's not who you are."

"That's what Brynn says."

"Well, I raised an intelligent girl, you know."

"I'd do anything to protect both of you and make sure you get out of here safely."

"I know, Ash, but for right now, we'll work with what we've got. Tomorrow night, the power will go out again. After tonight, they'll think there's a glitch in the system, so it won't be quite as suspicious. Someone will come in and release you. You can trust him. I'll get Brynn and meet you at the service entry door on the first floor at the north side. Noah will be waiting for us."

I shook my head. "I want to come with you and get Brynn. I need to see her. Please."

Anna's eyes were full of sympathy. "I know, but it will be faster this way. You'll see her soon. We'll have people helping us get out a back way. Don't worry about us, just get yourself to the service door."

I stared at her a moment longer, this woman who'd given me a mother's love even though I didn't belong to her. Finally, I nodded reluctantly. "I'll see you tomorrow night."

●　　　●　　　●　　　●　　　●

True to her word, the next night, the power went out again. Seconds later, a tall guy who appeared to be my age slipped into my room. I experienced déjà vu when this person's silhouette also seemed familiar.

Declan.

Rage rocketed through my body. I tugged at my restraints.

"What the hell are you doing here? Get out! You'll ruin everything."

Declan held up his trembling hands in surrender. "I'm here to help you, Ash. Anna sent me. I knew I did wrong, and as soon as I saw her here, I told her what I knew. I'm working to help you and Brynn. I owe you. I owe a lot of people."

Anna promised I could trust the person she'd send. And Anna was one of the few people in the world I trusted. With his head hung low and the way he shifted from side to side, Declan seemed sorry. If he released me, and then I found he couldn't be trusted, he'd pay for it.

"Release me, Declan. And don't try anything stupid."

He nodded as he unlocked my restraints. "I just want to help. Anna has everything arranged. I'm putting you on a stretcher, covering you with a sheet, and then transporting you to the morgue. After what you did to Dr. Everly, and then the fiasco in Brynn's room, your face is too recognizable.

Once I get you down there, you're on your own, but it's just a short distance to the service door where you'll meet Anna and Noah."

I rose from the bed, and he moved away from me, his stance wary.

"I won't hurt you," I said. "Thank you for helping us."

His posture relaxed slightly. "You're welcome. Anna has helped a lot of people here, and most of us would do anything for her."

When I lay down on the stretcher, he covered me with a white sheet. "Try not to breathe too heavily. If any of the guards see the sheet move, we're both done."

"Got it."

As he pushed me down the hallway, I heard people grumbling and complaining about the power going out again. Their inconvenience was our ticket out. I focused on breathing as little as possible. Everything depended on no one becoming suspicious of this stretcher. I heard the elevator doors opening and closing. Good thing for us they still worked on backup power.

"Doing okay?" Declan whispered.

"Yeah. How much further?" I inhaled deeply while I had the chance.

"A few more floors down, then two long hallways. Don't move. Looks like we're stopping for someone."

I returned to my barely breathing state, conscious not to move a muscle. As soon as the power came back on, they'd notice I wasn't in my room, and Anna, Brynn, and I needed to be long gone by then.

"Evening, Declan."

"Wes."

"What do you have there?"

"Stripped him of everything valuable. Just headed to the morgue."

The elevator stopped, and Wes exited. "Only two more floors. Hang in there."

Relief rushed through me. It was getting harder to remain immobile. My adrenaline level ramped up, my body tensed to move. I believed Anna, but I still needed to see with my own eyes that Brynn was still alive. And I wanted to see Anna again, partly because I'd missed her every day since I thought we'd lost her and partly to reassure myself it was really her I'd talked to last night. Brynn and Noah must be ecstatic that their mother had been returned to them. We could be a family again. But there would still be a Patrick-shaped hole in our lives that would never be filled.

Declan wasn't wasting any time getting down the two hallways. We moved swiftly, and all I could hear was the creak of the wheels and the soft scuff of Declan's shoes on the tiled floor.

The swishing of automatic doors and strong odor of formaldehyde indicated we were in the morgue, but I didn't dare move until Declan gave the okay.

"It's empty this time of night." He pulled back the sheet. The overhead lights were still dim from the emergency power, but they were bright enough to see my surroundings. "Go out the door, hang a right, then take the first left. It leads directly to the service entrance."

I stood and held out my hand, and Declan reluctantly shook it. "Thank you for helping us. I can't say I'll ever completely trust you again, but it's a start."

"Tell Anna I'm happy she's with her family again. She was always good to me."

"I will."

"And tell Paige I'm sorry."

I nodded, then Declan exited the morgue. He moved briskly, whether anxious to not incriminate himself or just anxious to get away from me.

I waited a couple of beats, and then stuck my head out the door to check the hall.

Empty.

Eager to get out of here and back to my family, I rushed silently down the corridor. No matter what, I'd never let anything happen to them again. Now that I knew what I was capable of, I'd use that ability to defend them and myself. Killing wasn't necessary, but I could seriously maim someone if they couldn't take a hint.

I reached the end of the first hallway, stopped at the corner, and took a quick glance down the next corridor. Again, it was empty. The left turn Declan mentioned was only a short distance away.

Nearly there.

I glanced behind me once more. Clear. My gaze returned to the last corridor.

A man was standing in my path.

I came to an abrupt halt, unsure whether he was friend or foe. He was older, probably a little older than Anna. His stance was confident, hands clasped behind his back, his gaze self-assured and appraising. Some deep instinct told me he was no friend to me.

A36's interest in this obstacle stirred inside me, and I moved into a fighting stance.

"Hello, Asher." If snakes could smile, this was how they'd look.

"Who are you?"

His reptilian smile widened. "I'm someone you'll no doubt want to kill in the next few minutes. But that wouldn't be a wise decision."

Neither I nor A36 liked the sound of that. I considered taking him out right now. Brynn and Anna were waiting. I moved toward him.

He held up his hands in a stopping motion. "If you value Brynn and Anna's lives, don't come any closer."

I froze.

"I know she and Anna are just beyond that door. In fact, I knew about their escape plan and decided not to interfere."

"You still haven't told me who you are."

"When you killed Dr. Everly—which I meant to thank you for, as she was quite incompetent—did you think she was the top of the food chain?" He chuckled. "She was intelligent, I'll give you that, but her scope was too narrow. She didn't possess the skill set to head The Colony. That's my job." The reptilian smile disappeared. His expression was superior, that of someone used to getting what he wanted.

"What do you want from me?"

"I want A36."

"You can't have him. Look, I'm getting out of here, and if I have to kill you to get to Brynn and Anna, I won't hesitate."

He reached slowly into his pocket, and I tensed, ready to attack. His other hand came up in reassurance. He brought out a comm unit. "See this? All I have to do is give the word, and snipers on the roof will kill Brynn and Anna. I believe Noah is also close by."

I shook my head. No. This couldn't be happening. We were getting out of here, away from The Colony. Going back to working against them, destroying them one piece at a time.

He tilted his head to the side. "I literally hold their lives in my hand, Asher. Fight me, and they die. Come back upstairs, and I'll permit them to leave safely. Make your choice."

He had me, and he knew it. I fell back against the wall, and ran my hands through my hair in frustration. So close. We'd been so close to getting out of here. "Do I have your word they'll be safe? Whatever that's worth?"

"Of course. You can watch them leave on the security monitor. I doubt they'll leave willingly without you, but they'll be told you chose to stay."

I shook my head. "They'll never believe you."

He placed his hands behind his back again. "It doesn't matter. I own you. You work for me now." From behind his back he brought out my old friend, the shock collar. "This is for insurance that you won't kill me once Brynn,

Anna, and Noah leave the city." He approached slowly, reached up, and fastened it around my neck. "By the way, my name is Silas Reeves. You can call me Director."

"I won't be your assassin. I'll kill myself first."

"And then I'll kill the three people I'm allowing to walk out of here. I can find them at any time." He turned in the direction of the elevator, paused, then looked back at me. "A36, if you think being an assassin was the only reason we pursued you for so long, you're mistaken. That's just the first part of Project Adam. I can't wait for you to learn the rest."

The weight of his words landed in my stomach like a boulder. Learning I'd been made in a lab to the specifications of The Colony, created to kill without mercy and without a conscience, was horrific. Discovering my parents and sisters weren't truly my family had been devastating. It had never occurred to me there could be something more beyond that, just as abhorrent. Or worse. And I was sure it was. Nothing that involved The Colony reeked of sunshine and rainbows, so why should this be any different?

"There's more? What is it?" I asked hesitantly.

He opened his mouth, then closed it. "I think I'd rather show you. It's quite impressive."

The director turned, hands clasped behind his back, and headed down the hallway toward the elevator. I had no choice but to follow, so I fell in behind him, our footsteps echoing down the corridor.

Freedom had been less than twenty feet away, so close I could almost smell the fresh air. Brynn, Noah, and Anna waited for me just beyond the door so we could make our escape. At least I knew they'd get away safely. All I had to do was play by the rules, follow instructions, and be a good little soldier.

Was their safety guaranteed if I ended my own existence? My gut told me the answer was no. The second I harmed myself, the director would hunt them down. I was sure of it. So there went that option. Maybe finding a way to remove the patch Dad added wouldn't be such a bad thing. I'd lose my humanity, but I'd also avoid the overwhelming guilt, grief, and sadness every time I took a life.

I knew if given the option, I'd never be able to give up my emotions. I'd rather be aware and live with the pain than be a cold, unfeeling murderer. And I wasn't ready to give up yet. I'd fight until the end.

The elevator ride was uncomfortable. Silas studied me openly, his narrowed, reptilian eyes never leaving my face. I had the feeling he could see inside me and knew every thought that crossed my mind. That he understood my weaknesses—which were the three people I prayed were making their way out of this godforsaken walled city.

Dread snaked through me, coiled into a hard pit in my belly. When the door opened on the thirtieth floor, I trailed behind him into an expansive room with two-story ceilings. Every other area I'd been in had long, white, sterile corridors in keeping with a lab or medical facility. But this room was filled with inviting couches and chairs and had a stunning floor to ceiling view overlooking the city below.

What was this place?

"It's a beautiful view, isn't it? Perfect. Just like the citizens below."

I grimaced in horror. "Their perfection comes at the expense of others. What gives you the right to steal Outliers away from their lives, strip away characteristics they were born with, then leave their bodies to be taken out like trash?"

The director blinked as if truly perplexed by my question, then his lips curled into a condescending smirk. "Colony scientists developed the technique that allowed Outliers and every other person on this planet to live disease-free. We provided a healthier life for them. It's only fair that in return, they show how grateful they are by making donations to our citizens."

My blood boiled at his arrogance. To him, all who resided outside these gates were second class citizens whose lives were inconsequential. I remembered Mom coloring Elsa's hair every few weeks. Cami wearing contacts to hide her sapphire blue eyes. Me throwing races at school so as not to draw attention to my speed.

If there was even a minuscule chance I could rip off this collar, the director would be dead inside of five seconds. Maybe less. My hands tightened into fists. A36 pleaded with me to give him a go at the collar.

"How can you live with yourself, knowing you're the cause of so many deaths? Especially children who don't understand what's happening? I've seen their terror and their tears, and I hope someday you feel every ounce of pain they've experienced."

"I live quite well. The fate of Outliers isn't something I give much thought to. And besides, we don't kill all the children. Many of them are here."

Wait. What? "What do you mean they're here?"

"That's part of what I wanted to show you, A36. Follow me."

Where he was leading me was a mystery. I cringed at the horrific image that flashed through my mind of children hung up in meat lockers like sides of beef. If that was the case, shock collar or not, he was a dead man.

I followed him through the two-story lounge area and down a wide hallway. No sterile white here, either. Instead, it boasted bamboo floors and glorious pictures hung on sage-colored walls. If you could forget where you were, it was quite appealing. Certainly more so than the compound with its dripping water leaks and aroma of rust.

But I couldn't forget where I was, and I'd give anything to be back at the compound right now.

We passed several doors, each with a plaque showing two names on the wall beside it. He stopped in front of a set of double doors and then turned to face me.

"Although it's the middle of the night, we have no regular time schedules here. We've found it works better that way. I think you'll be quite impressed with what we've accomplished so far."

The director swung open the doors leading into a glassed-in room overlooking a large enclosed area. Another observation room. I'd spent enough time in those to last me a lifetime.

I hung back, hesitant to see what was beyond the window.

"Come closer, A36. You can't see anything standing back there."

As I trudged forward, I heard the voices of children below. Not laughter or conversational tones, but sharp, clipped yells and retorts. The area beneath us was a large gymnasium with several different training areas. Children of all ages sparred each other in various rings using hand to hand combat. Others wore earmuffs while they shot at targets on the walls. Some threw knives at human mannequins.

"Amazing, isn't it? Some are quite skilled. We keep only the best and send the others to harvest centers."

Ice ran up my spine and spread through my limbs. I knew. I knew what this was before he said it.

"This is why Insurgents have never received any outside assistance. Why would anyone want to help destroy their supplier of executioners? No one suspects children. Other places may not be able to stomach training children themselves, but they have no problem paying the fees we charge."

Bile filled my throat, and I swallowed hard, unsure I could even get the words out. "You're training these children to kill and then selling them?"

Silas's brows drew together. "You seem surprised and, pardon me for saying so, a little judgmental. After a period of time when it became clear

Everly was incapable of bringing you in, we had to come up with a temporary solution. You, A36, are the original Project Adam. These children are lethal and deadly, but still flawed with emotion, no matter how hard we try to suppress it.

"Your father may have found a way for you to experience the normal range of emotions, but I promise you, it's only temporary. And because lack of empathy is built into your genetic code, those are the genes you'll pass on to your offspring."

My... offspring? What was he saying?

Silas sighed and clapped his hands together. "Ah, well, but that's talk for another day. I'd mentioned the children being flawed with emotion despite their programming, but we did come across one who's been quite successful since entering the program, with a list of confirmed kills far and above anyone else's." He pressed a button on his comm unit. "Send up C24."

Down below, I noticed one of the older children break away from a group. Silas continued talking, still going on about the child assassin's abilities. But I'd tuned him out. Something about the person's gait sparked a memory in the recesses of my mind, but I couldn't quite grasp it. Curiosity drew me closer to the window. Just before entering the elevator connected to this room, C24 unclasped her wheat-colored, untamed hair and shook it free from its ponytail.

"—We used donors for several enhancements, as she was lacking in athletic abilities and was quite clumsy."

I heard the words and yearned for them to mean what I suspected. But I also didn't want it to be true.

The elevator dinged, the door slid open, then a young woman stepped out and strode toward us. She gave a slight bow in Silas's direction, then turned to face me, hands clasped behind her back.

"I thought the two of you should get reacquainted since you'll be working together."

It had been a decade, but I'd never forget those cornflower blue eyes full of tears when they looked at me the last time I'd seen her. I now understood she really had been at our house. She'd been the bait used to lure me there.

"Elsa." My voice broke.

"Hello, Asher."

ACKNOWLEDGEMENTS

During the writing of this book, I was mostly secluded (except for Bond, my feline overlord) while begging these characters to tell me their story, which they chose to share in snippets and glimpses. I told someone this story would be the death of me. Luckily, I had the support of numerous friends and family.

Thanks to Staci Troilo, my rock star editor. You go above and beyond and elevate my writing to the next level. I'm still convinced you've cloned yourself.

Misty Swafford, I'm so glad you entered the Name My Character contest. The name Declan encompasses everything I envisioned for this character—thank you for allowing me to use it.

It can be difficult to find a beta who isn't afraid to be honest, but I struck gold the first time with Jo Anna Young. Your suggestions and critiques made this a better book. Because of you, a certain character will have a bigger presence in the sequel. Thanks for being there during my panic mode!

Thanks to C.J. Redwine for the first chapter suggestions and everything I've learned at your writing retreats.

I owe Susan Thomison endless gratitude for brainstorming and being there during the eleventh hour plot hole debacle. I'm fortunate you overlook my lack of interest in chick flicks, shopping, and anything pink and continue to be my friend. I'm determined to make you into a Marvel nerd eventually.

Mike, Tanner, and Reese, thanks for listening/pretending to listen while I go on endlessly about books. You can't fool me—I see those eyes glazing over in boredom.

Dad, Mom, and Jenn, thanks for telling anyone who will listen about my books.

To all the bloggers and friends who've read my books and helped promote them, I deeply appreciate everything you've done. Finding people who are just as passionate about books makes it all worthwhile.

Thanks to Reagan, David, Christopher, and Justin at Black Rose Writing for all you've done to help get this book into the world.

NOTE FROM THE AUTHOR

Word-of-mouth is crucial for any author to succeed. If you enjoyed the book, please leave a review online—anywhere you are able. Even if it's just a sentence or two. It would make all the difference and would be very much appreciated.

Thanks!
Teri

ABOUT THE AUTHOR

Teri Polen reads and watches horror, sci-fi, and fantasy. *The Walking Dead*, *Harry Potter*, and anything *Marvel*-related is likely to cause fangirl delirium. She lives in Bowling Green, KY with her husband, sons, and black cat. Her first novel, *Sarah*, a YA horror/thriller, was a horror finalist in the 2017 Next Generation Indie Book Awards. Visit her online at www.teripolen.com

Thank you so much for reading one of our **Sci-Fi** novels.

If you enjoyed our book, please check out our recommended title for your next great read!

Culture-Z by Karl Andrew Marszalowicz

In the year 2190, mankind has made great strides forward in the worlds of technology, science, and greed. However, when all three get together one last time, this oblivious generation may not exist much longer.